*"I underes____ ____ ____" he said.*

"This is my job," she responded. "I'm quite good at it."

"So I see." Reese stepped a little closer. Because she'd leaned against the door, Eva couldn't move away.

She had the sudden sense of being trapped. One of his arms rested against the door, near her face, and he leaned toward her as if to catch every word. His eyes devoured her, pinioning Eva as much as the arm that kept her from moving through the door to her escape. "Escape" was too strong a word, but it was the only one that came to mind—escape, as if from a jungle animal. Eva wondered if the danger she felt was obvious to Reese.

It wasn't. He heard only her clear voice, saw only her dark, serene eyes, and felt the urge to reach out and touch her lips with his fingertips, feel their softness and then cover her mouth with his....

Dear Reader,

When two people fall in love, the world is suddenly new and exciting, and it's that same excitement we bring to you in Silhouette Intimate Moments. These are stories with scope, with grandeur. These characters lead the lives we all dream of, and everything they do reflects the wonder of being in love.

Longer and more sensuous than most romances, Silhouette Intimate Moments novels take you away from everyday life and let you share the magic of love. Adventure, glamour, drama, even suspense— these are the passwords that let you into a world where love has a power beyond the ordinary, where the best authors in the field today create stories of love and commitment that will stay with you always.

In coming months look for novels by your favorite authors: Maura Seger, Parris Afton Bonds, Elizabeth Lowell and Erin St. Claire, to name just a few. And whenever you buy books, look for all the Silhouette Intimate Moments, love stories *for* today's women *by* today's women.

Leslie J. Wainger
Senior Editor
Silhouette Books

IMRL-7/85

# Anna James

# The Dream Makers

## Silhouette Intimate Moments

Published by Silhouette Books New York

**America's Publisher of Contemporary Romance**

SILHOUETTE BOOKS
300 East 42nd St., New York, N.Y. 10017

Copyright © 1986 by Madeline Porter and Shannon Harper

ISBN: 0-373-07167-1

First Silhouette Books printing November 1986

America's Publisher of Contemporary Romance

Printed in the U.S.A.

**Books by Anna James**

Silhouette Intimate Moments

*Edge of Love* #13
*Her Own Rules* #38
*Love on the Line* #65
*The Venetian Necklace* #104
*Nina's Song* #115
*Images* #135
*The Reluctant Swan* #147
*The Dream Makers* #167

## ANNA JAMES

spends most of her time either in Atlanta, Georgia, or Los Angeles, California. She has written many different kinds of romances—from historicals to contemporaries, as well as numerous Gothics. When she's not traveling or writing, she enjoys tennis, the theater, long walks on the beach, and her three incompatible cats.

# Chapter 1

This situation in Corinth is a hell of a mess." Gino Marchetti looked up from his polished mahogany desk and across the acres of off-white carpet to the doorway of his office where Eva Sinclair stood. While he waved around his cigar, she watched patiently, waited for the smoke to clear, then crossed the room to settle in a chair beside Gino's desk.

Watching him put the cigar back in his mouth and chomp down on it impatiently, Eva suppressed a slight sigh. Her dark eyes surveyed Gino calmly. She'd been through this sort of scene often in the seven years she'd worked for Marchetti Films International, and the stages were familiar to her. First came the cigar-punctuated outburst, followed by the long pause as man and cigar smoldered. Then Gino usually leaned back in his swivel chair, whipped off his dark gold-tinted glasses and wordlessly demanded Eva's response.

Before long the glasses came off, and Eva obliged smoothly. "I thought the location was perfect."

"Hmmph," came the not unexpected response. "We had people out scouting locations all over the blasted South—dozens of towns, hundreds of old houses. And I had to choose this one." Gino tugged at his blue silk necktie, puffed on the cigar and shook his head.

"From the photographs I saw, the choice was perfect—a house built in the 1840's near a town that still looks like the 1940's. It was exactly what you wanted, Gino. Nothing else came close."

Gino grunted again, leaving Eva the opening she needed to remind him, "It would have cost a fortune to build the house on a studio lot out here."

The telephone buzzer interrupted jarringly, but it barely disturbed Gino, who pressed a button, responded with a curt "Later" and turned back to Eva. "I know exactly what it would have cost, and I never had any intention of building the house on a set, Eva. That's why I sent the scouts down there to Carolina."

"*South* Carolina."

Gino shrugged. "Whatever the place is called. Somebody made a big mistake. We got the wrong house."

Eva could only hope that heads wouldn't roll over this one, but she saw a glint in Gino's eyes that meant someone was going to get fired unless she could undo the damage. Softening Gino's blows had never been part of Eva's job description, but she'd taken it on because she couldn't stand to see anyone get hurt, even in the vitriolic film industry. Eva had always suspected there was more bark to Gino than bite. But no one would ever know for sure, because over the years she'd always managed to keep Gino from making good his threats.

"What kind of a mistake was made?" Eva asked. She didn't want any names, but she needed the specifics.

She got them. "The contracts are a forgery." Gino glanced at the memo on his desk. "Our people dealt with some guy called Beau Benedict instead of going directly to his mother, who's the owner of the place. The kid signed her name, and no one bothered to double-check. Jerks," Gino added under his breath.

"And Mrs. Benedict has changed her mind?"

"Never made it up in the first place. She was still considering our offer when this Beau chump took it upon himself to forge the thing."

Eva searched her mind quickly. "Don't we already have an advance crew in Corinth?"

"Damn right. A whole second unit and the set designer, all cooling their heels on full salary. Wasting my money," he added, "and you know how I feel about that. Bad enough to have to wait for temperamental actresses to arrive or for bad weather to clear. But I'm damned if I'm gonna let a crew sit around and do nothing because some *kid* tricked my business people."

Eva realized it was going to be up to her to solve this problem. She crossed one long stockinged leg over the other, causing a faint rustle of her skirt's silk lining. She smiled slightly, her brown eyes flashing against her ivory skin, and waited for the challenge from Gino. Because he was still fuming, the challenge was slow in coming.

"I made the decision to shoot *Glory Road* at this place," Gino said, glancing at the memo again, "this

Diligence Hall Plantation. I don't have time to waste on more scouting, so I'm *gonna* shoot it there.''

Eva heard the threat. "What do you want me to do, Gino?"

"I want you to fix it, *cara*. Get on a plane to this . . . Carolina, and fix it, and do it quickly," he added, "because I plan to bring *Glory Road* in on schedule."

This time when the buzzer rang, Gino answered it.

Eva watched with a half smile as he tucked the phone against his shoulder and began speaking in rapid Italian. She listened long enough to get the gist of the conversation. It was another problem that caused no more than a lift of Gino's heavy black eyebrows as he confronted the creative chaos that was a daily part of his business. He was used to it and so, finally, was Eva. She'd survived a few trials by fire herself.

She'd gone to work for Gino knowing a great deal about production, very little about administration and only enough about her employer to realize that he was very protective of those he considered "family." And because of that summer in Italy seven years before, he'd considered Eva family. Since Gino was protective, she was loyal and determined not to question his motives; since Eva was a quick study, Gino was rewarded with a job well done.

Eva was neither the most highly paid member of his staff nor the most powerful, but when it came to difficult, sensitive situations, she was the one Gino called on. She went ahead, clearing the way as negotiator, and she had learned to bring compromise out of chaos. Her instincts were right; her intuition was flawless. If there was a solution, Eva Sinclair would find it; if pressure was needed, she would apply it without making good Gino's threats. Although he continued to threaten, she continued to find answers. The combination had worked well. So far.

While her integrity was taken for granted, her loyalty raised some eyebrows. As Gino and Eva traveled together over the years and across continents, they were followed by speculation about their relationship. Beneath the cool, sophisticated exterior she showed the world, Eva was a very private person. She'd been annoyed by the persistent gossip detailed in tabloids from Rome to Paris to London, but Gino had just laughed. The only problems that bothered him were those dealing with film production.

One was bothering him now as he completed his call with a groan and relit his cigar. "Those foreign crews...such a problem," he murmured while Eva smothered a smile. Since his move to the States, Gino considered himself a Californian; in fact, like many others who'd come from abroad in the very early days of movies, he had adapted with lightning speed, leaving behind everything that was European except the accent—an asset in the film industry.

"This shoot in Rome is going to give me gray hairs," he said. "I got gaffers over there who can't climb, if you can imagine..." Gino shook his head in dismay. "Some crazy fool—probably a graduate of that film school you went to," he threw in, reminding Eva that the only true lessons that could be learned about film were learned on the set, "fell off the light rigging. They give me a gaffer, and he takes a tumble. Can you imagine?"

"Was he hurt?" Eva asked with concern.

Gino shrugged. "I don't know. I guess he must have been. Stopped the shoot for half a day, and now we're looking at a lawsuit."

"We're fully covered, Gino."

"Yeah, yeah," he agreed, "but it's a pain. The paparazzi are all over the place, looking for 'foul play.' They even use the American expression." Gino ran a hand through his curly gray hair. "As if we've got some kind of intrigue going on in Rome. Intrigue," he repeated. "Hell, all we got is a gaffer who can't climb."

"Well, I hope he's going to be all right. Maybe I should go over and see about it," she offered.

"No, *cara*; I want you in Corinth. Tomorrow." He glanced at his watch. "If not today."

Eva smiled. She could make a late flight, she decided, taking into account Gino's concern, which seemed greater to her than the problem. "I've handled contracts more complex than this one in less than a day," she reminded him, sure his worry was unwarranted. "I'll probably still have time to fly to Rome just to make sure—"

"Don't count on getting away that quickly, Eva, until I tell you the rest."

Eva's eyebrows rose. A tendril of blond hair had escaped from the soft roll at the nape of her neck. She tucked it back into place slowly, aware that Gino planned to drag out his dramatic pause, and she determined not to show any overt curiosity.

"Until I tell you about Reese Benedict," Gino completed finally.

This time Eva *was* surprised and showed it. Her brown eyes flashed with interest when she heard the name that intrigued almost everyone; she was no exception.

"The mystery man, eh?" Gino asked with a grin. "The best foreign correspondent this country's ever put on TV. Bright, popular. He challenged people's minds, that one. The whole world listened to his opinions."

"Until a couple of years ago." Eva remembered with a little shiver the tragedy behind Reese Benedict's sudden retirement. "He vanished after his wife was killed in some nameless country by a car bomb that was meant for him."

Gino nodded, not thinking about fate but about his own problem. "Well, he's resurfaced just where we don't want him—in Carolina."

Eva didn't bother to correct her boss. "Do you mean that Reese Benedict belongs to the Benedicts of Diligence Hall Plantation?"

Gino nodded. "*Correcto*. And it looks like he's the one who threw a monkey wrench into my soup," he said, missing his intended metaphor by a mile, much to Eva's amusement. "He's the one putting pressure on the old dame to keep us away from Diligence. Damned strange name."

"Some of those old plantations were named after virtues like that. Patience, Fortitude..."

Gino shook his head, dismissing the Southern peculiarity that was beyond his Mediterranean comprehension. "Well, the man's got a lot of clout, and I guarantee you he'll use it. So you're my weapon, Eva, my beautiful and persuasive six-shooter. Use both barrels to make him see reason. This one is important." He picked up a folder and handed it to her across his desk. "I put down some concessions here. Hold them until last, though. I'm not too crazy about capitulating."

Eva couldn't help smiling at that understatement.

"If you need negotiating room, go ahead and add these to the contract. We'll restore the house, plant trees, landscape and up the fee for the use of their plantation. Beats me, though," he added, "why they're balking. Most people would be glad to have Marchetti Films shooting in their living room."

Eva didn't disagree. She imagined that Gino was right, although she certainly wouldn't welcome a film company into *her* home. Reese Benedict was obviously of similar mind. "What if he isn't impressed by our offers?" Eva didn't have to know the man to predict his response. The newscaster's strong opinions and unswerving courage were common knowledge. He was no pushover; far from it. He'd always gone where he wanted in spite of coups or wars and gotten his story whether from a beggar in a war-torn street or a dictator in an occupied palace. Nothing had ever stopped Reese Benedict, and Eva doubted if Marchetti Films would be an exception.

Gino seemed to be reading her thoughts. "But he has a weakness now, *cara*. He's tired of fighting. Fighting got him nothing but a dead wife."

Eva winced at the bluntness of that remark. She'd never gotten used to Gino's way of expressing himself but continued to hope that his words belied his feelings.

"There's a bottom line, which I guess you've already figured out," Gino added.

Reluctantly Eva nodded.

"We offered these contracts to the Benedict woman in good faith. If her younger son chose to forge them, and she chooses not to honor them, then we've also got a choice: to prosecute. Isn't forgery a felony?"

Eva stood up, and the folds in her cream-colored linen skirt fell perfectly into place. "You know it is, Gino." She flashed a smile that reflected in his tinted glasses. Eva knew what to do; it didn't have to be explained. A hundred times before she'd threatened on his behalf and always managed to avoid delivering. Sometimes Eva couldn't help wondering whether in Italy, before her time, Gino had carried out his threats. It wouldn't have surprised her. Gino Marchetti hadn't gotten to where he was on bluffs alone. Eva could only hope that if she ever failed in her negotiations the outcome would be less harsh than sending a young man to jail.

She turned and began the long walk to the door. "I'd better start clearing off my desk."

"Don't waste too much time on that. Delegate what you can and worry about the rest when you get back. I want you on the plane tonight. If you can make it."

Eva turned and flashed another smile. "I'll make it, Gino. I'll keep you posted."

"I'm sure of that *cara*." He chomped down on his cigar and picked up the phone, indicating he was ready to get back to work. Then he stopped and added an afterthought that was too patently casual not to have been planned. "Franco called."

Eva could feel the thud of her heart against her chest. Strange, she thought, that after so many years just the sound of his name had such an effect on her. They rarely discussed Gino's son because of the painful memories and unhappy thoughts.

Reaching the door, Eva wanted more than anything to open it and leave without asking the question that demanded to be asked. "Is he all right?"

Gino shook his head. It was in moments like this that Eva most clearly saw another side of this tough man. He'd looked long and hard at life and accepted the tricks it played. His son's fate hadn't really surprised him, but occasionally something in his face told her that he deeply wished it had turned out differently.

"He's alive; I guess in that way you could say he's all right. He's in a hospital in Austria this time. He calls it a health spa, but that doesn't fool me. I know the place. He's drying out from too much liquor, or too many drugs. Or maybe just an overabundance of the good life."

Eva wanted to get out of there, leave without another word about Franco Marchetti, but she couldn't. She had to soothe even though nothing could really help. "At least he's getting good care, Gino." She tried to keep her voice positive. "That counts for something."

Gino didn't respond, but Eva read his thoughts. He was concerned about her, worrying that she was still hiding behind her job to avoid being hurt again. It happened to everyone, he'd often told Eva, calling his philosophy realism, not pessimism. But she knew he fretted over her, keeping her nearby, never quite removed from the memory that haunted them both. She could sense he wanted to offer advice, as he often did, tell her to get on with that part of her life that had been interrupted seven years ago and never taken up again.

Eva broke the tense silence by opening the heavy walnut door. "I'll call from South Carolina, Gino," she said.

He waved the cigar in a smoky farewell, letting her go. "I'm counting on you, *cara*."

He *could* count on her, Eva thought as she walked down the hall to her office, her mind on Italy seven years before—the beginning, the end, and finally the new beginning. Franco. And then Gino.

She'd been a most unlikely girl to turn up in Rome, Italy. Eva knew that as well as anyone. The daughter of a dry-goods store owner, born and reared in a midsize Wisconsin town, she'd been expected by her parents to settle down like her older sisters, marry and be blessed—as they were—with beautiful strong children. That's what Eva had expected, too; she was as surprised as everyone else when she applied for the fellowship to study film in Italy, even more surprised when she won.

Or so she told everyone. But it wasn't exactly true. There'd always been a glimmer of hope that something wonderful would happen to her. She'd been bright, the smartest one in her class, and pretty, too, pretty enough to be a movie star. But that wasn't Eva's goal. She wanted *something* to do with movies, but she couldn't find the words to explain; she didn't even know if there were words for what she wanted. Confused, Eva took the few courses her school offered in photography and rudimentary filmmaking. Then, still doubting her skill and unsure of her goals, she headed for Italy, journeying out of the Midwest for the first time in her life and leaving behind a very confused family.

She never finished film school; she didn't even finish the first year. But because of Franco, his father and what happened that long ago summer in Rome, she found the place in film that she'd always been looking for. An often unkind and always uncertain fate brought her to Marchetti Films, where she became assistant to the renowned producer, Gino Marchetti. She traveled to locations and studios and conference rooms across the country and around the world. The next stop, less exciting than most, was Corinth, South Carolina.

Eva instructed her secretary to book a late flight to the East Coast, glanced at her watch and found she had plenty of time to bathe and pack and make it out tonight, as Gino wished. She pulled several manila folders from her desk drawer and flipped through information on the *Glory Road* project, discarding what wasn't pertinent and organizing the rest. The glossy location shots of Diligence Hall were as impressive as she remembered from the pre-production meeting.

One of the shots, showing a broad river running through the plantation, its black waters guarded by huge live oak trees that bent low to almost caress the water, was delicate if a little spooky. "Perfect," Eva said aloud as she flipped through the photographs, admired the wide lawns, rolling hills, sweeping gardens and stopped at a picture of the house itself.

It was an imposing Georgian structure, rectangular, with lead-paned front windows, a hooded door and a corniced roof topped by four tall chimneys. The red brick was generously covered by ivy, and the stately house glowed in a late afternoon sun. Eva smiled, remembering the screenwriter's expression when he'd first seen the pictures of Diligence—a place that had been nothing more than a figment of his imagination.

The inside would need work to accommodate the action of the film. Some stage dressing would be necessary. Though the antique furnishings had been little changed or even rearranged, Eva suspected, over the years. She shook her head in wonder. This was just the place for the story about two diverse characters caught in their own conflict after World War II, when an idealistic young soldier brings his new bride home to the place where his family has lived for generations. Diligence Hall offered just the right contrast with the woman's cacophonous life in a Northern city.

Eva remembered from research reports that the house had miraculously withstood the turmoil of the American Revolution and the Civil War, numerous hurricanes, the economic fluctuations from the days when cotton was king through the carpetbaggers and into the twentieth century with its flappers, bootleggers and a great depression. Still it stood, serene and beautiful, defying the mundane trivialities of the world around it, peaceful, a sanctuary—a refuge. Looking at the softly luminescent picture, Eva could almost feel the calm.

Two thousand miles across the country, it was already dark, but Diligence Hall was far from calm. It was ablaze with light, and angry voices floated out the library window into the hot summer air.

"What the hell were you thinking when you signed Mother's name to the contract, Beau? Of all the ignorant, ridiculous—" The speaker tried to maintain control; yelling wasn't his style. But even with his voice raised, he didn't lose the mellowness, the modulation that was famous all over the world and had come with many hours of network newscasts. The tone was ingrained in his voice now. "I just don't understand your motivation, Beau," he added. The control was back.

A woman's voice interrupted. "Now, son, I'm sure Beau—"

"Let him speak for himself, Mother."

"That's right, let me speak for myself," came the response, strongly Southern and obviously edged with tenseness. Beau turned toward his brother. "I didn't think having a film company here would cause any problems. And we need the money...."

Reese Benedict stiffened but didn't turn from the window, where he stood resolutely, looking across the vibrantly green lawn that sloped toward the river. "What do you mean by 'we need the money'?" he asked and then moved away, not toward his brother but to a corner of the room where his mother sat on a rose-colored Queen Anne chair, which her very presence seemed to dignify.

"What I meant," Beau tried to explain, "was that we could always *use* the money."

Reese's eyes sought his mother's questioningly. He tried to read something deeper than what she offered with her smile, but like everyone else caught in her gaze, he was struck by its glow. At fifty-six, Lacy Benedict radiated a lasting beauty. Her eyes were deep blue and set wide apart, giving her a look of mild surprise and good humor. Her skin, bathed in milk and honey and rarely touched by the sun, maintained its youthful clarity, and her strawberry blond hair had kept its soft color—with frequent trips to the beauty parlor on Main Street. Like her younger son, Beau, she was slim, almost fragile, but also like him, there was a wiry strength beneath this seeming fragility. Reese didn't return her smile. "I wasn't aware of financial problems here, Mother."

"Reese, darling, you know it's always difficult to keep Diligence on an even keel...."

"And just as difficult to come to me for help, it seems. What are the problems, Mother?" He sat down on the sofa opposite her.

"Well, there's nothing specific, darling. Our tenants are getting older, and none of the young people want to farm any more. Of course, we still have the timber, but I can't bear to cut our lovely trees." She smiled innocently. This time Reese returned the smile, noticing that his mother was coming dangerously close to batting her eyelashes. "I just can't imagine anyone these days who doesn't worry about money," she continued. "As Beau said, we could always use a little extra...."

Reese's brows drew together. "Don't tell me that means you favor this preposterous idea of letting an aggregation of charlatans overrun Diligence?"

"What do you mean by charlatans?" Beau interjected.

"Just what you think. They're self-important Hollywood types who care only for their movies—or films, as they prefer to call them these days—at the expense of everyone and everything else. I won't have them desecrating this house."

Beau's blue eyes were the exact color of his mother's, but they flashed almost purple when he was angry. He was much like his mother, although he often lacked her gracious Southern manner—especially tonight. "Why do you have to assume they're so terrible?" he asked, not waiting for a response. "That's a typically arrogant remark, Reese. The location people I've met with—"

"Spare me the details, Beau. I've dealt with television and film people for more than fifteen years, and I know exactly what they're like. Exactly." Beau's pale skin reddened to the color of his hair, and Reese knew it was time to temper any tone that Beau might interpret as condescending. He didn't want to hurt the boy or make a fool of him, but neither was Reese going to stand for his brother pandering to Marchetti representatives. That kind of life and those associated with it were just what Reese had come home to escape. "I've seen it all," he told his brother, "and I don't want any part of it here."

"But I do!" Beau shouted. "You've seen it all; I haven't seen anything. You've been gone since high school—first to get your journalism degree at Missouri, then an advanced degree at Columbia, then a job on television, and finally network newscaster. London, Paris, the Middle East—'' At that, Beau broke off, seeing the look of torture on his brother's face and realizing sharply that the Middle East was where Barbara had lost her life.

"Anyhow," he finished lamely, "I've been stuck here in Corinth, going to the local college and managing Diligence. Maybe if I'm lucky, I get a big weekend in Atlanta."

"I'm afraid that's my fault," Lacy interjected. "I wanted you here with me after Reese left...."

"It's not your fault, Mother. I chose to stay, but now I'm ready for something more. The Marchetti's proposal was a chance to get some excitement in my life."

"You certainly achieved that—by forging Mother's name," came the sarcastic reply.

"I didn't want to give you a chance to change her mind and ruin it for me just when I was ready to make things happen," Beau responded angrily.

Lacy, watching her two sons, one fair and blond and so like her, the other...the other so like his father. Physically different, they were equally full of emotion and determination and a bit too old for a fist fight, Lacy decided as she broke in once more. "Now, boys, let's be reasonable, and I'm sure we can work this out."

"There's only one way to work it out," Reese said, "and that's for the film company to pack up and leave. There's a handful of them around now, but do you know what it'll be like when the rest of the crew arrives? They'll invade every corner of our lives with cables and cameras and recording systems and scaffolding. Good Lord, just the thought of the noise and clamor, the take-out food scattered from one end of Diligence to the other... I just can't let you do this, Mother. We'll have no privacy left."

Lacy looked helplessly at her son. He'd come back to Diligence a changed man. Once he'd faced the world and all it had to offer; now he couldn't stand the thought of a little commotion. He wanted only to hide away—and Beau wanted to take up the gauntlet, taste the glamour and excitement that had once belonged to Reese. Unfortunately, Beau hadn't gone about it in the best way. But Lacy was sure everything would work out. She had great faith in destiny; it had always been on her side. Meanwhile, she might as well tell Reese the rest, Lacy decided.

"I'm not sure we can settle anything yet," she said with a charming smile in the direction of her older son, "since Marchetti Films is sending out someone from the administrative office to talk with us. We might as well wait until—"

"When was this decided?" Reese asked. "I seem to be getting a lot of delayed news."

"Well, son, you stay shut up in the guest house most of the time, and I can't keep sending the servants out there after you. I simply wait until you surface," she added with a demure smile. "The woman who's coming is Marchetti's assistant."

Reese's hand came down hard on the arm of the Sheraton sofa, and he just barely held back an expletive that would have seriously offended his mother. "That's all we need," he said, "some tough, hard-nosed woman who thinks she's going to push us into doing what her boss Marchetti wants. Well, whoever this special assistant is, she's got a surprise in store. No one is filming on Benedict property—not if I have anything to do with it."

"When's she coming?" Beau asked, his interest piqued.

Lacy glanced at her watch. "In about eight hours," she answered, ignoring Reese's scowl and rewarding Beau's smile with one of her own.

# Chapter 2

By the time Eva reached Corinth, South Carolina, it was nearly noon the following day. "I believe this is what's known as 'off the beaten path,'" she commented to Dan Morrow as she collapsed onto her bed at her motel.

Dan brought in her bag from the car, quickly closed the door and wiped his forehead with a bright blue handkerchief. "Forty miles from what's laughingly referred to as an airport and hundreds of miles from civilization as we know it." He fell onto the bed beside her. "I imagine you've been in and out of some remote spots in your career with Gino, but let me tell you, remoteness has met its match here. One forgets it's the twentieth century down *hee-ah*," he drawled, attempting to imitate the sound, which Eva agreed was unlike any other Southern accent.

"It's because this is the so-called 'low country,'" Dan explained. "These people have an accent all their own. But it's not the way they *talk* that drives me crazy, it's the way they *move*. Lord, it's maddening. My dear, slow motion was never so slow. Why, just the other day when I stopped by the Dairy Queen—"

"For an ice cream cone?" Eva asked incredulously.

"Even those of us who're fabulous set designers in the film industry are entitled to our sinful indulgences," Dan responded. "Well, I stood in line at the Dairy Queen for the better part of half an hour and listened to every detail of the graduation prom. I didn't know that it was possible to take *sooo* long to fill a cone from one of those machines. I think the appliances work at a different speed here in Corinth." Getting the laugh he expected, Dan continued, "However, I've figured out the problem."

Eva languidly dragged herself from the bed and began unpacking as she waited for Dan's explanation.

"It's the humidity," he informed her. "Walking outside in midafternoon is like making your way through molasses. Pretty soon we'll all be moving just like the locals and talking like them—all because of the weather. It gets you down, honey," he drawled, getting into his role. "You have to avoid the great outdoors at all costs."

Eva laughed as she recalled their mad dash from the airport at a speed nowhere near legal, which Dan had declared was necessary. "The heat comes right off the asphalt through the bottom of the car. The only way to keep cool is to outrun it."

"Well, we certainly tried," Eva said as she shook the wrinkles out of a linen dress and hung it in the closet.

"And what about the moss? It's everywhere," Dan said with a shudder. "I have the distinct feeling when

I'm out *ther-ah*," he said, gesturing dramatically beyond the curtained windows of the room, "that I'm walking right through the middle of an Edgar Allan Poe story."

"Think of it as 'atmosphere' for the film," Eva said with a grin, realizing how beautifully the moss-covered trees would photograph. The big line oaks sprang from rich black soil on each side of the roadways, their branches almost meeting overhead. She'd been fascinated as she looked up during the drive at the dappled sunlight shining through the delicate webs of moss. "Like light through the windows of a cathedral," she told Dan. "It was beautiful."

Eerie was Dan's word. " 'Let me out of here' is all I can think when I drive those narrow roads that tunnel through the moss. It's like some kind of bizarre jungle. But you don't dare leave because of the heat, so the challenge becomes the race from car to motel. Can't even venture outside at night," he added, "because of the mosquitoes. They're as big as elephants."

Eva laughed. "I can see you've gotten a lot of work done for Marchetti while you've been here, Danny."

"Won't let me in, my dear," he said simply.

"Who won't?"

"Reese Benedict, that's who, as I'm sure you know. I went out there and got my photos of the interior so I could start working on the set changes. Next day he was standing on the—whaddaya call it—veranda.

" 'There's been a mistake,' he says in that voice all America loves to hear. Or once did. 'What do you mean mistake?' I ask, and he tells me Marchetti isn't filming at his family home, as I believe he called it, so I should go along back to Hollywood. Obviously," Danny added, "he isn't aware that I'm the famous set designer, Dan Morrow, of East Eleventh Street, New York City. Anyway, I beat it. What was I going to do, challenge him to a duel?''

Dan fell back onto the bed, arms outstretched. "So I returned to this lovely motel with its green-and-yellow flowered bedspreads and matching curtains," he said sarcastically, "and waited for Gino to tell me what to do. Also in green-and-yellow land are a few kids on the advance crew and a casting assistant who's supposed to be hiring extras. They haven't done *anything*."

"Well, it'll all be over tomorrow," Eva promised.

"And we can go home?"

"Nope. You can go to work."

Dan groaned and then added on a more hopeful note. "Don't be so sure of that until you encounter the famous TV personality."

Eva drove out along Main Street toward Diligence Hall. The town of Corinth wasn't lacking in charm, only modernity. The buildings were old, some of them wood-framed, a few concrete. Grass peeked through cracks in the sidewalk, the stoplight was a relic from the past and a hound dog slept in the doorway of a store. Eva shook her head in wonder. Very little set decorating would be necessary to take Corinth back to the 1940's. It was basically still there.

The town wouldn't be a problem, but Danny was right about one possible impediment: Reese Benedict. For a moment, Eva felt a little thrill of excitement. Reese was a formidable opponent, but all the cards were in her hands; there was no way she could lose unless Reese allowed his brother to go to jail.

She wondered if that could be his plan and then shook her head. It wasn't possible. The man was courageous; he might well have gone to jail himself for a principle—even one as absurd, to Eva's mind, as this. But she couldn't imagine Reese Benedict allowing his brother to be arrested for forgery.

Then why was he challenging Gino when he obviously couldn't win? The answer was simple: conceit. Reese Benedict believed in the force of his personality. And she imagined that his confidence would grow even stronger when he found out that Gino had sent a woman to represent him. Seeing Eva, Reese might ease up, let his defenses down a little, use his charm. She smiled when she thought how useless that charm was going to be.

Eva made the turn off the main road that was indicated on the map Dan had drawn for her, put on her sunglasses against the afternoon glare and turned the air-conditioning all the way up. Danny was right about something else: the heat was stupefying.

Looming in the distance after a sharp turn in the road, the house surprised Eva. Something of the past, a sense of timelessness, hung over Diligence Hall. She could almost feel the decades drop away as she drove toward it. Following the circular gravel drive, she pulled the car up in front of the house. Two tiers of steps, bordered by a neatly trimmed hedge, led to the porch. On the top step stood a handsome young man, very blond, dressed in fawn-colored slacks and a sport shirt and looking cool and crisp in the heat.

"I'm Beau Benedict," he said in a voice that was a little shaky, offering a smile that was a little hesitant. Beneath the weather-defying exterior, he was less than confident. Eva didn't blame him. Gino Marchetti was nowhere to be seen, but his presence went with his representatives wherever they travelled. He was well represented here by Eva Sinclair, who was far more businesslike but just as cool as Beau—for the moment at least, Eva thought, hoping that the heat wouldn't wilt her before she got inside.

They shook hands, and Eva could feel nervousness in Beau's grasp. But she felt strength there, too. He was a proud young man from a proud family.

"Mother is on the veranda in back," he said, leading her up the steps and adding, "waiting with my brother."

The house was air-conditioned. Eva breathed a little sigh of relief that Beau interpreted correctly. "Yes, we've air-conditioned the downstairs and a few of the bedrooms, but Mother still prefers to sit out on the porch. It's shaded from the sun," he assured Eva. "She's just never gotten used to what she calls manufactured air."

Eva laughed, sure she was going to like Lacy Benedict.

She did, immediately. Lacy greeted her guest with a graciousness that was an unaffected part of her upbringing, but she didn't even try to hide the embarrassment. "I just can't imagine how all this happened, but I know you're going to be able to help us straighten it out." She smiled warmly and advised Beau, "I think we would like some refreshment. Would iced tea suit you, Miss Sinclair?"

"Perfectly," Eva answered.

Lacy then completed the introductions, indicating the third person on the porch. "This is my older son, Reese."

Eva hadn't failed to notice him even though she'd tried to concentrate on the charming old veranda, its porch swing, chintz sofa, flagstone floor, and ample green wooden chairs. But her gaze was drawn back to him; he eclipsed all the rest, filled her vision—and he wasn't even facing her.

He stood at one end of the porch, looking out over the river, almost as if he were simply another element of nature. Only when his mother spoke his name did he turn, and Eva knew immediately that she was going to have a problem. She'd been in many tight situations when negotiating for Gino, but no one had ever distracted her, no matter how powerful the personality or the position. Reese Benedict was the first exception. His eyes caught and held her in their gray gaze. She'd seen him on television enough times to remember the color, but not their depth or their intensity.

They nodded politely rather than shaking hands, sizing each other up as if to prepare for battle. He was tall, much taller than she'd expected, not so much thin as lanky. His dark hair had evidently been brushed from his face earlier in the day but had fallen back over his forehead. He reached up and unconsciously smoothed it back again, but a few strands were persistent. Eva suspected that the use of hair spray had been necessary when he'd appeared on television. It wasn't used now. Now his appearance was casual—the jeans, the polo shirt, even his stance—but not without flair. Eva wished she'd dressed more simply instead of choosing white silk and pearls.

Not more than a few seconds passed before she regained her composure, silently cursed herself for losing it and made a promise that it would never happen again. Lacy didn't seem to have noticed; Eva wasn't sure about Reese.

"Did you have trouble finding us?" Lacy asked.

"Not at all," Eva replied and rejoiced that her voice was as calm as she was now. "And please call me Eva," she added.

Beau returned and dropped into a rocker beside Eva. "It's not difficult to find anything in Corinth. Just go down to Main Street and turn left or right."

"Well, I must admit that I had a map, drawn by our set designer and I'd seen the location photographs, of course."

There was an obvious tensing around the porch. Lacy, who was elegantly arranged on the chintz sofa, sat up a little straighter. Beau planted his feet on the floor and stopped rocking. Reese turned toward the river again, but Eva saw his back grow rigid. She knew what she was doing; the mention of the film hadn't been accidental. She had an agenda, and it was time to get to it.

But there was a delaying tactic to contend with. The iced tea was delivered by a servant whose slow gait was part Southern, part age and part arthritis. Lacy poured the cold drinks into crystal glasses, and Eva realized that this refreshment pause had indeed been planned—not by Reese but by his mother, the slim, delicate woman who was running the show.

Eva was glad to have her in charge, for that meant her son would play only a minor role. Diligence, after all, belonged to Lacy Benedict; Reese, who'd been years absent from the plantation, was only a bystander and could do no more than make suggestions. Lacy was the one whom she had to convince. Eva hoped she could do so without even using Gino's threat.

After politely sipping the tangy iced tea and commenting on the beauty of the surroundings, Eva withdrew the contract from her briefcase. It was time for business.

"All of you are aware of the terms of this agreement," she said, "and what Mr. Marchetti would like—"

Reese interrupted, quietly but with authority. "The contract, as you know, Ms. Sinclair, wasn't signed by my mother at all and is therefore null and void." He was the only one still standing, but he seemed to be the most relaxed. He even smiled at Eva, and for a moment she thought he was toying with her, testing to see if she knew what she was doing. In the world he'd once been a part of, Reese had no doubt heard the rumor about Gino and his assistant; for all he knew, it could be true.

Eva decided to wait for Lacy. The pause was effective, and Lacy cooperated.

"Reese, dear," Lacy said with the slightest bit of reproach in her tone, "Eva has just arrived, and we do owe her the courtesy of listening. After all, we've caused a certain amount of inadvertent trouble for those people who flew out here from Hollywood—"

"Mother, for God's sake," Reese said, dismissing Hollywood with a shake of his head.

But Eva didn't let Lacy's remark go unanswered. "You're perfectly right, Mrs. Benedict. This misunderstanding has thrown us behind schedule, which is why we need to get it cleared up right away so that we can begin shooting."

"You can begin shooting any time," Reese said, "anywhere. As long as it's not at Diligence Hall. There are dozens of other plantations along the southeastern coast whose owners would probably be delighted to have Hollywood in their backyard."

Eva could feel her anger rising. The man was infuriating in his determination to keep her from making a point, but she was equally determined to have her say. "You're perfectly right, Mr. Benedict," she responded without a trace of anger. "But there's no place as perfect as Diligence for the filming of—" she smiled at Lacy and managed to keep herself from adding a sweeping gesture along with the film's title—"*Glory Road*."

"What a wonderful name!" Lacy said, as Eva had hoped she would.

"Is it about the war Between the States?" Beau asked.

Eva shook her head. "No, it takes place almost a century later, after World War II, when a young soldier brings his new bride home on her first visit to the South. *Glory Road* is more of a figurative than a literal title." Eva didn't dare glance in the direction of Reese Benedict, who, she was certain, had a look of scorn on his face. Lacy and Beau, however, were intrigued.

"Diligence Hall is the soldier's home?" Beau asked.

"Yes, his family has lived here for generations," Eva responded, and from the sofa Lacy nodded appreciatively. "Since the story is set in the 1940s, it was felt that the town of Corinth would be perfect. Its charm hasn't changed in so many years. Of course, that's part of the problem for the girl, who's so used to the bustle of city life. Diligence Hall is a difficult place for her to understand. She comes from a family that has no background—almost as if it began with her. Of course, this creates problems difficult even for their strong love to overcome."

"How does it end?" Beau asked.

"The ending's still unresolved," Eva answered, and then she caught Reese's eye and saw that he was smiling knowingly.

"How strange," Lacy said.

"That's Mr. Marchetti's style, Mother," Reese interjected. "But whatever happens, I expect there'll be an abundance of moody scenes with the heroine becoming almost suicidal."

"Not exactly," Eva said, aware that he had the right idea; Gino's projects were usually far from cheerful in their themes.

"That's all right," Lacy decided. "I'm sure it'll be very interesting."

"Mother, please don't be taken in by this artistic nonsense. No matter what the subject, it'll be total chaos to have a film crew at Diligence," he said firmly, "making a shambles of our home and our lives."

Eva spoke just as firmly. "Even with your contempt for the film industry—"

But she wasn't allowed to finish her thought. "Only that portion of it that takes advantage of the starstruck," Reese interrupted, causing Beau to react with a silent flush.

"—I'd appreciate it if you would at least listen to our offer," Eva continued as if she hadn't been interrupted.

"I've read the contract, Ms. Sinclair."

Eva came right back. "Mr. Marchetti has made further concessions." She thought she saw Reese's eyebrow lift slightly. "Which," she continued, "he certainly wasn't obligated to make. But understanding your concern about the disruption of life at Diligence Hall *when* we film here," she added, emphasizing the inevitability of the shooting, "we've added the following..."

Eva read from the new contract that detailed plans for restoration, landscaping and repainting. "Of course, we'll make any improvements you feel necessary, at our expense. Anything unsuitable to you will be restored to its original state when we complete filming." She paused for a moment. "The fee initially quoted for the use of the house during the weeks our crew will be here has been doubled."

Beau let out a low whistle, which Reese silenced with a hard look. But Eva was watching Lacy as she added, "All this will be possible when Mrs. Benedict signs the contract."

The emotions playing over Lacy's face were in turn doubtful, hesitant, eager. Clearly, she saw the possibility of refurbishing Diligence Hall. "I wonder," she said, "if the floor in the main kitchen could be replaced. Those planks arc pine, and oak would be so much more functional—and attractive."

"I'm sure that would be no problem," Eva said, making a note.

"Just a moment, Ms. Sinclair. Nothing has been settled here." Reese moved for the first time, just a slight shift of his weight, but Eva noticed and braced herself. "I can handle any improvements my mother feels are necessary at Diligence Hall without bringing in a film crew. That's why I'm here, Mother," he said, and there was an intensity in those words that made Eva back off. She was dealing with a man of great emotional depth. She had to avoid stepping on his pride.

"Mr. Benedict," Eva answered carefully, "what we're offering is no more or less than a good business deal. Your mother will be well compensated for the use of her home during the weeks of shooting." Eva had reached a quick conclusion: Lacy had pride, too, and this was her house. There were certain things she would accept from her son, but earning them on her own was much more appealing to her. Lacy didn't want Reese's charity; she was willing to work for what she could get for Diligence Hall—or bargain for it. With Gino, Lacy could bargain.

"Since your mother is an intelligent woman who certainly knows what she wants," Eva continued, "I imagine she can make her own decision based on the merits of the situation."

When that incited no response from Reese, Eva realized that she'd been right. Lacy made the decisions here; Lacy held the power.

But Lacy still wasn't quite ready to be pushed. Not yet. She had her doubts, too, which she expressed. "What will they be like, these film people? Will they be careful with my things, my antiques, my mementos from all the years that the Benedicts have been here? It's such a grand home," she said with obvious feeling, "and I wouldn't want anyone here who was impolite or inconsiderate...."

"Mother, are you serious?" Reese asked. "We aren't talking about weekend guests. We're talking about the kind of people you wouldn't have working in the yard, much less entering your home. Not only will your belongings not be safe from damage, they probably won't be safe from theft."

Before Eva could respond, Reese crossed to the sofa where his mother sat. Lacy was clearly confused, and he was prepared to end the matter quickly. "Our home is not for public display," he said to Eva with finality. "And now, if you don't mind, I think the matter can rest here. Beau, please be good enough to show Ms. Sinclair to her car."

"Reese—" Lacy began in embarrassment.

But Eva needed no protection from Reese Benedict's arrogant presumption. She was quite capable of taking care of herself. "We have more at stake here than you seem to realize," she said firmly. After first assuring Lacy that her antiques would be treated with respect and there would be no robbery at Diligence Hall, she directed the rest to Reese, and he knew what was coming. "I'd appreciate it if you would sit down and listen to me."

Their eyes met and locked. Although Reese didn't sit down, he returned to his place at the front of the porch and waited.

Eva let the pause draw out, not just for dramatic impact, although she realized its effectiveness. She also needed the time to gather her thoughts in order to present the ultimatum cleanly and efficiently. "I came here in good faith to talk to all of you, but especially Mrs. Benedict." She looked directly at Lacy. "I believe that Marchetti Films has been fair—more than fair." Eva's dark eyes cut quickly toward Reese and then back to his mother.

"We've dealt honestly and straightforwardly with you from the beginning," she reminded them. "On the other hand—" and this time her pause was clearly dramatic "—we have not received the same consideration." Eva didn't look directly at Beau, but out of the corner of her eye she could see his embarrassed face. "Your son is guilty of forgery, Mrs. Benedict. That's a felony as I'm sure you and your lawyers are aware. If Mr. Marchetti chooses, he can swear out a warrant for Beau's arrest."

There it was. The threat. Reese had known she had it; in fact, he'd forced her to use it. Yet he must actually have thought that he could intimidate her or charm her into refraining from making the threat.

Beau and Lacy were both speaking at once, Beau moaning that he didn't realize the consequence of his actions, Lacy wondering whether Gino would actually send her son to jail. Reese was silent. He must have known the game was over. Marchetti films would be shooting *Glory Road* right here, just as they'd planned. There was nothing he could do about it now.

Eva was answering Lacy's question. "Mr. Marchetti *would* have your son arrested, Mrs. Benedict. This isn't an idle threat, I assure you. Like any other businessman in this position, he'd have no other choice."

"Then I have no choice, either," Lacy said. "I'll sign the contract, and we'll make the best of having these people in our home."

"Mrs. Benedict," Eva said assuredly, "Diligence Hall will be treated with respect. I guarantee that you'll have no regrets at all about your decision."

"It might be expedient to have such a guarantee written into the contract," Reese said. This was his first statement since his mother's decision had been made.

"The contracts can't be changed at this point, Mr. Benedict," Eva answered. "You'll have to take my word for it."

Lacy was perfectly willing to do so. "I'm sure everything will be just fine," she said optimistically, and Eva realized that this was the decision Lacy had wanted to make from the beginning. And once she'd made it, Reese didn't need to stay around for further discussion; his part was over. He was clearly displeased, though Eva thought she saw a hint of humor in his gray eyes. It wasn't in his voice, however.

"I'm sure Mr. Marchetti will be very pleased with the outcome of this meeting," he said to Eva before he left. "You can tell him when you call that you earned your keep today."

Before Eva could respond to the implied slur, Reese turned and stalked out through the porch door, crossing the yard and disappearing into the trees.

"Reese has always been strong minded," Lacy offered in the way of an apology for her son, even though she hadn't caught the innuendo in his last remark. "He's been even more adamant since he came back to Diligence. He lives down there in the woods," she explained, "in our guest cottage. He really prefers it there. I argued with him at first, but now I'm relieved. With these movie people coming..."

While Lacy went on about her older son and his aversion to having strangers at Diligence, Eva handed her the contract and a pen. Lacy signed almost automatically, before any of them realized it. Then all three of them looked at one another with a collective sigh of relief, and Beau jumped up to pump Eva's hand with boyish enthusiasm.

"I'm sure no one will regret the decision," Eva said as Beau gave her hand a final shake before leaving the two women alone on the veranda.

"Regret it?" he called out from the hall, "I'm going to love every minute of it!"

Lacy wasn't quite so sure, as Eva could tell from the frown that creased her brow. "I know these people will be...different," she said after a pause. "Not like those we're used to associating with."

Eva nodded. "That's true; they'll be different, but I think you'll enjoy them. In fact, I'm sure of it." Lacy Benedict was a spirited woman. She wasn't going to sit by and worry about her mementos; she'd be in the middle of the action when *Glory Road* was filmed, having the time of her life.

"Tell me all about Marchetti Films," Lacy said, beginning to enjoy herself now that her sons had left and gesturing for Eva to join her on the sofa. "I've always been so curious about Mr. Marchetti."

Eva laughed and sat down beside the older woman. "He's quite a man," she admitted.

"Traveling around the world," Lacy said, "making deals, raising money for projects.... Oh, I've read all about him in the magazines. He'll be here, won't he?"

"Not right away. He's the producer of *Glory Road*, but—"

"The director will be here, of course."

"Yes," Eva replied.

"And he's very famous, too?"

"Quite famous—and talented," Eva added. "Our second unit director is already here. He and the crew will be shooting for some time before the others arrive, so things shouldn't be too disruptive for you."

"Oh, I won't mind, I'm sure," Lacy said, already into the spirit. "Now, Eva, can I just ask you about...well, about you and Mr. Marchetti. I don't mean to be rude, but I've read..."

Eva laughed, aware that she was beginning to find more amusement than pain in that old rumor. "I hate to disappoint you, but the gossip is unfounded. Gino's always laughed it away, and sometimes I think he even encourages the speculation for publicity. The fact is, he's been happily married for thirty years, and both he and his wife are very dear to me."

"Well," Lacy said, "at least it's exciting to travel all over the world for him. And now here you are at Diligence Hall. You'll be staying for the filming, won't you?" she asked.

"For a while, until the designer and second unit finish their work." Eva had made the decision to stay on just after she confronted Reese Benedict. Dan wasn't always on good behavior, and a run-in with Reese was likely. She'd need to be here as a buffer until the cast and director arrived and everything was in place.

"Then stay with us," Lacy offered suddenly.

Eva didn't have time to object. Lacy was already into her spiel. By the time it was over, Eva had agreed to be a guest in Lacy Benedict's home for the preliminary shooting and promised to abandon The Corinth Columns Motel that very night. Eva had never stayed in anyone's home on location, even when Gino insisted that she lodge with friends of his. Yet she found herself a willing guest at Diligence Hall. She put it all down to the effects of Southern hospitality, and as she left, she further agreed to call Lacy by her first name.

Returning to the motel to pack, Eva began to wonder if the spur-of-the-moment decision had been a rational one. Reese Benedict lived only a few hundred yards away from Diligence, and Reese Benedict had caused her to lose her composure. Briefly, it was true, but it had been the only time in the years she'd worked for Gino.

She had a job to do in the next few days, to make sure that the preliminary work was completed on time and without problems, and she had the feeling that Reese wasn't going to make her job either easy or pleasant. Being close to him in a social setting might not be a good idea. In a remote way, he'd tried to work his charm on her to achieve his purpose, and he'd failed. But he was no less charming for it, no less charismatic....

An hour later, the door of her motel room burst open to reveal a hopeful Danny. "Well? Are we getting out of this place?"

"Afraid not. The contracts are signed. I'm getting ready to call Gino with the news."

"Damn. And here it is dinnertime again, and not a good restaurant within fifty miles."

# Chapter 3

As Eva reached for the phone to call Gino, she remembered what Reese Benedict had said. *You can tell him when you call that you've earned your keep today.* She'd expected a man of Reese's professional acumen and personal sophistication to be above such rudeness. She'd obviously expected too much.

Waiting to get through to Gino, Eva recalled Reese's attempts to put her down. A man acting from ego, she'd thought at first; then she'd realized it might have been frustration, even despair. The haven that he'd hoped to find when he left the real world and returned to Diligence was quickly going public, and he considered her the cause. She'd seen the spark of anger in his eyes, but she'd seen something else—a pain—when he'd spoken of taking care of his family. He was a complex man and not one to be taken lightly.

Eva was glad she'd decided to stay. She would treat him fairly and honestly, not just to protect his psyche but to protect Gino's film. There wouldn't be time for strife.

Eva finally got through to her boss and relayed the news. It was just what he liked to hear; furthermore, it was just what he expected to hear. Failure wasn't in Gino's vocabulary, and it never occurred to him to expect anything but success from his staff since they were a part of Marchetti Films. Eva was always relieved when she lived up to his expectations.

"What's the story on these Benedicts?" was Gino's question.

"The boy, Beau, is a likable young man who let his desire for excitement almost land him in jail. The older brother is a different matter."

Gino grunted in agreement, and Eva waited for him to exhale the smoke from his cigar. "What about the dame?"

"She's lovely, a charming and aristocratic Southern lady."

"She owns the place, right? She's the boss."

"Yes," Eva agreed.

"Then get in good with her," Gino ordered. "Don't worry about the other two."

"It's already done, Gino. Because of the tension— not to mention Dan's sometimes crazy personality—I think it would be a good idea for me to stay around for a while. Lacy's invited me to be a guest at Diligence Hall."

"That's my girl. I've taught you well, Eva; you know whom to use."

Eva recoiled slightly at the description of what was actually a friendship developing between her and Lacy Benedict. But Gino was pleased and her job was done, and she'd just ignore his remark, which was more jargon than his true feelings, anyway.

"I was gonna tell you to stay on anyhow, so it works out well," he continued. "I got one more little job for you."

Eva was curious.

"Find me a piece of land down there in Corinth."

Her curiosity turned to perplexity.

"About thirty or forty acres." Gino went on to describe what he was looking for while Eva took careful notes. When he'd finished she asked the purpose of his request, but she had the feeling she wasn't going to get a straight answer.

She didn't. "You'll know in time, *cara*. For now, just do it, *capisce*? Do it for Gino."

As usual, Eva agreed, and she hung up knowing that she'd always agree. As different as they were, her affection for Gino was deep and lasting. In a very real way, he'd saved her life, taking her in when she'd been desperate, and in time becoming her mentor.

Love had brought them together—not Eva's love for Gino, but for his son, Franco Marchetti. He'd been her lover, and he remained a fragile bond between Gino and Eva, almost a specter. He was a man who'd tasted all of life and then when he'd finished, still wasn't satisfied. For a time, when she'd first met Franco, fallen in love and left film school to live with him, Eva, too, had met life with the same enthusiasm. But he'd very quickly left her behind. The pace became too much for her; she couldn't keep up. Soon, she no longer wanted to. Yet she'd desperately tried to hold on to him and what they had.

But it was too late for Franco. That realization had been hard to accept, but finally, at the end, when it was all over Eva went to his father. She begged Gino, the one person she knew she could depend on, for the fare to go back to the States.

Gino had declined. He wanted her to stay and re-capture her self-esteem, which had hit rock bottom; he wanted Eva to prove herself—to herself. She did. And her gratitude to Gino, who had believed in her and given her that first chance at Marchetti Films, would never end. She would continue to meet every challenge, even though at times she tempered her admiration with a realism that let her see Gino the man, not just the genius.

As Eva packed her bag for Diligence Hall, she looked toward this latest challenge, to get *Glory Road* ready for production—and to take care of Gino's other request. She'd never refused him anything, and there was no reason to start now. Besides, Eva was curious. Until she found what Gino was looking for, she'd never know *why* he wanted thirty acres of land in Corinth, South Carolina.

It had been another bad night. Reese drank the first sip of his strong morning coffee and looked through the trees toward the river as the early morning mists began to dissipate. He'd had a nightmare again. It had caused him to wake up in a cold sweat at four in the morning and not be able to get back to sleep. He'd lain in bed for more than two hours before dressing and going out for a long walk with his dogs. That always calmed him. The dogs were good companions, two Irish setters, mother and daughter. There'd always been setters at Diligence, and if Lacy had her way, there always would be. There was old blood in the dogs, just like in the folks at Diligence Hall, aristo-cratic blood, Lacy often commented. They were champions.

As usual, the walk helped, but when Reese re-turned to the cottage with Coleen and Bridget, depression fell over him again, as though it had been hanging around the house, waiting. This nightmare hadn't been any different from the others: Barbara in the car just before it exploded, her hand turning the ignition key as Reese raced across the endless street, the explosion that turned into blinding flames and shards of metal . . . another horrible reliving of what had actually happened. But it wasn't just the nightmares; it was their frequency. He'd thought they would stop when he got back home, but after almost a year at Diligence, they still plagued him. They were just as vivid as ever, and they left him just as shaken.

Coleen limped over to the kitchen table and nudged Reese out of his reverie as only she could do. She was getting old, Reese realized, and was perfectly willing now to sit at his feet when their walk was over and leave the cavorting to her daughter. Bridget was the youngest in a line that had begun with a puppy given to Reese on his sixth birthday. He'd been serious minded, even then, just as he was now, he admitted to himself, and old Casey had tried just as hard as Coleen to amuse him.

Reese stroked the dog under her chin as he looked out the window. Coleen perked up her ears and offered a disinterested bark. They'd both heard the sound of voices through the open window. The conversation drifted toward them before anyone came into view.

"The panorama is great here where the property is more elevated." With a sweep of his hand, Beau included the meadow, the woods and the river in the distance. He was an enthusiastic guide for the woman at his side, whom Reese recognized as they crossed the meadow.

Beau nodded toward the cottage. "There's where my brother lives," he commented without interest. "It's actually a guest house, but it hasn't been used for years because there have been enough bedrooms at Diligence Hall. Back in the old days, there were huge parties lasting a weekend or even a fortnight—neighbors coming in their carriages from miles around, the women with piles of dresses and petticoats and hat boxes," Beau went on, enjoying himself.

Eva's gaze was drawn toward the cottage as if toward watching eyes. She shaded her hand from the sun, looked again, saw no one and turned away. Yet as they walked, she nervously continued to glance over her shoulder from time to time. Even if Reese Benedict had been watching her, Eva couldn't think why that should give her such a strange feeling and make her quicken her pace.

"Wait," Beau called after her. "I'm not going to take you down to the river dressed like that." As Eva turned toward him, Beau's gaze took in the ivory-colored pleated skirt that just touched her knees, her trim legs, and feet clad in ankle-strap wedged sandals. "Too much bare leg and foot," he explained.

Eva put her hands on her hips and challenged, "I can walk amazingly well in these shoes, Beau, and I don't mind a few scratches on my legs."

"It's not the terrain or the bushes. It's the chiggers, the ticks and the poison ivy that'll keep you out of the woods."

Eva changed her mind quickly, not quite sure what "chiggers" were, but unwilling to risk an encounter.

"Come on." He grabbed her hand. "I'll take you over to the gazebo and tell you the story of how Diligence got its name. Does that pique your interest?"

"Very much," Eva admitted.

"Actually, when you know the background, the name isn't all that strange," he said. "During the Revolution, my ancestors were opposed to good King George and his taxes long before war broke out. Legend goes that the original Beauregard Benedict instigated a raid on the British ship *Diligence*, anchored up the coast near North Carolina. The expedition was a success, the ship was burned, and all the tea thrown into the harbor. Beauregard was so pleased with their success that he named his plantation after the ship. And that's no tall tale."

"Even if it is," she said, following after him and glad to be going in the opposite direction from the cottage, "it's certainly an interesting one, especially since I thought the house came by its name because of the generations of hard-working Benedicts who inhabited it."

"Well, in *this* generation, Reese and Mother still have the reputation for hard work, but if you want to know the truth, I'm more diligent than any of them ever imagined. After all," he added, "I brought Marchetti Films here."

"Well, I suppose you could say that," Eva answered with a smile. "Yes, in your own inimitable fashion, you are responsible."

When they returned from the gazebo half an hour later, their voices drifting away in the breeze, Reese was still at the breakfast table. He couldn't hear the conversation, but he could tell that Eva had completely captivated Beau.

Without it being quite so obvious, Reese had been captivated, too, the first time he saw her on the veranda. She'd looked younger than he'd imagined and more beautiful than he'd thought possible in that silk dress that managed to be both fashionable and businesslike, while still clinging seductively to her breasts and thighs. He wasn't quite sure how she'd achieved that effect, but he suspected that she'd worked at it, carefully cultivating her image. And some image it was. As soon as he'd seen her and heard her name, Reese had remembered. In the less than subtle words of the tabloids, she was Gino Marchetti's constant companion. She'd followed Marchetti across Europe, creating a buffer around him while faithfully carrying out his orders.

Now here she was in Corinth, where she'd done his dirty work again, but in her own style, without being intimidated. That in itself was a change for Reese. People were usually intimidated in his presence; even Barbara had been occasionally. He had a reputation for sternness that he'd always felt was unjustified. But the reputation obviously hadn't reached the ears of Eva Sinclair. He remembered the way she'd conducted the meeting, skillfully, efficiently, the way she hadn't backed down. She was an interesting woman.

Reese leaned back in the kitchen chair, disrupting Coleen's nap, and shook his head. It really was too bad Eva hadn't come to town under different circumstances. Reese allowed himself the momentary luxury of taking that thought a step further and wondering what might have happened if they'd met socially.

The attraction was there; he'd felt it during the meeting in spite of their mutual antagonism. Under different circumstances, he might have taken her out to dinner. There was a little restaurant on the beach where the intimate atmosphere and good food would have made a perfect setting, especially with the candlelight flickering in her startlingly dark eyes and highlighting the sheen of her golden hair.

Reese could hear their voices now as they chatted animatedly. Her face was turned up to Beau; he could see her flashing smile. Her body moved smoothly beneath the pleated skirt, and her hair glowed silvery in the sunlight. Beau's look was nothing short of adoration. Reese couldn't blame his brother for that.

Suddenly he felt a stab of quick and painful jealousy and wished *he'd* caused the glow on her face and the light he saw again in her dark brown eyes.

Eva's eyes were flashing because she was enjoying herself. They'd sat in the gazebo and watched Bridget frolic in the grass for Eva's benefit while Beau continued to regale her with stories from the past. She'd forgotten all about the cottage in the distance and the curious gray eyes that may or may not have been watching her.

Eva had never been in a gazebo before; she'd never even seen one, and she'd been charmed by the delicate building with its curved benches and turreted roof that filtered the sun in crazy, delightful patterns onto the wooden floor. But now as they crossed the meadow and the cottage came into view, she felt a sudden uneasiness and was glad when Beau suggested they return to Diligence Hall.

"You've probably seen nothing of the house except the veranda and your bedroom," he said.

"And a few hallways," Eva responded with a laugh. "So far everything has taken me back in time. Breakfast on the veranda this morning with Lacy was like a trip into the past."

"Unfortunately, Diligence Hall is too much in the past. Modern times have confounded the place. We used to be self-sufficient, living off our cattle and crops—truck farming and vegetables and selling corn and hay for feed. In the *distant* past of course, Diligence made a fortune for our ancestors from cotton and indigo. Even until recently we were self-sufficient. Not anymore. The old folks are still around, but their kids are leaving Corinth, moving into the cities, and I can't blame them...." His voice faded as they climbed the steps, and Eva felt sadness, even a bitterness emanating from the young man who was the last of a dying breed—possibly not out of choice.

"Come on," he said, cheering up quickly. "I want to show you our most interesting relic." Inside, Beau led Eva to the winding stairway, telling her, "You've no doubt walked right up the staircase and not even noticed its significance."

The banister was intricately carved mahogany, Eva *had* noticed that. She's also noticed the wide sweep of the stairway, the grandeur it gave to the marble foyer, but its "significance" escaped her. "You're right," she admitted.

"Here," Beau said, "see these marks in the mahogany." He pointed out two long slashes in the burnished wood of the railing. "Well," he said with a glint in his eye, "these are saber marks made by a Yankee soldier who rode his horse across the marble foyer."

Eva raised one eyebrow, a little doubtful but still interested.

"It's true," Beau declared. "Experts have determined the age of the slashes—almost a hundred years—and that they were in fact made by a saber. Just about everyone agrees that the Yankee officer rode his horse into the front hall and slashed away at the banister. The rest of the story is highly disputed, but I believe every word." Beau sat down on the red-carpeted stairs while Eva examined the marks on the banister and waited to hear what happened next.

"Still waving the saber, he rode his horse right up the stairway," Beau reported.

Eva raised her eyebrow again.

"Remember, this was the end of the Civil War and the victorious Yankees were behaving in very ungentlemanly ways. However, this one got his comeuppance, as they say. The horse balked at the top step, reared back and dislodged the rider, who fell to his death on the marble floor," Beau finished with relish. "And I do hope," he added, "that you can find some way to incorporate that fascinating story into *Glory Road.*"

*Glory Road* had a few obstacles to overcome first, the most bothersome of which was Reese Benedict. It didn't take a lot of insight to reach that conclusion. Even the postmistress knew it, Eva found out when she drove her rented car to Corinth to mail the contracts. She waited patiently while the package was weighed and the postage attached and realized that Danny's theory about Southerners was all wrong. They weren't slow; they simply eliminated all motions that might tend to tire them. Trying to suppress a smile, she made a mental note to tell Danny to avoid the post office if he wanted to keep his sanity.

As Eva paid for the stamps and extended her thanks, the postmistress pushed up the sleeves of her blue-and-white flowered dress and leaned forward with her ample arms folded on the counter. "You're with those movie people, aren't you?" she inquired with no sign of shyness.

Eva nodded.

"Well, what I wonder," she said, having received the expected information, "is just how you all managed to get permission to make a movie at Diligence Hall." She shifted her round flowered body on the stool and added, "What with Reese Benedict out there now."

Eva chose not to respond, hoping that when the postmistress received no answer, she would have more to say about Reese.

She did. "He's like a hermit, that one. Never even comes into town if he can help it, while Beau and Miss Lacy are coming and going all the time like regular folks."

Eva returned her wallet to her purse and remained silent.

"Yes, I'm just surprised," came the follow-up, "that he'd let you folks out there. It's all I can do to get him to come to the front door of the cottage when I send my mailman with a registered letter. He used to get a lot of special delivery mail when he first came back, but it's kinda petered out. I guess folks decided he wasn't gonna answer, so they stopped writing."

Eva, by contributing nothing, was learning a great deal.

"He's awful stuck-up, you know," the woman continued.

Eva made a sound that could have been taken for confirmation.

"Bullheaded, too," was the final assessment, which Eva found only hours later to be absolutely on the mark.

Reese Benedict was standing near the driveway with the two Irish setters at his heels playfully begging for a walk. He ignored them and watched as Eva drove up and got out of the car. "I understand you have a little problem here," he said without moving from where he stood.

Because she couldn't hear what he was saying, Eva was forced to walk a few steps toward him. He followed each step carefully with a look that she couldn't interpret. "What kind of problem?" she asked.

"The house faces the wrong way," he stated flatly.

"What?" Eva asked incredulously.

"Oh, yes, it seems your people can't get the sunset footage they want without losing the light. I suggested that since we can't turn the house around for them, they might try to find another place more suitable."

Eva smiled. He was joking, but just barely. "I'll talk to them," she said. "I'm sure we can try a variation of day-for-night shooting and solve the problem."

Reese raised one eyebrow, and Eva realized he knew what she was talking about. "Possibly," he said and then turned abruptly and with the dogs barking at his heels, walked toward the woods.

Eva watched him go and decided that the postmistress was right. He was infuriatingly "stuck up." He was also one of the most attractive men she'd ever met, and by far the most mysterious. Eva couldn't help wondering what was going on inside that mind that had once interpreted the news from around the world with such insight. Surely he was more than just an arrogant man who had chosen to be a hermit. Yet everything so far proved otherwise.

When Reese arrived at the house at five o'clock the next morning, well before sunrise, Eva and the second unit cameraman had already set up and were filming the shot. He walked across the dew-covered grass and stopped nearby under a live oak tree, where he stood quietly watching. The cameraman left the camera running while the sky changed.

"I think this will work, Eva. All we'll have to do is reverse the film and put the actors in over it. Yep," he said, as he watched through the viewfinder, "it'll be perfect. Won't even need a filter."

Eva, unable to avoid glancing toward Reese, thought she saw the flicker of a smile in his eyes.

That filler shot became the easiest job she confronted during the first long day of work at Diligence Hall. Not to her surprise, Danny was at the center of most of the trouble, and to her *great* surprise, so was Lacy Benedict.

Lacy had accompanied Eva and Dan upstairs, proudly showing off her home for Eva, who responded with appropriate enthusiasm, and for Dan, who saw it all as something that needed to be ripped out and changed to meet his needs.

"We're all right when it comes to the period of the film. This interior can pass for any year after 1840," Dan said, but without any of the admiration Lacy surely expected in his voice. "My major problem is with space. The main halls work fine, and so do most of the doorways. And I love all the space above; the ceilings just go on forever," he said, delivering his first compliment that a by now wary Lacy hesitated to accept as such.

"But this interior hall," Dan said, moving along the second floor, "won't work at all unless we tear out the wall opposite when we make the turn into the master bedroom."

"Oh, you couldn't!" Lacy objected.

Dan turned to look at her as if that were the last thing he expected to hear. "And why not?"

"Why, some of those oak panels are the original woodwork," Lacy said, incredulous that Dan hadn't noticed.

"But Mrs. Benedict," came the equally incredulous response, "what does that matter?"

Eva, aware of what Dan was getting at, almost intervened before deciding to see if the two mismatched people could work this out on their own. After a full five minutes of parrying, during which Lacy kept quite composed and Dan became red-faced, Eva stepped in.

"Lacy, I believe what Dan's trying to say is that he can put the wall back without causing any damage." Of this there was no doubt; Eva had complete trust in Dan.

"Oh, I don't think that's possible."

Dan had examined the wall carefully and nodded to Eva, indicating that there would be no problem, while Eva explained the capabilities of the Marchetti carpenters to Lacy. It took time and finesse, but finally Lacy was convinced.

She wasn't as willing to give in to the next problem, the one that ended their long day. This time Eva and Reese were alerted at approximately the same moment by Dan's raised voice. Once more, the set designer was confronting Lacy; once more, she was calm and gracious, belying her inner, agitated state.

"The wallpaper will *have* to be covered, Mrs. Benedict," Dan was declaring. "It says 1980, not 1940. May I just ask when you papered this wall?"

"Why, about two years ago, I believe."

"See?" Dan all but shouted out. "It's eighties' paper. We need forties' paper in here—vines and berries and what have you . . ."

Eva, joined by Reese, headed for the dining room. She was momentarily uncomfortable at having him observe another contretemps; then it occurred to her it wasn't all that bad to show her skill in negotiating and problem solving in the great man's presence.

"There seems to be a little trouble in paradise," Reese observed wryly.

"Problems are a natural part of progress," Eva responded as they entered the room.

"This time I'm not backing down, Eva," Lacy said. "He can't possibly make this change without damaging my paper—"

"That's true." Dan shrugged disinterestedly.

"Can't you tape the other paper over this one?" Eva asked Dan.

The set designer shook his head. "The tape would pull off this pattern."

"A very expensive pattern," Lacy added, "which is out of print."

Eva had the notion that Lacy really *wasn't* going to back down, and she didn't blame her. "I wouldn't want the paper damaged, either, Lacy; it's perfect for this room," Eva said. "Danny and I will have to figure out another solution."

Eva managed to get Dan out of the room into the hall so that Lacy wouldn't have to be upset further. But Reese Benedict remained by the door, observing. What he saw no longer surprised him, and it still pleased him: Eva, slim and straight, listened to Dan. She nodded her head, absorbing everything he said while remaining calm and neutral. The serenity that she exuded seemed first to quiet the strident voice of the designer and then to stem it altogether as he decided to hear her out.

"Matte photography could work," she suggested but then agreed that it would be an unnecessary expense. "How about cheating the shot and picking it up in the studio?"

Dan considered that for a moment, walked back down the hall, checked out the angles and then finally agreed. All the while Eva watched Dan while Reese watched Eva, his admiration at its peak by the time she took his mother aside to explain exactly what was happening.

"We won't have to touch the wallpaper," Eva told the relieved Lacy. "Instead, we'll photograph the scene with the camera at an angle that avoids this wall. Then when we have to change angles, we'll insert a shot made at the studio using the paper Dan chooses."

"But what about the people in the room?"

"We'll put the two scenes together, and it'll look just as if they're in the dining room."

"Well, I declare," Lacy said. "Isn't that tricky...."

"But amazingly simple," Eva answered, following with a suggestion that surprised not just Lacy and Dan but Reese, as well. "Why don't you go through the rest of the rooms with Dan and let him explain just what he's trying to achieve? Understanding the process certainly helps, and he can clarify everything so much better than I," Eva said with a glance at Dan, who raised an eyebrow but refrained from comment. He knew as well as Eva that they'd solve all the major problems in his designs. Dan smiled; when he wanted to, he could be a charmer. Eva had the feeling he'd liked Lacy Benedict from the beginning, and she had no doubt they'd return from the tour as friends.

As the two went off, Eva turned to find that Reese was still looking at her. She tried to read his expression and thought she saw a trace of admiration there; she definitely saw humor.

"I underestimated you," he said.

"This is my job," she responded, "I'm quite good at it."

"So I see." Reese asked a few questions about the filming, and she answered him briefly but succinctly, and as he listened, Reese stepped a little closer. Because she'd leaned back against the doorjamb, Eva couldn't move away.

She had the sudden sense as she talked of being trapped by him. One of his arms rested against the door, near her face, and he leaned toward her as if to catch every word. His eyes devoured her, pinioning Eva as much as the arm that kept her from moving through the door to her escape. She realized that "escape" was too strong a word, but it was the only one that came to mind—escape, as if from a jungle animal. She shivered a little and felt her heart quicken and goose bumps race across her skin. Eva wondered if the danger she felt was obvious to Reese.

It wasn't. He heard only her clear voice as she spoke, saw only her dark, serene eyes, inhaled the scent of her, a perfume both expensive and sophisticated and yet light, fresh and airy. It was perfect for her, just like the white crushed-cotton sundress and the cool white sandals. Her hair was pulled into a loose knot at the back of her neck, and for a strange irreverent moment he considered reaching out to loosen the ribbon that held it and to bury his hands in the silky shining mass of her hair as it fell free to her shoulders.

That moment of desire held in check seemed to last for an eternity. She'd stopped talking and stood motionless beneath his gaze. Her lips were parted slightly, and once more Reese felt the urge to reach out and touch them with his fingertips, feel the softness and then cover her mouth with his....

But he didn't move, and neither did Eva. Everything was quiet around them, and they were immobile, as if caught in a moment when time stood still. Outside, life must have gone on, but they were oblivious to its existence, two people suspended in nothingness until Dan's voice invaded their world.

"I think we've gone through every room that we'll be filming, Eva."

Reese dropped his arm, and Eva stepped away; the moment was over.

"It all looks good to me," Dan continued in a chatty tone that told her Lacy had won him over.

Somehow Eva walked away from Reese with no more than a nod, accompanied Dan to his car and arranged a schedule for the following day.

"Fine, boss," Dan agreed, checking Eva's clipboard and then adding, "I like the Benedict woman a lot, and the kid is all right, too, but the great Reese Benedict... He hasn't said much yet, but mark my words, dear, if there's trouble in Corinth during this shooting, it'll be caused by that one."

Eva, who'd once felt the same, almost objected but stopped herself just in time to keep from looking like a fool.

"And the way he looked at you," Dan added as he got into the car, "I call it a look of real hunger. You better be careful, my dear; the man's dangerous."

For Eva, the danger she also had sensed had been replaced by another sensation that she tried to ignore.

But she couldn't ignore the opinions of others, and everyone seemed to have an opinion, not just Dan and the members of the advance crew. Everyone in the town of Corinth had something to say about Reese Benedict. Eva sought them out, fascinated by their comments, which were very mixed. Not all of Corinth shared the postmistress's views.

But they knew all about the filming, Eva learned when she stopped at the General Store later in the afternoon. The clerk began an assessment of Reese with a wordless scowl, and Eva thought that would be the end of it, but she hadn't noticed the two men firmly ensconced over a chessboard in the corner—or if she'd seen them, she must have assumed they were statues. Motionless on opposite sides of the board, they were quite verbal.

One of them declared in no uncertain terms that he thought Reese should have stayed up north where he belonged. "'Stead of hiding out over there and not giving the time of day to nobody."

His opponent in the chess game, a black man who was as tall when he was sitting as the clerk was when standing, declared, "That's just the man's way. He likes Corinth, or he wouldn't have come back. He likes the old ways and the easy life we got here, Ed."

"Yeah," Ed replied with scorn, "it's that life that's killing the town. There's no progress here, which suits Benedict fine. And why shouldn't it? He's rich and can just sit out there on his backside doing nothing. What he should do is use all his high-powered influence to get some business brought into this area." Ed's narrow face became even more rodlike as he pursed his lips.

"It's not his responsibility to get people jobs, Ed."

"Well, if he likes Corinth so much that he's come back here to live for good, he oughta *make* it his responsibility." But no final decision was reached, and by the time Eva had found everything she needed for her extended stay in Corinth and paid for her purchases, the conversation had returned to baseball.

Beau met her at the door of Diligence Hall and helped her unload while Eva told him about the faces of the General Store threesome, avoiding mentioning their comments. "This town is a casting director's dream," she said as she walked up the stairs beside Beau. "The faces of those men, and the postmistress, are classic. Especially the one named Ed."

"He's what my mother calls 'mean as a snake,' and he has snake eyes to prove it. But you're right; Corinth is a town of interesting faces."

"I bet you know them all."

"Are you kidding? I know every face in the country. I've even sketched a lot of them."

"Really?" An idea was forming in her mind.

Beau, unaware of the way Eva's mind worked, answered, "Yes, I'm a frustrated artist. Fact is, I majored in art at the local college but never did much with it except draw for my own pleasure. Faces are my strong point, my professors always said."

"Do you keep the sketches?"

"Sure, I never throw anything out, no matter how bad."

Eva's mind continued to click away. She'd hoped from the beginning that Beau's enthusiasm could be rewarded with a job of some sort on the film. Now she had the answer. "You probably know where they all live, even where they work." She and Beau crossed the cool marble hallway.

"Naturally," Beau said, adding, "There's iced tea on the veranda."

Eva followed him down the hall. "And I expect you know who's reliable, who can be counted on."

"Down to a man." Beau was catching on. "Do you have something in mind for me, Eva?" he asked with a deceptively uninterested voice that was completely negated by the excited look on his face.

"Possibly."

"I've been wondering whether I could do something on the film. Are you thinking about my helping hire the extras?" he asked.

Eva smiled. "Yes, I believe the casting director would welcome the kind of assistance you can give her, especially if she could begin with your sketches. Besides, you deserve a reward, Beau."

"Oh?" he asked as they walked out onto the porch.

"Sure. If it weren't for you, we wouldn't be shooting at Diligence, remember?"

Beau laughed, and Eva realized that she now had two allies at Diligence—Beau and Lacy. The third Benedict was an unknown quantity.

# Chapter 4

Eva remained unsure of Reese's attitude toward her and the company. He'd accepted their presence at Diligence out of necessity; there'd been no other choice for him from the moment Lacy had signed the contracts. That didn't mean he had to like it, and as far as Eva could tell, he didn't like it at all. Yet the trouble that Dan had predicted never occurred, as Reese continued to keep his distance, an observer whose critical grey eyes seemed to assess everything while he refrained from comment.

He was the only silent one. Everyone else in Corinth and its environs had questions about the film, which were inevitably followed with comments about Diligence and Reese Benedict. Eva heard them all as she accompanied Dan on his photography forays into town. Thinking that Dan's flamboyance, together with his outspokenness, wouldn't appeal to the locals, Eva had gone along at first as a buffer, only to find that he was warmly welcomed.

"They appreciate an *artiste*," he told Eva with a triumphant smile. As for Dan, he was quickly adapting to Southern ways. While he worked, photographing street settings for the art director who was still working out of the Los Angeles office, Eva found herself lingering and listening. The subject was still the same. Reese was the real celebrity among them. The pending arrival of the cast and crew of *Glory Road* elicited far less interest than their attitude toward the renowned Reese Benedict.

The talk still fascinated Eva just as the man continued to intrigue her. She'd begun to sense a kind of envy in some of the negative comments; in the positive ones she heard respect, admiration and even pride that he was one of *them*, that he belonged to Corinth and had returned to the place he loved.

"When it comes to love of his hometown, Reese Benedict has more of that than anyone." That comment and variations on it were frequent. The consensus, even among his detractors, seemed to be that Reese would put Corinth above almost everything else, right up there next to his own family.

However, he still stayed away from the crowds and kept to himself in the guest cottage or on walks in the woods nearby. After the initial filming problems had been solved, he'd become a distant figure, but the more he remained in the shadowy background, the more Eva watched for him, hoping for a rare appearance. When he did appear, she couldn't keep her gaze from wandering toward him. Each time her eyes met his directly; he was always watching.

Beau was far more obvious; there was nothing subtle about him as he dogged Eva's footsteps around the plantation and all over town. "The more I stick by you, the more I learn" was his theory.

Finally Eva gave him the script to read. It only served to fill him with ideas for extras, each of which he offered to Eva for her approval, following after her with his pad and a stack of sketches that were constantly spilling out of his folder as he rummaged through it in search of the right one.

Soon Eva began to wonder *when* the casting director would arrive and take Beau off her hands. Yet she couldn't object too strongly because Beau was serious, devoted and very bright. And his artwork was excellent. Beau had an eye for detail that would have been the envy of any serious artist. He was going to be a good addition to the production staff of *Glory Road*.

As Eva could have guessed, Reese didn't share the enthusiasm about his younger brother's new job, and when Beau told him the news, it was with a hesitancy that was justified.

"You mean to say that you're going to work for her?"

"If you mean by *her* Eva Sinclair, well, not directly." Beau and Reese made their way along a path that led to the stables where their horses were saddled and waiting. "But if you've asked me to go riding just so you can berate me, then I'll pass, Reese. It's been weeks since we rode together, and if I recall that was the occasion of another one of your lectures. I like to ride for relaxation, so..."

Reese put his arm on his brother's shoulder as they approached the stables. "I'm not about to lecture you, Beau. You're a grown man and perfectly capable of making your own decisions, but you also have a job here at Diligence."

"Which I handle quite well, by the way. I might remind you that I've been managing Diligence affairs since I finished school, and doing a damned good job." Beau swung expertly into the saddle of his bay gelding, and Reese mounted his own horse with equal ease. "God knows, you should be aware of that since you've gone over the books with a fine-tooth comb."

"I don't doubt your ability, Beau."

"I should hope not," Beau said, giving his mount a touch to the flanks. "But I think you're also aware that operating Diligence is hardly a full-time job. Maybe if we still had the tours—"

"I won't discuss that, Beau." Reese shook his head stubbornly.

"Well, at least they brought in some income, and—"

"I said that I don't want to discuss it." Reese urged his horse forward toward a low hedge that was the first jump on the hunt course they'd ridden since they were boys. He cleared the hedge cleanly, followed by Beau, and soon they were riding abreast again.

"Then tell me," Reese said in a voice that didn't attempt to hide his irritation, "exactly what you'll be doing for Marchetti Films."

"Assisting the casting director. She just arrived, and I'm meeting with her this afternoon. Eva arranged it. Of course, the major roles will be played by professional actors," Beau told Reese, who didn't bother to remind his brother that he knew something about the process. "But all the extras can be taken from Corinth people. They might even be used in some small parts, Eva said."

"Eva said," Reese repeated.

"What do you have against Eva?" Beau asked defensively.

They came up to another jump and took it together. Not until they got back on the trail and slowed down did Reese answer his brother's pointed question. "I don't have anything against her personally; I just don't care for the way she's disrupting things at Diligence."

"Well, I like her. She's given me a real break—which I deserve, I might add."

"I realize that, Beau, and I also realize that you've been stuck here in Corinth while I've been off to the ends of the earth, but I thought that was your choice, what you wanted."

"Once I suppose I did, but now I'm ready for something more."

"But not this, Beau, and not with an outfit like Marchetti. It's all make-believe nonsense."

"It's exciting," Beau insisted.

Reese smiled. "Yes, I suppose it is. But take some brotherly advice. Don't get hooked like I did. I didn't mean to stay overseas forever...." Reese said, his voice drifting off as he remembered what it had been like, living abroad, following the action wherever it led him and his news team. It had been a tonic at first and then a necessary drug. He hadn't been able to do without the adrenaline that the news stories pumped through his blood, and no matter how much Barbara wanted to come back to the States, to a home of their own so they could begin a family, Reese kept putting it off— one more month, one more year—until it was too late, and there was no one to come home with. So he'd roamed over Europe for almost a year before returning to Diligence alone...to stay. "Don't get hooked," Reese repeated to his brother.

Beau grinned as the horses picked up speed. "Well, if I do get hooked, I hope it's on Eva. Isn't she great?"

Before Reese could respond, Beau added, "Smart, sensitive, aware. And boy, is she good-looking."

Even as he answered, Reese knew his words sounded pedantic. "She's older than you are, Beau."

"Not much," came the quick reply. "Just a few years. Besides, it's a known fact that women like younger men—because of our incredible sensuality," he bragged.

Suddenly Reese found himself experiencing another of his fantasies, seeing Eva dressed not in her pale creams and whites, efficient and businesslike, but with her hair flowing around her shoulders, wearing something black and lacy and diaphanous. A man was bending over her...and he was that man. Angrily, Reese pushed the image from his mind, confused by this constant invasion of his thoughts by the woman who was also invading his home, a woman who could mean nothing to him.

"Forget her," he said sharply to his brother. "She'll leave as soon as the filming is over. She'll leave, and without a thought about you or anyone in this part of the world. This isn't her stomping ground; she's an international woman, not the one for you." Or for me, he thought as his horse picked up speed.

Beau glanced over at his brother as they neared the next jump. Reese leaned forward, digging his heels into his mount's flanks, pulling ahead. Accepting the challenge, Beau urged the gelding on, and the horses raced for the jump, landing in a gallop, neck and neck.

The Corinth Columns Motel would never be the same again, or so the manager said. Eva didn't dare tell him that he hadn't seen anything yet. So far only a few members of the advance crew were ensconced at the motel; the others were coming in slowly, one by

one. They brought their life-styles and habits with
them. Nothing ever changed, no matter what the location. They were a group, the Marchetti production
team, that turned every motel anywhere in the world
into a home away from home. Somehow, the rooms
immediately reflected their style as they managed to
create an atmosphere that never varied. The card tables went up, the food was ordered in, and the motel
changed its face overnight. Other guests were confounded; the management was frenzied. But rarely
were there any real problems; trouble was kept at a
minimum, while the staff of Corinth Columns Motel
could only stand aside and watch in wonder.

Mary Eammes, the casting director, arrived amid
the chaos with her omnipresent boyfriend. Then came
the groupies—girls who followed after grips or gaffers or electricians on the crew, turning up wherever a
film was being shot; Eva never had quite figured out
what sort of antennae sent them word of each new location.

A settling in began, which Eva always thought of as
"phase one." She planned to stay through the beginning of "phase two,"—when the actors, director and
the first unit arrived. By then, Eva hoped, all the preliminary work would be completed, the Benedicts
would be used to the change in their lives, and Marchetti Films would have assimilated into Corinth—and
vice versa.

Eva arrived at the motel at noon to meet with Mary,
and found as usual that everyone had congregated in
two double rooms already filled with smoke and the
odor of Italian food.

"Where in the world did you find an Italian take-
out restaurant in Corinth?" Eva asked in amazement.

"We didn't," came the answer. "We ordered this from Luigi's in Beaufort."

"Is Joey the auditor on this film?" Eva asked, her hands on her hips.

"Oh-oh," someone mumbled, "here comes the lecture."

"I don't know, Eva. I think so," another voice volunteered. "But he's not here yet."

"Well, when he gets here, I imagine he'll have something to say about ordering take-out and having it delivered fifty miles!"

"But, Eva, that's the nearest Italian restaurant."

"Then you'll have to forgo Italian for a while," she ordered. The moans came from every corner of the room.

Ignoring them, Eva managed to find Mary in the crowd and get her into a relatively quiet corner. "Sorry I threw Beau Benedict at you with practically no explanation and sent you out to the house cold, but I was in the middle of a meeting when you got in."

Mary lit a cigarette. "It was something of a surprise to find the kid listed on my first day schedule. But your instincts were right, as usual, Eva. He's going to make my job a lot easier. The sketches are wonderful. I can practically cast from them. Of course, the Benedict name is not high on Gino's list at the moment. If he gets wind that the boy's on the payroll..."

"I'll talk to Joey about that. Besides, when we bring this picture in on time and under budget, Gino isn't going to be reading financial sheets. Meanwhile, what he doesn't know won't hurt him."

"I often wonder if he knows what a miracle worker he has in you?"

"Probably not," Eva said with a laugh. "But I've got a pretty special prize in him, too, just remember."

Mary took a long drag on her cigarette and squinted her blue eyes as she exhaled. "How it works, I'll never know. He's a tough old reprobate, and you're a real classy dame. Yet the two of you have a weird kind of harmony going."

"We go way back, and over the years we've learned to trust each other. I know he just wants to get the job done."

"Well, that's why we're here. With this kid's help, I should be able to get the extras and bit parts cast in record time. I'll go over the lists with Beau at dinner tomorrow."

"What's wrong with tonight?"

"I need a day for jet lag." Mary ran one hand through her tousled brown hair.

"Mary, what kind of jet lag can you get traveling from L.A. to the East Coast? You make up time; you don't lose it."

Mary stifled a yawn. "Not me. I lose time whenever I get on a plane. Oh, by the way," she added, "would you clue me in about that older brother, Reese?"

Eva hesitated a moment before she answered, wondering how to couch her words. "He's something of a problem."

"Well, he's about the best-looking problem I ever set my eyes on. He was walking across the lawn when I drove up. That house was fantastic enough, but when I saw this gorgeous creature coming toward me, I could've fainted. He had on fawn colored riding pants and a polo shirt that just *clung* to his wet skin. And there were these two red-colored dogs—"

"Irish setters, Mary," Eva said, aware that Mary's interest in animals was as limited as her interest in people was boundless.

"Anyway, they made a great addition to the picture, barking at his heels as he walked toward me. I just stood there mesmerized. Of course, I was hoping he'd be the kid who was going to work with me. Somehow, he didn't look like he needed work, though. Those smoldering gray eyes. Unbelievable." Mary put out her cigarette and lit another. "Finally, when he got right up to me, I recognized him as the guy who used to be on the network news. But he's about a thousand times better looking in person. Does he have a thing for you?"

"What in the world are you talking about?" Eva asked in a puzzled voice.

"I don't know. Just a feeling. I only talked to him a minute or two before Beau came down, but he managed to keep turning the conversation back to you— how long had I known you, what were you like to work for, all that stuff."

"He's probably looking for my weaknesses." Eva was a little confused but tried not to show it.

"Maybe he's planning to do an exposé on us: what happens behind the scenes on a movie location. All the dirt."

"No, I don't think the man's planning a media comeback. He's out of television for good, which is too bad because he was so talented. Remember those reports he did from the Middle East?" Eva couldn't hide her admiration. "He was incredible."

"Now you're beginning to sound like you have a thing for *him*. This is very confusing," Mary said, "but I have a feeling it's going to be interesting."

* * *

"Hurry in; there's a storm brewing," Lacy said as she greeted Eva at the door the next evening. "I gave the cook the night off since there'll only be the two of us for dinner." They walked into the foyer together as Lacy explained, "Beau is having dinner in town with Mary Eammes. She certainly does seem like a nice young woman. But *so* young. I never imagined that a person her age could have such a responsible job."

"She's very talented," Eva explained, "and Mr. Marchetti pays no attention to age. He has cameramen, who in any other profession would have been retired for years, working alongside kids just out of film school. Talent and dedication are his only requirements."

"Well, she's a pretty young thing..."

Eva saw where Lacy was leading. "Unfortunately," she told her, "Mary's boyfriend is here, too." Eva had decided to explain some of the facts of life of location shooting. "The film crew tends to travel like families, bringing along whoever they're living with at the time."

"My goodness," Lacy said. A little shocked, she recovered with curiosity. "What does the young man do for a living that he can just take off and travel with Mary?"

Eva smiled. "Lacy, I don't ask. Sometimes it's better not to know all the details."

Lacy shook her head. "Well, you promised they'd be interesting people. Now about dinner, Eva. Since Beau's not here and Reese... well, Reese hasn't been coming over for meals lately, not since..." She hesitated, a little flustered.

Eva saved her. "I know, Lacy, not since we arrived at Diligence."

"I just hate for him to be so rude."

"It's all right; I don't blame him at all. Your son wasn't in favor of the arrangement you made with Marchetti Films, and he doesn't feel that he has to welcome a crew that he didn't want here in the first place. I certainly understand that."

"I don't understand *him* sometimes. Oh, well," Lacy said, not about to bother herself with her son's problems. "I thought we'd take potluck tonight. The cook's left a wide choice for us out in the kitchen."

"Lead the way," Eva said. "I'm an expert at pickup dinners."

As they headed for the kitchen, a huge peal of thunder cracked across the sky, causing Eva to jump and grab Lacy's arm.

"Don't worry," Lacy said with a laugh. "We get these storms frequently in the summer. They sound terrible, but rarely do very much damage."

Before she finished the sentence, the sky lit up with lightning, startling Eva again. "Don't mind me, Lacy. I'm just not used to this."

"Do you mean to tell me that you don't have storms in Los Angeles?" Lacy couldn't believe that.

"As a matter of fact, I really can't remember the last time I saw lightning in California. Of course, I run into all kinds of weather when I'm traveling, but I just try to stay indoors during storms."

"Well, don't worry. We'll be warm and cozy in the kitchen," Lacy assured her.

The kitchen *was* both warm and cozy, a big comfortable room with a wooden floor, an old oak table and ladder-back chairs with flowered pillow seats. "This is one of the oldest rooms in the house," Lacy told her. "That's the original cooking fireplace. Very little has been changed over the decades except the appliances. We don't prepare dinner over an open fire any more!" she said with a grin as she looked into the big refrigerator and took out a cooked ham. "What about ham sandwiches?"

"Sounds great," Eva agreed.

"There's cheese and lettuce and maybe some turkey slices in there, too, if you can find them."

"These are going to be regular Dagwood sandwiches," Eva said, searching for each of the ingredients as Lacy called them out.

Together they made iced tea and a tossed salad and decided to eat in the kitchen. Lacy spread a checkered cloth over the table, and they piled their sandwiches high. "This was always Reese's favorite meal when he was a boy. He could make the most enormous sandwiches. His father and I always marveled at how he managed to bite into them."

Every time she turned around, Eva came face-to-face with a conversation about Reese Benedict. As before, she now found herself listening with fascination, and even more so, because this wasn't town gossip.

"He was his father's son, though, more than mine, when he was growing up," Lacy told Eva. "I came here as a young bride of nineteen. Reese was born the next year. I was so busy learning how to be the mistress of the plantation that I left Reese's upbringing to the servants and to his father." She said this almost apologetically. "As he got older, Reese went everywhere with his father—hunting, riding, even to the legislature meetings in Columbia. For one term my husband was in the state legislature," she explained. "I imagine that's where Reese began to get his interest in politics and government.

"I often think if I'd been more involved in his up-bringing, Reese wouldn't have gone off so soon. He might even have stayed here with us, content to live in Corinth instead of roaming all over the world. But his father gave him an abundant supply of ambition and a hunger for knowledge. He wanted to know everything, to go everywhere. That's what took him so far away to college and kept him from ever coming back—until now."

The wind had intensified. It whistled eerily down the chimney, and Eva found herself shivering.

"My, you certainly aren't fond of storms, are you?" Lacy asked. "I just love them, especially late at night. They put me to sleep, but I expect this one will keep you awake." Lacy filled the coffeepot and set it over a gas burner on the stove.

"I'll get used to it," Eva said just as another bolt of lightning cracked nearby, and she jumped again. They both laughed, and Eva hoped the laughter and the lightning wouldn't keep Lacy from continuing to talk about Reese. She wanted Lacy to go on, and at the same time she was embarrassed at her own fascination with the subject.

The wind died down a little, and Lacy began to reminisce again. "By the time Beau was born, I was a lot older and found that the role of mother came quite easily. Of course, Reese had missed out, and Beau got more than his share." Lacy smiled sadly. "I'm afraid things were never quite equal for them in any department. Beau seemed to love it here at Diligence, but I'm beginning to wonder if keeping him here wasn't a mistake. And Reese—of course, he loved it overseas. Yet here he is back again. Children will continue to be a puzzlement no matter what their age."

Lacy took the coffeepot off the burner and got two cups from the cabinet. "Well, I do go on," she said, "but I was trying to explain away some of Reese's rudeness. He's had a hard time since what happened overseas..."

"It must have been a terrible blow, losing his wife like that. I'm sure he loved her very much." Eva couldn't imagine what had prompted her to make such a remark, but Lacy didn't seem to notice the boldness.

"They were devoted," Lacy said. "Barbara was a Corinth girl, you know. Born and reared here. I expect traveling was very difficult for her, but she went with him everywhere; she was crazy about him."

Eva experienced a moment of jealousy even though she'd expected to hear just what Lacy had told her. Only a devoted wife would have traveled to the hot spots of the world with her husband, undergoing all the discomfort and danger. Eva had known all along how strong their love must have been; it was because of that love that he was in seclusion now.

Lacy suggested that they take their coffee into another room, and Eva followed, walking along the hall where the windows were illuminated by the lightning and lashed at by the pounding rain. "It's not letting up," Lacy commented. "Looks like it could turn into a real big blow."

"Not a hurricane?" Eva wasn't at all interested in becoming part of a local disaster.

"Oh, no, not this early in the summer," Lacy assured her. "It'll just be a big wind and more rain than we need, frankly, unless we want the crops to float away this summer." Lacy led Eva into a lovely room with an old spinet in one corner. On the piano was a flute, and leaning against the wall was a cello.

"How did I ever miss this room?" Eva asked herself aloud, charmed as they sat together on the Queen Anne sofa.

"I can't imagine," Lacy answered. "Dan was very taken by our music room and said he even hoped they could find a reason to film one of the scenes here. It's really our favorite gathering place. We often played family concerts here, Beau and his father and I, before my husband died."

"How lovely. Are you the pianist?"

"No, my husband played the spinet, I played the flute and Beau the cello. We still have our evenings when we can get Reese to come over from the cottage. Of course, he plays the piano, too, just as his father did."

"I'd love to hear you play some time," Eva said, aware that such a request might be taken as an intrusion, but again Lacy wasn't in the least offended. In fact, she promised to have a musical evening. "But without Reese, I'm afraid. He's adamant about performing for an audience. He'd simply die if he knew that Beau and I once entertained a house tour!"

"Really?" Eva said, a little surprised herself. "I didn't realize that you gave tours of Diligence Hall."

"Well, we don't any more, not since Reese came home. But we used to have tours once a week during the summer. We enjoyed them, and so did everyone else, I think, and we made a little pin money at the same time. You should have heard my spiel," Lacy said with a laugh. Then she sighed and shook her head. "But Reese—well, you can guess. He wasn't interested in the slightest; certainly he wasn't amused."

Lacy waited for the thunder to quieten and then said suddenly, "Let's have a little brandy, shall we? That would surely make you sleep better tonight."

"Sounds fine to me," Eva agreed. "Shall I get it?"

"Oh, no," Lacy objected. "It's in the kitchen cellar, and only I can find it. You just stay here and try to ignore the storm," Lacy said with a reassuring smile as she headed down the hall, leaving Eva sitting on the sofa waiting for the next bolt to shatter the sky. When it came, it cracked like a gunshot from point-blank range. Instantly the lights sputtered and went out, leaving the room in darkness and leaving Eva huddled on the sofa.

In the silence that followed, Eva forced herself to get up carefully, step by slow step, and open the door to the hall. Necessity quelled her fears, and with one hand trailing along the wall she made her way toward the kitchen, remembering that she'd seen candles in one of the cabinets.

The rain pounded against the windows as she passed them, and lightning flashed, illuminating her way. With each flash Eva hurried down the hall as far as possible until it was dark again. Just ahead she saw what she thought was the kitchen door.

"Lacy!" she called out, reaching for the doorknob as lightning lit the sky. "Oh, great," she fumed. She'd tried to walk into a closet.

The next crash struck nearby with a crack that seemed to split the whole house open. In the light, Eva spotted the open kitchen door and ran for it, flinging herself inside and across the room to the counter. Opening the doors, she rummaged around in the cabinet until her hand touched a box of candles. In her haste she knocked a glass candlestick off the shelf onto the floor, where it shattered. But she'd found the candles, and the matches were right beside them.

With shaking hands Eva struck a match and held it to the wick until it caught. She breathed an audible sigh as the whole room brightened from the light of the candle. Not about to take any chances, she slipped the box of matches into her pocket.

"Lacy," she called out again, "I have a candle. I'll bring it down."

The stairway to the cellar was lined with shelves full of canned fruit and vegetables, each carefully labeled. As she made her way down the steep stairs, Eva noticed that on one of the shelves the jars were all pushed together and several of them were turned over. She held her candle out and saw others broken on the steps, spilling out the contents of jams and preserves.

Suddenly she knew what had happened. Lacy, losing her footing, had reached out for a handhold and knocked the jars off the shelf. Eva hurried down the stairs, knowing what she would find at the bottom.

Lacy was crumpled near the staircase. Eva saw the blood first and barely held back a scream. "Lacy!" she cried as she knelt beside her. The blood on the floor made a puddle beneath her cheek.

Holding the candle in one hand, Eva reached out the other and touched Lacy's face, turning it slightly. "Thank God," she said aloud. Lacy's skin was warm. She wasn't dead. The blood had come from a gash on her forehead. The bleeding had stopped, but there was something else—the position of Lacy's right leg. Eva saw immediately that it was broken. She didn't dare try to move her, knowing that she couldn't have carried her up the stairs even if it were safe to lift her, though she tried to make Lacy as comfortable as she could.

For a moment Eva almost panicked and then forced herself to keep calm, to think straight. She couldn't handle this alone; she had to get help. Standing up slowly so the candle wouldn't go out, Eva made her way back up the stairs and down the long hall. She didn't dare leave a lit candle behind, and desperately hoped Lacy would remain unconscious until she returned.

There was a telephone on a table in the foyer. Eva rushed for it, and the candle went out. But she didn't need any light to get through to the operator. She dialed O and put the receiver to her ear. It took a full two seconds for Eva to realize that in the storm the telephone lines had been blown down, too. But she dialed again, willing it to work. The phone was dead. She hung up slowly, trying to think of her next move.

There was no one in the house, no one anywhere around, except Reese. Eva opened the hall closet and pulled out the first coat her hand reached. It was a lightweight beige raincoat. She pulled it on, buttoning it as she moved toward the front door.

Far in the distance among the trees, Eva could see the single light of a lantern blazing in the window of the guest cottage. She would have to run through the woods toward the light. But when she tried to open the front door, the force of the wind blew her backward into the hall. As the thunder roared around her, Eva trembled as much in frustration as in fear before gathering all of her energy and pushing against the door.

It slammed behind her as she raced across the porch and down the stairs, stumbling, falling and picking herself up. She had to get to Reese.

Whipped by the wind, the rain stung her face and low-hanging branches slapped against her as Eva dashed toward the cottage blindly, unable to see anything except the light in the distance. Halfway there, the heel of one shoe caught in the mud and slipped off her foot. When she reached down to put it back on, a limb landed in the path in front of her. Struggling into her shoe, Eva made her way around the branch through the thick undergrowth until she found the cleared path again and started to run, heading for the cottage, not even hearing the storm now.

When the storm began, Reese had taken out his lantern, expecting the inevitable electrical failure. It didn't bother him in the least; he was used to hardship far greater than being without lights. In fact, he'd always enjoyed a stormy night in the South as a time to relax with a glass of brandy and read in the light of a lantern, an easy time, but a lonely time.

When the lights went out, he'd turned the stereo to battery power, put on a symphonic tape and turned the volume up to compete with the noise of the storm. Then, putting the book aside, he'd watched the rain through the living room window.

The lightning flash that broke open the sky when Eva stepped onto his front porch seemed to light up the whole universe. In that flash, Reese saw her standing on the porch, her hair plastered to her head, her eyes huge with an emotion that at first he thought was a need like the one that was raging through him. For an instant he gave himself over to the crazy notion that she'd come to him with that need—come through the storm wanting him as he'd been wanting her.

Reese gave his head a shake, dislodging the fantasy and knowing the look in those huge eyes was panic. He pulled the door open, and she fell into his arms. He allowed himself to hold her for an instant, feeling the throbbing of her heart through the oversize raincoat, before he asked, "What's the matter? Is it Mother?"

Eva nodded against this chest. "She fell—"

Reese let go of her only long enough to grab a raincoat and put it on. Then with his arm firmly around her, he opened the door. Suddenly Eva was in the storm again. But this time Reese's arm steadied her, and in spite of the driving wind and rain, she didn't fall or even stumble as they made their way to the house.

Once inside, Reese asked, "Where is she?"

"The cellar," Eva managed to respond.

"Do you have a candle?"

"Yes," she mumbled. It was still on the hall table.

Carrying the lantern, Reese headed toward the kitchen, and Eva, calmer, her panic over now that Reese was here, began to think more clearly. Before he'd reached the end of the hall, she was on the porch again, heading for her car.

She drove around to the back of the house and across the lawn to the kitchen door where she parked so that the lights blazed a path from the car to the house.

Reese appeared at the door with his mother in his arms. "Good thinking," he called out through the rain as Eva went around the other side of the car to help him stretch Lacy out on the back seat. "Watch her leg," he told Eva, "It's broken." Gently Eva lifted Lacy's legs and Reese settled her on the seat.

"I'll take her to the hospital," he said. "Go back into the house and get yourself dried off before you catch pneumonia."

"No," Eva said, "I want to go with you." Before he could object, Eva was in the car, and they were on their way.

But it was slow going. The road, narrow and barely accessible at best, was already waterlogged, and Eva found herself trembling as she reached into the back seat and grabbed hold of Lacy's hand.

"It'll be all right," Reese assured her. "I've driven this road in worse conditions. What happened?" he asked Eva as he drove.

"She went down to the cellar to get a bottle of brandy. I imagine the lights went off while she was on the stairs, and she lost her footing. Reese, will she be all right?" Eva asked.

"I think so. Her pulse is strong. It's probably just a slight concussion. I'm worried about the leg, though." At that moment, a sapling bent low and was uprooted in the wind, blocking the road. "Damn," Reese cursed under his breath as he pulled the car to a stop.

"I'll help." They got out, trudged through the mud and together managed to pull the tree off the road. Reese looked over at her when they got back into the car and smiled. It was the first real smile she'd seen— the others had been half smiles, wry and often sarcastic. This was different.

By the time they reached the highway, the rain was falling in sheets, but Reese stepped on the gas, and the car roared through the night. "It's not much farther," he said, reassuring Eva, who was once more holding on to Lacy's hand.

Just as the hospital's lights came into view, Lacy stirred, moaning softly, and Eva squeezed her hand. "It's going to be all right, Lacy; we're at the hospital, and you're going to be fine."

Next to her, Reese smiled again.

## Chapter 5

Eva and Reese had been sitting uneasily in the emergency room for almost an hour. But there was a tenseness in the air that had nothing to do with the accident. Now that the rush to the hospital was over, they were left with empty time that could be filled only by waiting. It was obvious they were uncomfortable waiting together.

Reese was concerned about Eva sitting in the large chilly room for so long with wet shoes and still-damp hair. Since the rain was letting up, he'd suggested she take the car and return to Diligence Hall. Stubbornly she'd refused and then wondered if her refusal had angered him, feeling suddenly out of place in spite of her concern for Lacy.

After all, she wasn't a member of the family. Reese was Lacy's son; Eva was a guest, and not even a welcome one.

Yet they'd gone through a long night together, arriving at the hospital emergency entrance to find a young paramedic reading a book behind the desk. He'd roused himself, called for a stretcher bed, and they'd wheeled Lacy into the examining room. The intern on duty had immediately realized that Lacy's leg would require more than a simple set.

"I think surgery is indicated," he'd told them after explaining the nature of the complicated break. "I'm going to send for the doctor on call."

They'd waited another half hour until the doctor arrived, agreed with the diagnosis and ordered that Lacy be prepared for surgery. He assured Reese, "She has the constitution of a woman half her age, and I don't foresee any problems. However, it will be complicated, Reese. She'll be in the operating room for an hour, possibly two, and there's no need for you to wait." But the doctor gave that advice knowing full well that Reese wasn't going anywhere that night, not until he knew that Lacy was out of danger.

They'd stayed with her as long as possible, chatting and laughing and keeping Lacy—and themselves—in good spirits. But as soon as she'd been wheeled into the operating room, and they'd taken seats side by side on the uncomfortable green plastic chairs to wait, the atmosphere that had been jovial for so long became suddenly strained.

There were no further attempts at conversation until Reese suggested that Eva go into the lounge and dry her hair. She managed to comply with the help of an automatic hand dryer and a supply of coarse paper towels. Then she shed the soaked raincoat, took off her torn stockings, got most of the mud off her shoes and returned to the waiting room looking almost presentable.

Presentable wasn't the way Reese would have described that look. With her hair hanging down to her shoulders, Eva had the scrubbed-fresh appearance of a beautiful young girl. He turned away to avoid even the first careless fragment of another fantasy as she sat back down beside him.

Eva had gone to the lounge as much to get away as to get dry, and the few minutes apart had given her a chance to breathe a little easier. But when he'd looked away from her so quickly when she returned, Eva had been afraid they'd lapse into tenseness again.

She'd started to talk, and Reese responded. Soon they'd dispelled the uneasiness.

"I'm finally learning what it's like to wait in a hospital corridor while a broken bone is being set," Reese said. "I guess the tables get turned eventually. My parents spent many long hours here when I was growing up."

"Don't tell me you were accident prone," Eva said, pleased that he was sharing this recollection with her, but unable to imagine Reese Benedict as a less than perfect child.

"A broken nose, leg and ankle," Reese listed, "not all at the same time!" he added. "I was a studious kid, but that didn't keep me from taking my share of tumbles off bikes and out of trees and, of course, off horses. Later, when I went to school and managed to keep myself in one piece, Beau carried on the tradition. So Mother spent her share of time in this waiting room. I doubt if she ever imagined I'd be waiting here while *she* had a broken leg set." He smiled, but Eva knew that he was worried when he added, "Of course, it's more serious when you're older. Bones are more brittle, and they don't heal as quickly."

While they'd been driving to the hospital with Lacy lying in the back seat, Reese had assured her that everything would be fine. Now Eva realized that he was far from confident. It was her turn to reassure.

"I'm sure she'll be all right. As the doctor said, she's a very strong woman. I felt that the first time I met her."

Reese agreed. "Yes, the strength has evolved over the years. When I was a child, she was very shy; timid, actually, and not at all outspoken. But there was always that grit at the center, where it counted. She was so young when she married my father that I think Diligence and all it entailed confounded her. The years have made Mother strong and given her a good sense of values, as well. She filters the important from the trivial better than anyone I know. She's also developed a pretty good sense of humor."

Eva agreed, but she couldn't help thinking about the house tours—which Reese objected to so vehemently—and Lacy's other recent decision, to let Marchetti Films into her home. Evidently, Reese was thinking along those same lines.

"She's gotten a bit stubborn over the years, too," he said with a twinkle in his eye, which told Eva that maybe, just maybe, he was beginning to change his mind about having the film company at Diligence. Certainly, as they sat together, relaxed and even friendly, he didn't seem to be harboring any objection to this one member of the film company. Eva hoped his acceptance would continue after they got through this crisis together. Everything would be easier if they could keep the rapport that seemed to be developing between them.

It was easy for Eva to maintain a friendly atmosphere: she *felt* like talking and was soon telling Reese about her childhood and her lack of broken bones. "Maybe we were made of stronger stuff in the Midwest," she teased, "but I was a real tomboy and never even sprained an ankle."

"Wait a minute," he said, not hiding his confusion. "*Where* in the Midwest?"

"A little town near Madison, Wisconsin," Eva answered, knowing that he was surprised.

"Good Lord, I thought you were born into this sophisticated life."

Eva laughed. "Hardly. My father owned a dry goods store. I never left Wisconsin until I was sixteen, and that was a summer vacation to visit relatives in Chicago."

"I'm dumbfounded," Reese said, shaking his head. "How did you end up with Marchetti?"

"That's a *very* long story," Eva answered.

"Well, let's go down to the cafeteria for a cup of coffee, and you can tell it to me."

Eva willingly got up, welcoming the thought of another setting besides the fluorescent-lit waiting room. "But I'm not sure I want to go into my life story."

"Just a little of it," Reese suggested, "enough to satisfy my curiosity." He was unable to hide his delight at being proven wrong in his assessment of her.

The cafeteria wasn't much of an improvement over the waiting room, and the coffee was barely drinkable, but they drank it anyway, joining a small group of people waiting at the end of a stormy night that had left its share of accidents.

Sitting at a table in the middle of the room, Eva thought that they could have been just another couple waiting out a crisis—except they weren't just another couple. Eva was assistant to Gino Marchetti, a woman who'd crossed the world many times before reaching Corinth, South Carolina; sitting across from her was a world traveler equal to none.

"But underneath it all, you're just a country girl," Reese said, still amazed, "even though you seem like nothing of the sort."

"Deep down, you'll find pure Wisconsin," Eva informed him.

"That sounds like my wife," Reese commented. "No matter where we lived in the world, she always called Corinth home." He rarely talked about Barbara any more, even to close friends, and surprised himself by mentioning her to Eva.

Eva felt his discomfort and quickly added, "And now here you are, disproving Thomas Wolfe's contention that 'you can't go home again.'"

Reese nodded and then became aware that he wanted to tell her more about himself, about what had made him come back and even about the fact that he still hadn't been able to find the peace he'd been searching for.

And she wanted him to tell her more, to explain why he'd come home to this life, and how, after seeing what he'd seen, Reese could be content with the view of the river from his cottage.

But neither of them got a chance to continue the probing, because the doctor was crossing the room toward them. Two hours had passed, and the surgery was over.

Reese stood up. Eva could tell he was apprehensive, but the look on the doctor's face as he reached their table quickly turned the apprehension to relief.

"She's going to be fine," the doctor said. "It took time because there was shattered bone as I'd anticipated. It's all cleaned up now, and her leg is set. She had a slight concussion but didn't even need stitches."

"Can we see her?"

The doctor shook his head. "Why don't you wait until morning, Reese? She's just coming out of the anesthesia. There'll be some initial pain that I'd like her to sleep through. In the morning she'll feel more like seeing you."

"You're sure she's going to be all right?" Reese asked. "No possible complications?"

"Not a one. Guaranteed. The problems will start when she wakes up tomorrow and decides she's ready to walk out of here. Which she'll try, if I know Lacy. Be here then, Reese," the doctor added with a wink as he shook hands with both of them and sent them off.

Outside the rain had stopped. Eva and Reese stood for a moment on the concrete steps of the hospital and breathed the clean air. There were tree branches scattered everywhere, but the wind had died down, and the moon had appeared to light up clouds that were motionless in a calm sky. The whole world seemed to have been washed fresh and pure.

Reese reached for Eva's hand as they walked to the car. It was the first time he'd touched her since their run from his cottage to Diligence Hall. Even then, the touch had been one of necessity as he'd led her through the storm. This time he wasn't helping her or comforting her. Eva didn't try to interpret it further; she simply kept her hand in his.

Reese drove Eva's rented car fast through the night toward Diligence with the windows open and the wind blowing her hair. As the car shot through the darkness along the wet road, Eva was reminded of the long night rides with Franco coming home from a trip or a weekend away. He'd driven fast, too, and there'd been the same scent in the air, the fragrance of a night washed clean. She felt familiarity as they raced along, and a sort of strangeness, too.

Reese sensed both and wanted to ask why she was so quiet. Yet something prevented him from intruding. He turned on the radio, and the sound of the music brought her back. Then he spoke. "Now tell me," he said gently, "how it happened that a girl from Wisconsin ended up with Marchetti Films."

Eva shook her head. She could tell him some of it, she convinced herself. They'd been so close during the long night as they waited for the doctor that it seemed appropriate to let him know a little more about herself. "I met him in Italy."

Reese smiled. "Let me rephrase my question: how did a little girl from 'a little town near Madison, Wisconsin,' end up in Italy?"

"I won a grant to study films in Rome."

"Ah-ha," Reese said. "And after you graduated, the school sent you for an interview with Marchetti."

For a moment Eva thought about letting that explanation suffice. It was certainly a logical one, and the real story wasn't something she was proud of. Yet the closeness remained, and because of it, she answered, "No, I never finished the school. I hardly even started. I met Gino through his son. Well, not through him so much as because of him."

"Was it Gino's son you were thinking about just now, when you were so silent?" Reese asked.

Eva tried not to show surprise that he'd all but read her mind. She tried not to think of their closeness, which two people usually shared only after years of being a couple. She tried to regard his remark as a guess, a coincidence, when she answered.

"Yes, I was remembering how Franco used to love to drive at night. Often we'd go to Naples or to the

Riviera for the weekend, and we'd always come back very late. He drove fast, too," she added for no real reason.

"He was very important in your life," Reese stated, and once more it was a fact that assumed the truth. Eva could only nod. "Did you meet him at the film school?" She shook her head. "Or on the Via Veneto?" It was obvious that Reese was going to continue asking questions until she answered with more than a nod or a shake of the head.

"The Via Veneto's close," she said finally, trying to keep her voice light and not let him hear any despair. For despair was the word she most often associated with Franco. "I was the proverbial small town girl arriving in Rome, and anyone meeting me in those first weeks would have been able to see right away that I wasn't going to last. I was too naive and far too romantic. Franco sensed that immediately."

Eva smiled and then said, "Actually, I did meet him near the Via Veneto, in a little café. I thought it was pure happenstance, but in fact he often went there—to meet women for his collection."

Reese looked over at her sharply, and she could see a sting of pain—pain for her—in his eyes. She tried to keep her voice disinterested. "Franco collected women the way some men collect art."

Eva turned to look out the window. The wind was still whipping in her hair, and she liked the feeling it gave her, a feeling that was close to freedom and close to release; it was a feeling that allowed her to tell the rest.

"I didn't know about the collection then," she said softly. "Even if I'd known, it might still have happened. I was young and in love." Eva remembered the day she made her decision to move out of the dorm.

She'd packed up her clothes and her books and waited there on the steps for Franco, not giving a thought to anything but him, knowing that she loved him and he loved her, and in time they'd marry. She'd thought she might even continue her classes at the film school....

Of course, that hadn't been possible, and marriage had never been a consideration for Franco. But Eva knew none of that as she waited for him, bright-eyed and excited, thinking her future would consist of nothing less than the love and laughter they'd shared so far.

"Anyway," she said, not dwelling on the way it had ended, even in her mind, and certainly not telling any of that to Reese. "My time in the collection was over, and there I was alone in Rome—no school, no place to live—wondering what to do next. I'd met Franco's parents and liked them very much, so I girded up my courage and asked Gino for a loan to get back to the States."

Reese found himself frowning. "I'll bet Gino Marchetti doesn't lend money to just anyone."

"In fact, he didn't even lend it to me," Eva said with a laugh. "He did something even better. He gave me a job, and here I am."

"Yes," Reese said, reaching over and touching her hand, "here you are." The touch was more personal than his hand holding hers as they'd left the hospital, even though that had lasted much longer, and this was fleeting.

They rode on through the night in silence, and when they reached the house, Reese pulled the car into the drive and turned off the ignition. He sat quietly for a long moment before he got out. Then he opened her door and led her up the stairs, leading without actually touching her. Yet even the lack of touch was compelling.

At the door he waited beside her with no move to open it. As far as Eva could tell, he might have been planning to stand beside her indefinitely.

If Reese had a plan, it might have been just to stand there, so close in the night air that the freshness of Eva seemed to be mixed with the freshness of the night. Their bodies were only a heartbeat apart; only a kiss separated their lips. Reese leaned toward her to make that kiss a reality, his face so close that she could almost feel the touch of his whiskers. She knew what his day's growth of beard would feel like on her skin, but she wondered how his lips would taste. Soon, she would know that, too. She closed her eyes, and the front door burst open.

Beau dashed out of the house. "There you two are," he said, oblivious to everything. "I got home about an hour ago, and all the lights were blazing. The back door was wide open," he rattled on, "the cellar light was on, and there were broken jars all over the place. What's happened? Where's Mom?"

Reese couldn't sleep. He'd stayed at Diligence Hall long enough to explain the night's events to his brother and come home as the first light of dawn was making its way over the live oak trees beside the cottage. He was tired, but he didn't even bother to undress and get into bed. Reese knew himself well enough to know that there'd probably be no sleep this night—or what was left of it.

He poured himself a brandy and returned to the chair where he'd been sitting when Eva had turned up like an apparition on the porch. He'd been watching the storm and thinking of a woman whom he'd expected to be nothing more than a nuisance to him. Suddenly she had become an obsession.

Reese Benedict had never been one for fantasizing, certainly not one for romanticizing, yet he'd done both—and not just during this night. He'd thought about her during most of his waking hours, watched her from the distance and finally, knowing that he was getting involved in something he neither wanted nor needed, forced himself to stay away from Diligence Hall and Eva Sinclair.

Then she'd come to him in the storm, and for that one paradoxical moment he'd thought his need had somehow been transferred through the woods and across the fields to Eva, drawing her out into the storm. Of course, he'd realized immediately the absurdity of that thought. Still, it had stuck with him for that long moment and created a turmoil inside unlike anything he'd ever felt.

It tore at him now as he sat staring out into the approaching dawn, thinking of Eva, forgetting the disruption she'd brought to Diligence, not caring because she'd penetrated a part of him that had lain dormant and that he'd thought could not be touched again.

At last when he began to feel exhausted enough to sleep, Reese finished his brandy and walked down the hall to his bedroom, past the rows of photographs from a lifetime of travel across continents. He hadn't intended to hang the pictures, hadn't even meant to keep them, but Lacy had other ideas. As soon as he'd moved into the cottage, she'd insisted on putting up the pictures.

"They're a part of your life; you can leave it behind, but you can't pretend it never happened," Lacy had insisted as she rummaged around in a drawer for hammer and nails and then marched into the living room, prepared to start hanging. He'd convinced her that they weren't meant for the living room but couldn't convince her to stop wielding the hammer. Finally he'd agreed to hang the pictures in the hall.

When Reese first moved back to Corinth, he'd had plenty of visitors. Old newsmen who'd worked with him in the States and overseas had dropped by to reminisce; others had come with offers of work. Reese hadn't wanted to reminisce, and he didn't plan to return to work. Finally they'd stopped coming. But they'd seen that hall filled with photographs, and they'd thought he'd be back again some day.

Reese looked at the pictures, many of them actually taken when he'd been under fire. In one shot a helicopter was landing nearby, and the wind from the propellers had almost blown the script he was reading out of his hand. Only moments later, machine-gun fire had strafed the area, and the helicopter had blown up as it touched the ground, killing the two men inside. No, he'd never go back.

When he went to bed, Reese was still thinking about Eva. They'd been together through an evening of anxiety that had made the shared hours seem intimate. Not only seem; they'd *been* intimate. He'd felt close to Eva, and she must have felt close to him; otherwise, she wouldn't have told him about Franco Marchetti.

Reese remembered the little she'd shared with him— it wasn't all, he suspected—and his heart ached for the memory of an infatuated young girl and a man who'd brought her a little happiness followed by much despair. She'd been young, though, and she'd gotten over it. Or he imagined that she had. But something he'd seen in her face told him she was carrying that hurt with her still.

As he fell asleep, Reese ached to soothe her hurt.

A little before noon he got up, drank a cup of coffee and showered. There was something very different about the way he felt as he stepped from the shower, toweling himself dry. Thoughtfully, a frown creasing his brow, he walked naked into his room, pulled on a pair of khaki trousers, brushed his damp hair and then stood motionless in the middle of his bedroom, wondering what was different. Abstractedly he walked over to the chest of drawers, opened one and pulled out a cotton camp shirt. He unbuttoned the shirt and, still frowning, put it on.

After another cup of coffee, Reese went for a walk with the dogs. As he walked, he realized that he felt good, rested and refreshed. He couldn't remember when he'd last waked up without a tight feeling in his gut, without the dread of today and the guilt of yesterday hanging over him. That was the difference. And even after the strain of the previous night at the hospital, he knew the reason for that difference was Eva Sinclair.

It was very quiet at Diligence Hall when Reese went over after his walk. Beau was nowhere to be seen. He'd left early to visit Lacy first thing, as they'd arranged the night before. Afterward he was to meet with members of the *Glory Road* crew. The gardener was busy at work trimming the hedges and picking up the debris from the storm of the night before. Inside, the cook, after a night off, was planning the day's meals.

"I don't know who's going to eat them, though, with your mother in the hospital," she told Reese. "Beau went off with nothing but a cup of coffee. I went up to Miss Sinclair's room once, but she's still in bed."

"Let's just play it by ear for a couple of days until Mother gets home," Reese suggested. "I doubt if Beau will be back for dinner, certainly not for lunch, and I also have plans—for Miss Sinclair and myself."

Shaking her head, the cook put aside her menus. "Well, let me fix you some breakfast," she said hopefully.

"No, thanks, Alma," Reese responded. "Coffee was enough for me, too. But I imagine Miss Sinclair's awake by now. She'd probably like breakfast."

That pleased Alma, who busily prepared a tray with soft boiled eggs, toast, juice and marmalade. "Do you think that'll be enough?" she asked as she added one of Lacy's prize roses in a crystal bud vase to the tray.

"Looks great," Reese said.

"I'll take it right up," she volunteered.

"No," Reese found himself offering, "let me do it."

As he climbed the stairs he couldn't help smiling at the look he'd left on Alma's face when he took the tray from her. This was an uncharacteristic gesture on Reese's part, to say the least. He tried to remember if he'd ever done anything comparable in his life. The answer was no. It had never been expected of him; he wasn't the type. Such gallant gestures were Beau's style, not Reese's. Barbara, always the attentive wife, had usually brought him coffee in bed. Well, a man could change, he told himself as he knocked on Eva's door and heard her call "Come in."

She was just waking up, curled in the sheets, her hair a blond mass that covered her face so that she looked out at him through a yellow cloud. The look was one of pure surprise. He noticed it only in passing as his eyes went on to take in the creamy skin of her shoulders and breasts, barely covered by black lace. He'd imagined her as she was now, except that in his imaginings Eva wasn't nearly as desirable as the flesh and blood woman who stared wide-eyed at him and belatedly gathered the covers around her shoulders.

Reese put the tray on her bedside table and tried to slow the steady pounding of his heart. It seemed so loud that he moved back quickly, afraid she could hear it. A flood of desire had built from within him from the moment he'd entered the room and seen her snuggled in the rumpled sheets. It rushed through him now, flooding his limbs until he wanted nothing more than to reach out and touch her, hold her in his arms. He forced himself to take a half step back.

"I thought you were Alma," she said.

"Yes, I imagined as much." For a man who was usually so glib, Reese could barely articulate the words. Suddenly he seemed to come to his senses, and realizing how out of place he was, moved away from her to the other side of the bed. He couldn't imagine what had possessed him to bring her the tray or why he was still in the room, looking at her like some infatuated adolescent schoolboy, but he couldn't bring himself to leave.

If Reese was confused, Eva was confounded. She'd never expected to wake and find him in her room. To see him standing there, so tall and masculine, carrying the tray with the rose vase had surprised her; it had also excited her. When he'd stood so close to the bed, looking down at her, she'd thought for a moment that he was going to reach out. Then he'd quickly turned away, and something about that was disconcerting, too. She couldn't be sure whether he wanted to leave or whether he wanted to stay—or whether he, like Eva, wanted both at the same time and couldn't handle the resulting confusion.

"Would you like for me to open the curtains?" he asked suddenly.

Eva looked at him and nodded. He pulled the sash, letting the sunlight into the room where the silence was almost palpable. If he couldn't bring himself to leave, Reese knew that before he embarrassed both of them any more, he'd have to end this wordless dilemma.

"I wanted to thank you," he said finally, with some of the presence that was more typical of Reese Benedict, "for what you did last night."

She nodded, her recovery less apparent.

"I certainly appreciated your quick thinking," he added.

Again Eva nodded.

"And going with me to the hospital, waiting with me—I appreciated that, too. You didn't have to—"

"But I wanted to..."

"I'm glad you did..."

Their words overlapped, and in the confusion, they both managed to laugh, nervously.

"I'm going to the hospital this morning," Reese said. "Would you like to come with me?"

"Yes, I would," Eva answered almost without thinking.

"Does the crew take Sunday off?" he asked.

"Yes," she responded equally as quickly.

"Then maybe we can go for a drive so you can see something of our countryside in daylight. Last night, I'm afraid, you didn't see the low country at its best. We could spend the day together, what's left of it," he added, and Eva realized that the Reese Benedict she'd gotten used to since arriving at Diligence wasn't always forceful and demanding. He could be gentle, and he could smile—that wonderful smile she'd seen twice the night before and was yearning to see again.

She knew something had changed between them during their night in the storm. Right now she didn't want to analyze it. Instead she was going to reach out for it and enjoy the day. "I'd like very much to go for a drive," she said.

She got the smile she'd hoped for.

At Reese's suggestion, Eva lingered over her breakfast. Since it was going to be a long lazy day, she could take her time. But as she drank the fresh orange juice, she realized that she didn't want to be alone any longer. Reese had gone downstairs to wait for her, and she suddenly missed him.

Eva got out of bed, lingering over the choice of what she would wear. She chose a pair of tight pink-and-white checkered pants and an oversize yellow shirt that she'd bought on a whim before leaving Los Angeles. Eva usually dressed more conservatively, but she told herself that the all-cotton outfit would be comfortable in the heat. When she put it on, she knew she didn't want to resemble Eva Sinclair, the business-woman.

Reese caught his breath when he saw her, more because of the colors of her outfit than the style. In the days she'd spent at Diligence, Eva had worn pale tones—beiges, creams, white—and here she was in a splash of bright pink and yellow.

"So this is how a film executive dresses on her day off," he said, taking her arm.

She answered honestly. "I don't know what got into me."

"Whatever it is, I like it."

Lacy liked it, too. "You look refreshing," she told Eva when they arrived at the hospital. "Just what I need to brighten my day."

"Has it been bad?" Eva asked seriously.

"Not really, just boring," Lacy answered with a smile. "Thank you for coming and for rescuing me last night. The last thing I remember is tumbling down the stairs with all those jars of preserves crashing around me! Beau told me what happened." Lacy looked up at Reese. "Wasn't Eva marvelous to go out after you when she's so afraid of storms?"

"I thought she was remarkable last night, Mother, but I had no idea Eva was afraid of storms." He looked at Eva questioningly.

"Well, I'm not any more," she said, trying to make light of what had been a legitimate fear. "Last night was all I needed to get it out of my system!"

"I'm just glad you were there. I *knew* having you at Diligence Hall was a good idea." Lacy flashed a look at Reese, who saw it was one of those looks that demanded an answer.

He was happy to give her one. "I totally agree with you, Mother," he said as Eva blushed and Lacy beamed.

"We're certainly glad to find you looking so good," Eva commented to change the subject.

"Beau brought me my makeup, thank heavens, but I told him I'd need a little something for the inside, as well. He's going to ask Alma to fix up some barbecue for dinner. The hospital food is inedible," she informed them in a voice she purposely projected as far as the doorway.

"I heard that, Lacy Benedict," the doctor said as he walked into the room. "And I'll allow outside supplies only if you promise to share the barbecue with me."

More seriously, he explained the details of Lacy's surgery and assured Reese that if she behaved herself there was no reason why his mother's leg shouldn't heal perfectly. "She can go home in a few days, and she'll be as good as new in about eight weeks..."

"Eight weeks?" Lacy repeated incredulously.

"That's how long you'll be in the cast."

"But how will I get around?"

The doctor's response was directed to Reese. "I've been trying to slow her down for years, and when I finally succeed, she's ready to be up and at it again." He turned back to Lacy. "I imagined you'd be asking that. I've put you in a walking cast, but we're going to move slowly—first a wheelchair, then crutches and then a cane."

"Well, let's get started," Lacy said. "Bring on the wheelchair. I'm ready to go home."

They all laughed, but Lacy was serious. "You wait," she said, "I'll be out of here by nightfall."

Reese grabbed Eva's hand. "We better hurry if we're going to have time for that drive!"

## Chapter 6

Late in the afternoon, the huge trees along the roadside cast shadows that left Eva and Reese in near-darkness as they drove toward the sea.

"This is the unearthly time of day," Reese said, "when the South you imagined really comes to life."

"The South I imagined?" Eva was only half listening. She'd relaxed in the convertible, her hair blowing in the wind as she looked up and watched the sun trying to reach them through the massive trees.

"Yes, when Gino told you to get on a plane for Corinth, you imagined a mysterious, shadowy place, didn't you?" He glanced at her out of the corner of his eye, watching as the faint glimmerings of sun caught like gold dust in her hair.

Eva laughed lazily. "Actually I imagined *Gone With the Wind*, which is the way most people think of the South until they confront the real thing."

"And then?"

"In many ways it's what I pictured," Eva admitted, "with beautiful homes like Diligence, slow-moving rivers and lush greenery."

"And what about the people?" Reese persisted. He found himself interested in everything she thought and felt, and for the first time in a long while, his reporter's instinct was alive.

Eva laughed. "Most of them are pretty slow, too, as if they're still in the past, resisting change." When Reese didn't answer, Eva realized that she'd unintentionally included his feelings in her assessment and quickly added, "The biggest surprise was the weather. I expected hot, but—"

"'It's not the heat; it's the humidity', as they say down here."

"They're absolutely right," she agreed. "I'll never know how Scarlet and Rhett managed without air-conditioning."

"Managed what?" Reese asked with a grin.

Eva didn't respond to the sly innuendo except with a twinkle that she couldn't keep from her eye. It had been like that between them all afternoon, light, amusing and totally enjoyable.

"But all of this," Eva said more seriously, indicating the scenery around them, "is magic to me. I've never been anywhere quite like it."

"Sometimes for brief flashes I'm reminded of places I've passed through. There's something here that's reminiscent of the countryside of Vietnam during those rare peaceful moments that happened when I was there. The same rich black soil, tropical foliage, little houses along the roadside with naked kids playing in the yard while their mom sweeps the porch with a homemade broom."

Looking out the window, Eva saw such a scene as they went by, and the children in the yard grinned, white teeth flashing in their black faces. She found herself smiling back.

"As you mentioned, it's like a land that time never touched." With that, Reese acknowledged that he'd understood her remark and was, indeed, a member of that group that had left the modern world behind. The difference, Eva thought, was that he'd done so out of choice; some of the others hadn't been given alternatives.

"Let me show you a good example of our past," he said, turning onto a narrow washboard-rutted road and driving through thick foliage that scraped against the car. He pulled to a stop in front of brick remains that had once been a towering edifice.

"It must have been magnificent," Eva said, looking up at the huge chimneys that still stood like sentinels guarding the ruins.

"The owner was killed during the Civil War. His family couldn't keep it up, and eventually the house was abandoned. Slowly, over more than a century, the elements had their way with it."

They walked around the brick shell of the house. From the stones wildflowers sprung in profusion as if they'd been meant to grow there in this monument to the past. "It's a past that's still alive, isn't it?" Eva asked.

Reese rested his hand against the brick wall. "Yes. Only in the South do you still see such evidence of the toll left by the Civil War. This was destroyed by the war just as surely as a house razed by Sherman on his march to the sea. In its way, Heyward House paid the ultimate price." His hand on the wall was affectionate. "The South was a defeated land, and defeat leaves behind its scars."

Eva looked from the house to the man standing near her, and she wasn't thinking of that long ago past any more; she was thinking of *his* past and wondering what kind of scars were hidden within him. He'd mentioned his wife the night before at the hospital, but Eva knew there was much more that he hadn't mentioned. He might never tell her about it, but it was still there beneath the scars.

"They're all covered now," Reese said, and when Eva frowned, he explained, "The scars, they're covered by all this verdant green." She nodded, still thinking of Reese's scars and wondering if they'd ever heal. He'd walked a little ahead and then stopped to look over the land with a gaze that was almost tender. It reinforced what Eva already knew: the love he carried for his place of his birth, the place he called home after years of roaming the world, was a deep love. Clearly, this land was his sanctuary.

They sat side by side on the stone steps. Above them, vines grew over the brick, springing up wildly with no pruning hand to contain them and covering everything in sight. A moss-infested tree beside the house had reached out decades before and pushed its gnarled limbs through the gaping hole above their heads that had once been a dormer window.

A sudden hot breeze sprang up and then quickly died, but it had caught in the moss and blown it against Eva's face, tickling her cheek. She brushed it away with her hand, her fingers trailing through the lacy gray tendrils.

"Of course, there's a legend about the moss," Reese said.

"Of course," Eva repeated. She leaned back against the bricks, staying in the tree's shade. Out of the sun, she could still feel its midday heat on her skin.

"When the first settlers came to this land and built their great plantation houses, one of the planters, an older, cruel character of ill repute . . ."

"Brought a beautiful young bride to be mistress of the plantation," Eva finished.

"And since you guessed that, you probably also deduced that she soon fell in love with someone else, a handsome young man, who was foreman of the vast plantation. When the cruel husband found out about the illicit love affair, he heartlessly killed the foreman. His young wife became so distraught that she hanged herself from the limb of a live oak tree." Reese paused, waiting for Eva to finish the story. When she remained silent, her lips curved in an expectant smile, he continued. "Her long blond hair, blowing in the wind, slowly turned gray, and the tendrils spread from tree to tree, always the reminder of unrequited love. And don't tell me you didn't guess that ending."

"Yes, I did," Eva admitted, "but I was also thinking that it's too bad these stories always end with unrequited love."

"No different from the movie you're making," he reminded her.

Eva countered, "We're not sure of the ending, remember? But I expect you're right. Our heroine may not be able to cope with her new life here in this land that's so strange to her."

"Just as it's strange to you," Reese remarked.

Eva had to agree. "Let's just say it's different. Different from Wisconsin where I grew up, and from any other place I've ever seen. It's so steeped in history and tradition and old ways, as if anything new would be harmful." She challenged him to respond.

This time he did. "Maybe it *would* be harmful," Reese said as they got up and started to walk toward the jungle of flowers that had once been a formal garden. "Change can be a spoiler of things," he commented, and Eva thought again how unlike the energetic, probing newscaster he'd become.

The flowers grew in untamed masses, choosing their own paths toward sunlight, lazy, carefree as the land from which they sprung. As they walked along the overgrown paths, Eva could feel the heat soaking through her, turning her shirt dark with dampness. With a hand that seemed weighted down by the heat, she wiped the perspiration from her forehead.

Reese noticed the gesture. "Ready to put an end to the sight-seeing?"

"No," she protested. "I just need a few minutes of air-conditioning before we move on to the next adventure."

"You're actually ready for more, even after the church, the old slave market and the ruins of Heyward House?"

"I'm just beginning to get interested," she said with a laugh.

Encouraged, Reese took her hand. They were both hot, sticky; she could see the damp glow on his skin, feel the heat in his touch. As they walked toward the car, the sun slipped through the trees, baked down on them. Eva felt a lethargy that almost overwhelmed her. She reached out to hold on to the door of the car as he opened it for her. Reese, seeing Eva grow suddenly weak, caught her in his arms.

They stood together, her damp body against his, and for a moment Reese forgot Eva's fatigue and let himself hold her, feeling her supple, pliant body pressed innocently and wearily against his. He could hear the beating of her heart and wondered if she could hear the accelerated racing of his. Then he returned to the moment, touched her hair and asked, "Are you all right?"

Eva nodded. "I don't know what happened."

"It's just the heat. Sometimes it hangs too heavily on the air to withstand." Eva had found her footing again, but he still held her firmly. When he finally took a step back, he kept his hand on her arm to make sure she wouldn't fall.

Eva could feel the yellow cotton shirt sticking to her skin. Reese had noticed it, too. His gaze, at first concerned for her as he watched to see if she could stand alone, slowly took in all of her, lingered, then stopped. The oversize shirt was roomy and unrevealing—except in the heat of coastal South Carolina. It clung to her damply, provocatively.

Eva could feel her nipples straining against the wet material. His touch had excited her, just being in his arms for a moment had her blood pounding. Once again she had a premonition of danger.

"I'm fine now," Eva managed, ducking her head and getting into the car. There she waited, her eyes avoiding Reese, until he stepped forward almost reluctantly and closed the door.


Far down the highway that led back toward Diligence, Reese turned off the road again and stopped the car. He wasn't sure why he had done it, why he had brought her to this special place. He left the engine running so that the air-conditioning would continue to cool Eva as he spoke. "This is a favorite place of mine...a nice panorama," he finished lamely, understating the beauty of the scene that stretched before them.

Eva followed his gaze. Sloping gently up from the road were acres of meadowland bordered by stately pines and magnolias. Along one side, the land rolled gently toward a riverbank. Through the trees that hugged the bank, Eva could see a wide black river. "Is this the same river...?" she began.

"Yes, it's the Sagamaw, which runs along one side of our property. In fact, we're just a couple of miles south of the border of Diligence. This land touches ours for a short span. It's quite beautiful, isn't it? So unspoiled..."

Eva nodded. "But I can't believe someone at some time didn't build a house here. The view seems too perfect to waste."

"There was a house over a hundred and fifty years ago..." Reese began.

"Of course, there's a legend about that, too."

"Of course," Reese agreed. "The daughter of the original owners was left standing at the altar by her prospective bridegroom. When her parents finally urged her to leave the church and return home, she locked herself in her room. She never came out again. Almost two decades passed. One holiday season the family went on a trip, and she stayed behind, as usual. There was a fire. Some say she started it to end her suffering at last. Anyway, the house burned to the ground, and she died in the flames. Her family built a big home in town and continued to farm the plantation, but as each generation passed, no one seemed inclined to rebuild."

"Are the remains still standing?"

Reese shook his head. "It was clapboard—built from timber on the land long before Heyward House.

There's nothing left of it; even the brick chimneys have crumbled away."

"Another sad story of the past," Eva mused aloud and then caught herself, determined not to let these tales of woe blight the sunshine of her day. "What happened to the succeeding generations?"

"The Graydons' house in town is now used as the county library. Charles Graydon is the last of the line. He and his wife retired to the North Carolina mountains, but they still hold on to the land."

"I can understand," Eva said. "It's wonderful property. In fact, I like it better than Heyward House."

Reese glanced at her. Her face looked pure and serene in the sunlight. Her eyes followed the rise and fall of the land, drinking it in with deep appreciation. He was glad he'd brought her here, he decided. She seemed to understand. With an unaccustomed burst of frankness, Reese shared a confidence with her.

"I'd like to buy this land some day, but the Graydons have never been inclined to sell."

The eyes that Eva turned to him were truly perplexed. "I don't understand, Reese. You own so much land at Diligence already, more than enough for ten families."

"But that's not the point, Eva," he explained a little tersely. "I want it as a buffer around Diligence to protect what we have."

"But Diligence seems well insulated." Sufficiently insulated, she thought, to provide a sanctuary for Reese.

"Would you suggest putting a string of trailers on the land or clearing the trees for tract housing—"

Eva thought at first that he was teasing; then she realized he was serious, voicing his worst fears. "Of course not," she interrupted, her own voice showing her impatience with his assumption.

Reese shook his head. "But what you're suggesting is that the Benedicts have enough land and don't need any more."

Eva, accustomed to being conciliatory and feeling compelled to find the right words, struggled inwardly for a moment before she spoke. "I guess it's because I'm an outsider and really don't understand what the land means to people around here." It wasn't an apology, but it did have the desired effect.

"It's really not important," Reese said flatly. "This is only a piece of land." He shrugged and in that shrug dismissed his earlier thoughts. "We still have some more time left before dark. I can show you something more interesting." He realized it had been a mistake; she didn't understand. But why should he expect her to? He didn't really know the woman, though he knew that he wanted her; he'd felt that before. When she'd been in his arms today, the desire had grown even stronger. That wasn't what he'd planned when he first met her. . . .

Reese was very quiet, and Eva was aware that the buffer around him seemed to have widened considerably. He'd been threatened; somewhere deep inside his unprotected psyche he'd been reminded of his dedication to keeping the world away. The whole county probably wouldn't be enough of a buffer for Reese Benedict. Eva felt angry with him for wasting his talent and turning away from life.

Even knowing the tragedy that he'd suffered, Eva still couldn't understand how a man of Reese's great talents and even greater perceptions could turn into a hermit. There seemed to be only one answer: Reese's view of the world situation as a newsman was more analytical than his understanding of himself and his place in that world. What he was doing wasn't fair to himself or to others; in fact, Eva felt it was selfish and could even be damaging. But she was the stranger here, so she kept her thoughts to herself.

Reese quickly assumed the role of tour guide again, stopping at a turn-of-the-century one-room schoolhouse before driving out to the levee where barges once loaded sea island cotton for shipment to the North. After assuring him that she was fully recovered, Eva trekked along with Reese and listened to more of his Southern tales, happy not to be shut out any longer. His mood had passed.

As the day ended, they drove across the inland waterway toward the sea. The road was straight and narrow, and all around them stretched the marsh, its tall grasses swaying in the late afternoon breeze. The undulating movement of the grasses was somehow haunting to Eva, and a little sad.

Reese saw that she was looking out on the lonesome scene and commented, "At this time of day when the shadows are long, the grass seems to go on forever, and the marshes appear very forlorn."

"Almost spooky," Eva agreed, "and yet so beautiful. I don't believe I've ever seen anything quite like these marshes."

"They make man seem very insignificant," Reese said, and again Eva had the feeling that nature preempted life for him. "But they're still incredibly beautiful," he said with a smile.

He seemed determined to be pleasant after his earlier change of mood, and they reached the pier laughing and enjoying themselves again. The restaurant at the end of the high rickety structure was bright, cheerful and bustling with activity.

"I guarantee that the pier will remain standing through the meal," Reese said. "Believe it or not, it's survived every hurricane that's rolled through here in the past fifty years. I also guarantee that the seafood's fresh," he added as they were taken to a table by the window. To prove his statement, the fishing boats tied below bobbed in the surf as the fishermen hauled in the last of the day's catch. "But the picture's not quite complete since I can't offer you a sunset over the ocean."

"I can see that anytime in California," Eva responded.

"Then you might be interested in our sun*rises*," Reese said. He looked at her for a long time before adding, "That is, if you're willing to get up early. You film people keep strange hours, don't you?"

"As I'm sure you remember from your days in broadcasting," Eva said.

"Touché," he answered with a grin, not perturbed by the mention of his past.

They turned to look out over the water that was pearly gray as darkness set in. A faint crescent moon rode over the sea, and beside it the evening star appeared. Nature was again dominating the scene, but now there were people in it, and Reese seemed happy to have them around. He was clearly pleased, judging from his next words, to have her beside him.

"I can't think of anyone I'd rather share this time of day with," he said thoughtfully, and Eva felt real pleasure. He was a complex man who at times had confused her, even worried her. But now his innate charm had surfaced, and Eva decided simply to enjoy the evening and not try to understand him, doubting if she ever could.

"My father used to bring me here when I was a boy. It's an old family restaurant that has changed very little over the years." Reese picked up the menu. "We always had the seafood platter with the catch of the day," he remembered aloud. "How does that sound?"

"Perfect," Eva agreed.

"It comes with hush puppies and coleslaw, and of course the fish is fried, I might warn you. Don't expect any French sauces."

Eva nodded in agreement. "I've always been one for sampling the local dishes. When in Rome—"

"Good. I knew you'd be game. Have you ever had hush puppies?"

"Never," Eva admitted. Remember, this is my first trip to the South."

"You'll like them," he decided.

A chatty waitress came, then took their order, flirting a little with Reese. When she left, Eva admitted, "I don't think I understood half of what she said. Slow doesn't necessarily mean comprehensible."

Reese agreed. "I admit that it took even me a little getting used to when I came back. But to clarify the main points: she's adding extra hush puppies, just for you, to the fish platter with scallops, shrimp, crab, and the special catch today, which is pompano; she wanted to know if we liked all the choices and hopes we enjoy our dinner."

"I caught a little of that. I must admit I'm learning more about the South and Southerners by the hour." Then she remembered something she'd meant to ask Beau. "What are chiggers?"

Reese laughed. "You're asking all the right questions. Chiggers are mites, actually, that bite like crazy and are the bane of every little kid who spends the summer running through the woods with bare legs. As a child, my legs were covered with red welts from May through September. Now for the next lesson." The dinner had arrived. "That," he said, pointing to her plate, "is a hush puppy."

Eva sank her fork into the doughy round ball and took a bite. "It's delicious."

"Nothing more than deep-fried cornmeal dough. Guaranteed to add a few pounds."

"Well, I could get addicted," Eva admitted. She took another bite before recognizing something else on her plate. "Oh, no," she said firmly. "I'm not eating soft-shelled crab."

"I thought you always sampled the local fare."

"I was lying," Eva said with a laugh.

"Eva, these are the best crab in the world—and I've tasted them on every continent."

Eva wasn't impressed. "I've never tasted *soft-shelled* crab on any continent, and never will. Now, the rest of this looks marvelous," she went on, trying to change the subject.

"I do believe you're a coward," Reese said. "Scared of thunder storms and squeamish about exotic food."

"Gino calls me a sissy."

"A good word," Reese responded, cutting a piece of crab, spearing it on his fork and holding it out to her. "Today the sissiness ends. Eat," he demanded.

Eva hesitated.

Across the room the waitress watched with what was clearly a smirk. Reese urged the fork closer; Eva glanced at him and then at the waitress, closed her eyes and opened her mouth.

Reese watched her eyes open in delight and knew he'd won.

She ate the rest of the crab and everything else on her plate with gusto while Reese looked on in amazement. She had a damned good appetite. Then he remembered that she was just a country girl. And he was a country boy, Reese reminded himself. In many ways, their lives were similar. They'd both emerged from small-town beginnings to be thrust into the middle of things, willingly and with excitement. Eva had stayed; Reese had not. That was the difference.

As their coffee was served, they talked on, easily, like two people who'd known each other forever. The night descended, its black curtain barely illuminated by the sliver of a moon. The lights dimmed in the restaurant, and even the candles flickered and threatened to go out. It was an easy time, a spontaneous time. Once he touched her hand, often he laughed.

"I like to hear you laugh," Eva told him.

"It's been a long time," he acknowledged. "You're good for me, Eva." He smiled ruefully, and Eva began to think that she'd been wrong. He hadn't isolated himself; he'd just gotten used to being lonely. "Yes," he admitted. "I never thought I'd say that about anyone."

The moment that followed his words seemed to go on forever. He'd touched her hand again and then left his hand there, covering hers. His lips spoke her name softly. "Eva."

The bright-eyed waitress materialized, and the intimacy passed. But for Reese it wasn't over. He was determined to recapture it. "Let's take a walk on the beach," he suggested on their way to the car.

Eva pulled off her shoes, and Reese did the same. They left their shoes side by side near the car. The tide was low, leaving a wide and hard-packed stretch of sand for them to walk on, barely lit by the moon and softly perfumed by the scent of the sea, which was carried on the hot, sultry breeze.

It was natural for him to slip his arm around her waist and just as natural for Eva to put her arm around him. Their bare feet left prints side by side in the sand as they walked at the water's edge, their steps, their heartbeats, their breaths in rhythm. Neither of them spoke; no words were needed.

Far down the beach they climbed a sand dune and then turned to walk back, and still no words were spoken. A warm silence had fallen like a blanket in the night, holding them close and giving them peace.

As they reached the steps that led back to the car, Eva found her voice. "Thank you for a marvelous day," she said. "I hate to see it end." Not until she spoke did Eva realize how deeply she meant the words that seemed to linger in the air.

They'd stopped walking, and she waited for him to answer, uneasy, wondering if he shared her feelings. She couldn't have known what was happening inside Reese as he heard her speak, couldn't have imagined that her words were the same words that he'd almost uttered and actually thought he *had* uttered until he realized it was her voice, not his. But it didn't matter who'd spoken; they shared the same thought. It mustn't end. Not now.

He leaned toward her, and the moon turned his eyes to silver. His arms tightened and pulled her close, so close that her breasts were crushed against him, so close that her thighs were molded to his. Even in the moonlight, heat still permeated their skin, but now it wasn't the heat of the air but a heat that came from within, a shared fever that rushed through them and overcame them, melding them together in each other's arms.

Then, as if it were too much for them, they each took a step back, a step away from the heat that was their passion. She turned; he reached out, caught her hand, held it. For an instant they were motionless, their lips breathing a shared breath, until his mouth came down on hers and took her breath away, drew it from her and left her weak and clinging in his arms. As soon as his lips touched hers, Reese knew that this wasn't going to be the gentle, feathery kiss he'd planned, but a deep demanding expression of the passion that infused him.

Eva was no more able to draw back or stop than Reese. She tightened her arms around his neck and gave herself to the moment, a magic moment on the beach, alone in the stream of light from the moon. It was a moment that stretched back in time to the day they'd met at Diligence Hall. It had been interrupted often as they'd waited and watched each other from a distance until the night of the storm and their frantic rush to the hospital. That night had begun the unraveling of the past, the stripping away of layers of reserve until they could see each other clearly.

She didn't want it to end. It forced her heart to race with immeasurable speed; it took her breath away and weakened her knees and turned her skin as cold as her blood was hot. It screamed in her lungs and filled her heart and mind with his name. Reese. Reese.

When he freed her lips and let her breathe again, her breath flowed on the night air, and his name flowed with it, spoken softly. "Reese."

"Eva," he answered. "You're more..." His lips strayed across her cheek and to her chin so lightly that Eva felt herself tremble to find that after the fierceness with which his lips had first claimed hers they could be so gentle now. "More," he repeated, "than I imagined..." His lips trailed to her neck, and again Eva trembled. "More than I dreamed..."

Reese enclosed her in his arms, wishing that his lips could taste all of her, that his hands could feel all of her. "More than..." he began but couldn't finish the rest, for his words, led by his thoughts, were transmitted into a tightening in his loins, a stab of desire so powerful that it almost frightened him. When his voice returned, the words were blunt and filled with his great need. "I want you," he said hoarsely. That was all; it told her everything.

Miraculously, her words, hesitant at first, echoed his deep feeling. "I..." she stumbled, "I want you, too, Reese."

The kiss that followed reignited the already blazing flame, and when he released her lips again, Reese knew that he couldn't get in the car and drive back across the marshes to his house. The fire within him was raging and had to be put out. "There's a motel next to the restaurant," he said. "Go there with me, Eva. Don't make me wait."

He'd added the latter because Eva had tensed slightly in his arms when he'd mentioned the motel. But he held her close, not letting her escape, pleading with her. "Eva, come with me," he begged.

The time that elapsed before he had her answer was only seconds but seemed like hours to Reese, until at last she raised her face to his, her beauty luminous in the moonlight. "Yes," she said simply. That and nothing more.

Once inside the room, Eva's gaze took in their setting and found that it was just another motel room, more modern and attractive than the Corinth Columns but not the sort of place where such feelings as those that were within her now belonged. It was far from being a romantic setting.

Reese read the look on her face and took her gently in his arms, holding her, kissing her forehead, softly caressing the suppleness of her back, reassuring her.

"It's all right, Eva," he said. "It's going to be fine." He tilted her head back with his fingertips and looked deeply into her eyes. "You're so lovely that you make any room you enter special just by being there." He kissed her lips tenderly. "Think of this as our room; what happens here will change it from an ordinary place into a rare and beautiful one. You'll see," he added, and his loving touch on her face made her believe.

Reese smiled, and Eva returned the smile, knowing that everything was going to be all right. She'd just begun to unbutton her shirt when Reese caught her hands and forced them to her sides. "No," he said. "Let me."

His head was spinning; the blood was raging through his body, and yet Reese managed to speak softly in a voice that didn't waver and to begin unbuttoning her shirt slowly, with care. When they'd stood in the moonlight and he'd kissed her for the first time, his passion had been so great that he couldn't have imagined it would be slowed into gentleness. Yet that was what he wanted now because he knew Eva would want it. He ran his tongue over his dry lips and swallowed hard, giving himself time to find and hold on to gentleness.

He'd reached the third button when her shirt fell open just enough to reveal the lacy edge of her bra. It was pale, pale blue and very thin, the material not quite covering the tops of her full breasts. He resisted the impulse to pull the shirt open in one harsh gesture. Instead, with his breath coming in gasps, he finished unbuttoning it and let the shirt at last fall from her shoulders onto the floor.

Eva could feel her breasts straining against the flimsy bra, almost bursting the material. Her nipples became taut beneath his gaze, and when he reached out and pulled the front of her bra down, her breasts spilled into his eager hands. Reese almost lost the last vestiges of his control. Reaching around her back, he tried to unhook the bra, and when that failed, pulled at it until the elastic snapped apart in his hands.

"I'm sorry," he said, "I—"

"It's all right," Eva told him. "It's all right." As she spoke, she quickly unbuttoned his shirt with nimble fingers that somehow remained calm.

He shed the shirt, and they gave themselves to an embrace far different from the ones that had come before. Now for the first time, they were skin to skin, flesh to flesh, and her breasts pressed against the dark hair matted on his chest. She buried her face in his neck and held on to him with all her strength, wanting nothing more at this moment than to hold him with her hands, bury her fingers in the hair on his broad chest and feel his taut skin quiver beneath her touch. It was enough.

But it wasn't enough for Reese, who bent over and in one motion picked Eva up and carried her to the bed. What happened next was a blur for him. As he rushed toward the moment he'd yearned for so long, he wasn't aware of his movements. Suddenly they were on the cool white sheets of the bed, and they were both naked, and he was above her looking down at her slim yet curving body stretched out beneath him.

He tried to keep his hands gentle as they reached out for her and inquisitively roamed her body, exploring every part of her—from her wide soft shoulders to her

breasts and her waist before continuing downward
over the soft mound of pale hair to caress the tender
skin of her inner thighs and her long supple legs. Then
he reversed the exploration of her body, his mouth
joining his hands in search of all of her.

Eva trembled almost violently beneath his touch,
gasping as his hands, his lips, his tongue explored her
inch by careful, erotic inch. "Reese," she called out,
and his name caught in her throat. She wasn't sure
whether she wanted to tell him to stop or never, never
to stop. He sensed her feelings and knew that he *must*
stop—for both of them, to let their senses calm a little.

Reese's hand lingered on her hip. Eva turned, and
he still held on to her, but she was reaching out now to
explore his body, so new and exciting, as he'd explored hers. She wanted to give him the same pleasure, to bring him as close to the peak of ecstasy as
he'd brought her.

But the moment Eva's hands lifted, he caught her in
his arms, and they rolled over together on the bed until he was above her and she was moving to meet him.
The journey was ending. The moment of discovery
was upon them.

As soon as he entered her, Reese knew that he
couldn't hold back, couldn't move slowly, couldn't
touch her gently any more. She was like liquid fire,
and she burned brightly for him. She was more than
he'd expected—more responsive, more exciting, more
fiercely loving, as her fingers dug into his back and she
met each deep plunge with her own sensual rhythm.

For Eva, neither memory nor imagination had prepared her for this. Nothing she remembered had ever
equaled the feelings she was experiencing now; nothing she had imagined had given her a hint of this pas-

sion, impelled by Reese's power and strength within her. Wildly she gave herself to him, swept away in a torrent of emotion, fierce, unrelenting. As he exploded within her, they cried out together above the roar of passion's tornado that was passing through them.

When it ended, when it was all over, it *was* as if a tornado had gone through the room, leaving behind spent, weakened forms tossed across the bed. They remained silent and still for a long time until finally he reached out for her, touched her first and then gathered her back into his arms, just as loving—more loving—than he'd been before at the height of his ecstasy.

"I meant to be gentler," he said, "I'm sorry if I—"

"No." Eva reached over and pressed her fingers against his lips. "Don't be sorry. It was perfect. Wonderful." There were no words.

He kissed the damp edge of her hairline. "I'm so glad. I'd meant to stay in control. I don't know what happened." Then he corrected himself. "Yes, I do." He kissed her lips. "I know exactly what happened." He smiled at her. "You bewitched me, and I lost myself in you."

Eva propped herself on her elbow so she could look down on him. "I'm glad, because the same thing happened to me." She paused and shook her head. "That's so unlike me. I'm usually in perfect control of myself and everything around me. It felt so good," she said, returning a kiss he'd given her between words, "to lose control at last." She laughed. "But only here, only with you."

"Everywhere else you can continue to be the cool, efficient Eva Sinclair." He kissed her again, more passionately. "But not here, not with me. With me, you're not Eva but Eve, the temptress who gives herself with abandon and turns an ordinary motel room into her own special paradise."

Eva looked around. The room had changed, and seemed more welcoming. "Yes," she agreed. "It *is* different now, this room."

"Our room," he corrected. "Our paradise." When he kissed her again, there was passion in his lips, and it was met with equal passion in hers, which surprised them both. "Eve, the temptress," he whispered in her ear when the kiss ended, and he moved so that her body melded into his.

Eva felt the pressure of his manhood against her again. Her head began to swim with the dizziness of her desire, and the room—their room—once more turned into paradise.

## Chapter 7

The next morning Eva awoke in another room—her room at Diligence Hall. As the sun sneaked through the blinds and teased her eyes open, she looked around from her canopied bed and thought of the room where she'd lain with Reese until nearly dawn. She remembered every detail of it, from the modern blond furniture to the tiny basket print of the wallpaper and the muslin sheets, stiffly ironed and rough against her skin. She yearned for that roughness now; it represented the passionate feelings that had lain dormant in her for so long, only to be unleashed in one wanton night with Reese.

Suddenly Eva's mouth felt his kiss, damp and hungry. She reached up and brushed at her lips with the back of her hand, and with that gesture erased the kiss that had been too vivid for her emotions to handle. Yet she still longed for the taste of him. Eva turned over and, burying her face in the pillow, buried herself in the memory of those hours together in a motel room at the end of what would always be the most surprising day of her life. She'd been surprised to find that the complicated and aloof man who'd watched her from the distance was also witty and warm and eager to find joy in what had become a joyless life. She'd been surprised at herself for so intimately sharing that joy.

Again she felt his touch, this time with a heaviness that weighted her down and caused her to turn over as if to dislodge his body from hers and get hold on her emotions again.

Eva forced open her eyes and let the bright day greet her. Its light vividly separated her from the events of the night before which began to fade and become unreal, like a dream. But it hadn't been a dream at all. What had happened between them had been very real. Reese Benedict had made love to her. Only one other man had ever stepped so daringly into her life to fill his arms with her. That man had been Franco Marchetti, and with him, as with Reese, the attraction had been immediate and overpowering. She'd lost control with Franco, given herself to him openly and willingly; she'd moved into his life and his world and, in the end, been left helpless, hopeless, alone.

Eva burrowed farther into the sheets, but she couldn't find comfort there. What was done was done. Franco was over, behind her, but with Reese she'd given herself again, willingly, to a passion that not only equaled but surpassed the feeling she'd shared with Franco. And wasn't Reese Benedict in his way as unsuitable as Franco?

Before she could prevent it, another image descended on her with a force that was almost palpable. She felt his hands at her breast, so eager that her nipples enlarged, and she had to lift the material of her gown away from her tender breasts to stop the trembling that raged through her body.

With a mixture of reluctance and relief, Eva unfolded herself from the sheets, sat up in bed, puffed the pillows behind her and leaned back, determined to think clearly. Everything was different now, she told herself. She wasn't an eager, inexperienced young girl anymore; she was a grown woman with a sensible, organized life-style. She could handle her emotions now. She knew better than to get involved.

She knew better, Eva repeated to herself, sitting up a little straighter. Once she'd been not only inexperienced but malleable, eager to be led. That wouldn't happen again. Now, as before, the setting was all wrong. Eva had seen enough location romances, and avoided her share, to know better. Italy had helped seduce her; Diligence would not. Yet here she was, sensible but still head over heels...

No, she corrected herself as she got out of bed, pulled off the short teddy that served as her nightgown, picked up a towel and went into the adjoining bathroom. She wasn't head over heels, not after one night in a motel with a man she hardly knew. She'd mentally outlined all the reasons not to be susceptible to that sort of romancing, and as she turned on the water and let it wash over her, Eva reviewed them again carefully to convince herself of their validity. To the list she added the most sensible reason of all: if it happened again, she would get hurt again.

Obviously it was possible to have a romance without being devastated. Other women did it every day. Eva thought of Mary and her present boyfriend. They knew it was only for now, and wouldn't last. All she needed was a logical outlook such as theirs, and the hurt would be avoided. Eva was mature enough to understand that, and she'd often thought of finding such a relationship for herself. But somehow, no one since Franco had been interesting enough; certainly no one had come near fascinating her.

Until Reese. Her attraction to him was so great that it frightened her all over again. There didn't seem to be room in her life for a casual love affair. When Eva Sinclair fell, she really fell. Before, she hadn't been aware of the hurt that could follow; before, she had been accompanied in her love affair by the wonder of innocence and youth. This time she saw clearly, and still the wonder persisted. It frightened her.

Well, Eva told herself as she shampooed her hair, Gino always said she was a sissy, afraid to take a chance, afraid to try anything new. She hadn't been afraid last night. Eva let the hard stream of water rinse her hair and continued to stand under it long after the soap had been washed away.

Reese had been an eager lover, overwhelming her not with force but with a gentle kind of power that led, directed and at the same time responded to her. The night had thrilled her so that she'd been overcome since waking with those erotic flashes of him. Now as the water continued to pour over her, hot at first and then warm and finally cool, she let herself relive every moment from the first touch at the car to the glances and the later, more meaningful, touches in the restaurant until the kiss on the beach that had been the real beginning. And finally...the magic moment of their blending. Her skin tingled at the thought of him, and only the stream of water that was now icy brought her back to reality.

Eva reached out and turned off the faucets, hoping that Beau already had his shower. During her vivid memories of that long night with Reese, she'd managed to use all the hot water!

Drying off, Eva wondered what it would be like when she saw Reese today. She *knew* what it would be like; they'd both be shy and evasive. The shyness had started when they'd left the motel to drive home in the hot, dark night, so uneasy that even talking was difficult. That silence, broken only by occasional words of concern, had continued until they had driven up to the doorway of Diligence Hall.

"Are you all right?" he'd asked once, knowing the answer. All right! She'd never been better. But she'd just responded softly, "Yes." He'd smiled, and she'd smiled back, and then she'd slipped into the house like a schoolgirl coming home late from an off-limits party.

Back in the bedroom, Eva stood in front of the closet and considered the selection of clothes, all off-white, beige and businesslike except for the outfit she'd worn the day before. She wished she had another splashy something, but that wasn't her image. She pulled out a blousy variation of the same old thing and put it on. Back to work, she thought wryly. Maybe she'd be able to confront Reese without embarrassment by stepping back into her familiar persona.

Downstairs she confronted not Reese, but an effusive, ebullient Beau.

"Well, this is the big day," he said as he poured a cup of coffee from the dining room sideboard. "I've been up since five this morning getting my extras together. Today's the party scene," he added.

Eva smiled. "Yes, I know."

"Oh, that's right. I guess you would know," he responded sheepishly. "But do you know I got seventy-five people, all with the right clothes, the right hair, the right *look* that will pass for the forties? A few of them are in makeup now. They'll be in the foreground wearing those bouffant, rolled, on-top-of-the-head hairstyles. Mary said we couldn't have gotten a better crowd of extras if she'd hired an agency." Beau smiled proudly. "The first unit and the principal actors arrive tomorrow," he added.

Eva glanced at him over her coffee cup.

"Oh, I guess you know that, too," Beau added with a grin. "Well, I'm pretty excited. Louise Ross has always been a big favorite of mine," he said, referring to the star of *Glory Road*.

"Then I might as well warn you that she's not what we call 'accessible.' Off the set, she stays in her trailer—alone."

"That's all right," Beau said, not about to be deflated. "At least I can watch her work."

Eva raised her eyebrows, and Beau burst out laughing. "Okay, okay," he admitted. "I have designs beyond watching. I hear she likes younger men."

"She very well might," Eva reminded him teasingly, "since she's only twenty-five herself."

Beau laughed again. "Well, some of those starlets go for the more mature types. Like Reese," he added, "although I won't have to worry about him since he's no more interested in women than he is in *Glory Road* itself."

Eva took a bite of cantaloupe to prevent the necessity of a reply.

Beau didn't seem to notice as he gulped down his coffee and stood up. "Got to make sure everyone's in place for the rehearsal," he said. "This will make a spectacular shot. Mom's furious that she's going to miss it."

Eva started guiltily. She'd almost forgotten about Lacy. "How is your mother today?" she asked, making a mental note to send flowers to the hospital.

"I just talked to her a few minutes ago. She's going strong and raring to come home. But her doctor still says it'll be a few more days. By then, I'll be a well established member of the *Glory Road* crew, assuming everything goes well today. Well, here I go—into the breach," he said, disappearing out the door, taking his clipboard and his excitement with him.

From his cottage, Reese watched the film crew set up the party shot as he'd watched other less involved shots during the early stages of production. He was aware of a change of pace now, a liveliness and determination in the air that had been missing before. The film was cranking into gear. Soon Eva's job would be completed. Soon she'd be on to another assignment, walking out of his life just as precipitously as she'd walked in—and it would be over. That last thought was accompanied by a moment of relief. Once it was over, he'd be free again, free to be alone as he'd been before she came, alone, nursing his guilt.

Reese pushed away the dog that had been nuzzling him for attention. The gesture was almost one of anger. Bridget barked sharply in confusion and looked up at her master with sad eyes. Reese smiled and gave her an affectionate pat, and he realized that his dogs and his memories weren't going to be enough for him now.

He watched as Eva appeared at the front door of Diligence Hall. The director looked up, saw her and broke away from the crowd. They moved aside, their heads close together, talking intently. Reese watched motionless and finally ran his tongue over dry lips. He knew that he wasn't looking forward at all to the time when it would be over.

She'd done something to him that no woman had ever done: she'd caused him to act irrationally. He hadn't expected that, and he wasn't sure how to handle it.

Reese tore his eyes from the scene outside and looked around the kitchen of this cottage where he'd come to be alone after life had begun to be too much for him. He thought about the reason for his retreat. He thought about Barbara. They'd had an unusual life together, but it had been good in many ways, and their lovemaking had always been a natural part of what they shared. But it had never been like last night, never stunned him with an earth-shattering pleasure. That had happened only with Eva.

When he looked out the window again, he saw her still deep in conversation, but as he watched, she looked up and glanced toward the cottage. Her eyes seemed to squint against the sun, and he thought he could see a smile form on her lips before she looked back at the director. With one hand she brushed her sunny hair away from her face, and Reese felt his heartbeat quicken. He wanted to go out and see her, talk to her, but he forced himself to stay inside. He didn't want to disrupt her work. More than that, he didn't know how he was going to react to her, what he was going to say after last night.

He was apprehensive, and Reese Benedict couldn't remember that he'd ever felt apprehension. She'd caused him to feel many sensations that he'd forgotten or never experienced. Angrily he shook his head, put her out of his mind and sat down at the kitchen table with a book, determined not to go out there but knowing that he couldn't stay away.

* * *

From high on the boom, the director of *Glory Road* checked his first shot, a wide angle of guests arriving one by one and in small groups to the party that would open the film. Off to one side, Beau and Mary stood with Dan Morrow.

"Well, I'm damned," Dan said with a grin, "if these extras don't definitely *say* '40s."

"Take that as a compliment, Beau," Mary chimed in. "In Dan's inimitable fashion, he's admitting you did a good job."

"Even though I wondered if he'd make it through the past few days," Dan observed.

"I know," Beau admitted, "I was a little hysterical, worrying about whether the clothes would be ready and the releases would get signed and everyone would actually show up on time."

"And if I'm not mistaken, Danny," Mary declared, "you have been known to experience moments of panic in your time."

"Please, darling," Dan said with a crooked grin, "don't give away my foibles to the uninitiated."

"If you're talking about my assistant, Beau Benedict, he's just about to become initiated, Danny, and if this scene films as good as it looks, he'll soon be a member of our questionable fraternity."

The call of "speed" from the sound man drifted across the lawn, the director yelled out "action" from high up on his boom, and the party began.

Half an hour later, the cameraman and director climbed down from their perch. "Looks good; now let's have the people for the tight shot."

Clipboard in hand, Beau headed across the yard, calling out the names of the extras who'd been through makeup, hair and costume and whose faces had appealed to Mary and the director.

Eva watched Beau work and realized not just how much he liked his job but how effective he was. He'd been particularly good at fending off the extras who'd hoped for more work, except for one man who was still tagging along persistently. Eva had first seen him at the general store where he'd bitterly denounced Reese. She watched and listened now as he unsuccessfully tried to worm his way into the shot and was handled effectively by Beau, who passed by Eva with a grin as the relentless little man followed close behind.

"I went out to see your Mom in the hospital," he was telling Beau. Eva wasn't surprised to hear that; everyone seemed to be privy to the assorted accidents, illnesses and problems in Corinth.

"Thanks, Ed. That was kind of you."

"Well, I didn't do it to get a part in this movie; I did it because I wanted to, but still—"

"I'm sure you did, Ed, but still," Beau repeated, "the director had certain ideas about what he wanted for this scene, and you just weren't right. That doesn't mean he won't use you later," Beau reminded him.

"I don't care about that, just so some of the folks who really need the money get chosen. This movie's good for us—good for Corinth, Beau. Business is booming in town. It's just what we need, in spite of your brother's feelings. Where is Reese, anyway?"

"He's at the cottage. Reese isn't too crazy about all this, as you might have guessed."

Eva saw Ed look toward the cottage. "Well, he can't spoil this one for us, not if I have anything to say about it."

"And I'm sure you'll have lots to say," Beau commented with a grin as the assistant director quieted everyone for the next scene.

Reese didn't appear until late afternoon and by then Ed had left. Most of the extras were slowly heading down the driveway to their cars, and Beau, exhausted, sat with Mary and Eva on the steps of Diligence Hall. The last scene of the day was being set up.

"Look at his face," Beau said as Reese approached, "It's taut. That means trouble."

"It's trouble that looks good to me," admitted Mary, who'd left her boyfriend in a card game at the motel.

Eva wondered whether the look they referred to was trouble or just uneasiness, the same uneasiness she was feeling. But Reese Benedict was too sure of himself to give in to a case of nerves.

She was wrong. He'd waited this long so that he could face her without the crowds around them, thinking that would be easier. But seeing her close up, he realized that it wasn't going to be easier at all.

Before he reached them, Reese was waylaid by the assistant director, who'd once worked on newscasts at the network. Eva could tell that Reese didn't want to talk with the AD. She saw his face tighten even more, and then unexpectedly, she saw him smile, shake hands with the man and listen attentively to reminiscences that couldn't have interested him. Then, after politely turning to chat with Mary and Beau, Reese approached Eva, touched her arm lightly and led her a little distance away. The touch had been easy, familiar, but once they were alone the familiarity disappeared.

"About last night," Reese began, unsure of what he planned to say next.

"Yes, I've been thinking about it, too," Eva answered. She didn't know what was coming, either.

"I'm sorry," Reese found himself adding even though he wasn't sorry at all and hadn't meant to apologize. "I know how it must have looked." He cursed himself inwardly, aware that he didn't give a damn how it had looked—then or now. He'd wanted her too much, still wanted her. And yet he moved his hand from her arm, losing the physical contact.

When his hand dropped away, Eva felt the distance and answered, "I was certainly to blame as much as you..." She knew the mention of blame made what had happened between them seem like a crime, when it hadn't been a crime at all; it had been a joy.

"I guess we were both carried away by the moonlight and the wine." But he'd been carried away by *her*, Reese realized. He reached out to touch her arm again, and she seemed to move slightly—or perhaps he didn't complete the gesture. Reese couldn't be sure; all he knew was that he didn't touch her and now he wouldn't touch her, not with the straggling film crew nearer, not when she looked so remote and efficient, not when his usually clear mind was so muddled.

Eva had missed the touch, or the attempt at a touch; she'd missed the confusion in his look; but she'd heard the words. They'd been clear enough. It wasn't her at all; it was the wine and the moonlight, the loneliness and the need for a woman—not Eva, but any woman. She looked away so he wouldn't see her face. "Maybe we should pretend it never happened. That might be easier since we'll be seeing each other for the next few days, and I wouldn't want things to be awkward between us."

Reese wondered how it could be any more awkward than this. They were like strangers, complete strangers, who only the night before had been fierce, passionate lovers. Now it seemed as if the intimacy had never happened. If only he could look into her eyes, but she insisted on looking away from him, as if something held her interest on the set. The shooting was over; there was no activity at all. She'd turned away because she didn't want to look at him, and Reese had no idea whether she was as confused as he was, or just disinterested.

"I can understand how you wouldn't want things to be awkward during the shooting; I wouldn't want that, either," Reese said and then reminded himself that he was allowing her to avoid his eyes. By God, he *would* see the look on her face, Reese determined. Instead of reaching to turn Eva toward him, he walked around, still keeping at a distance, to place himself directly in her view. That's when the AD called out to her.

Reese didn't hear the question; he didn't even hear Eva's reply. It didn't concern him because he'd seen her face finally, and there was nothing to read in her eyes; they were blank.

"Excuse me," she said, "I have to…" As Eva tried to explain, she realized that he wasn't listening. She stopped and waited, hoping that he would make some sign for her to stay—or to come back, for her to talk to him again. Any sign that this wasn't the last of what they had to say.

Instead he nodded his head. "I understand, Eva. The film comes first, of course." He walked ahead of her, quickly, somehow anxious to be the one to leave and thereby show his disinterest when, God knows, he'd never felt more interested. Yet he'd allowed himself to sound pompous, conceited and cold. He'd been all of those things all of his life, and he'd usually admitted them freely and even taken a kind of pride in them. Now, when he'd meant to be different, to be sensitive to her feelings, he was walking away.

Eva waited until almost midnight to return Gino's call. She knew he'd still be at the office working late, and she wanted a chance to have a long talk with him, uninterrupted by the vagaries of business that—by nine o'clock in Los Angeles—would have finally run their course. Gino would be at his desk, a glass of Soave in one hand, a cigar in the other, relaxing after a long day.

Gino's time would be her time at this hour, and Eva was ready to talk. After her unsatisfactory encounter with Reese, she sought the comfort of Gino, who'd always been there when she needed him, assuring her that nothing had changed between them. He was her rock, and his voice came over the line clear and comforting.

"*Cara*," he said with affection, "how's it going down there in Carolina?"

"As well as can be expected, I think." She tried to put some enthusiasm into her voice but failed dismally, and Gino heard the flat tone.

"Is it business or pleasure that's getting you down?" he asked pointedly.

Eva knew she'd better get to the business aspect and turn him away from what really mattered. She wasn't ready to talk about Reese to Gino—or anyone. She reacted quickly with a run-through of preproduction and the first day's shooting. "I think we're ready. I shouldn't have to hang around more than another few days. Everyone's getting the job done, and the problems I envisioned with the owners of Diligence Hall haven't surfaced. In fact—"

"I know, you gave the kid a job. Do you think that was smart?"

Eva wasn't surprised that Gino had gotten wind of Beau's position on the film; somehow, he always knew everything. "Yes, in fact I do, Gino. He saved us a lot of time and money and has actually put us a day ahead of schedule. Mary'll be on her way back to the coast in a couple of days to start casting for the new film."

"She plans to leave any problems that might come up to him?" Gino was ready to huff and puff a little.

"Yep. He can handle them."

"You think I should put the kid on staff or is he limited to Southern types?"

"I don't believe he's limited at all, Gino," she reassured him, "but you'll need to check that out for yourself."

"I plan to, *cara*, when I get there. Now tell me how you're doing with the other job."

"The other job?" For a moment Eva was confused.

"My land, *cara*, my land."

"Oh, that," Eva said, a little embarrassed. "I've been so busy, I..."

"Eva, Eva," he said impatiently, "no matter how busy you are, you always manage to do as I ask. So what have you got for me?"

"I've been reading the papers," she evaded as she juggled the phone and reached for a manila folder. "There's a twenty acre lot for sale near the highway just a few miles from town, and fifty acres down closer to the coast." Eva's eyes scanned the newspaper ads she'd circled, trying to come up with more information since she hadn't called on either ad. Uncharacteristically, she'd neglected to put her full effort into one of Gino's requests.

"What have you *seen*, Eva? That's what counts. What have you actually looked at?"

Eva tried to think of an excuse he'd accept for her inaction and knew there wasn't one. She'd have to go with the truth; that's the way it was with Gino. "I haven't looked at either of them, Gino," she admitted, "but to be perfectly frank, I didn't see any reason to go roaming over all that acreage when I don't know what I'm looking for..."

"You walk the land, Eva, tell me what you see, and I'll tell you if it's what I want. Simple, eh?" Gino's voice was curt, but Eva knew he wasn't angry yet. He depended on her, and if sometimes she needed a little prodding, he didn't mind.

But before he got really agitated, Eva agreed to look at both plots of land and report back to him. Just as she was ready to move on to other subjects, she remembered that she had, inadvertently, seen one property. "There *is* a place near Diligence..."

"You saw it?"

"Yes," Eva told him. "But I don't know whether it's what you want or not since I don't know why you—"

"Eva, Eva," Gino interrupted. "You'll know when I'm ready to tell you. Now describe what you saw. Just describe."

Eva tried to remember details that would interest Gino. "It's right on an access road," she said, "and very beautiful, a sloping valley bordered by trees and overlooking the river."

Gino grunted favorably. "How much acreage?"

Eva closed her eyes and tried to conjure up the dimensions of the property, using the river, the road and one side of Diligence as boundaries. "At least twenty-five acres," she decided, "maybe thirty, I'm not really sure."

"Sounds good," Gino said.

"But it's not even for sale, Gino."

"Everything's for sale, *cara*, at the right price. Do you know who owns it?"

"Graydon," Eva said, "I think that was the name. They don't live here, though. They've retired to the mountains."

"No problem," Gino said.

"Gino—"

"Don't ask," came the laughing response. "Just keep your eyes and ears open and have a look at those other lots for me. Keep a file, Eva, the way you always do. When I come out there, I can go right to each property, have a look for myself and decide."

"Decide what?" Eva sneaked in.

"My little busybody," Gino said with a laugh. "I'll tell you soon, but not now, and not over the phone." Eva smiled wryly to herself. Gino could make anything sound like a conspiracy. "Right now, do the work for me and stop the questions, *capisce*?"

*"Capisco,"* she replied. Sometimes she could get what she wanted out of Gino; other times it was impossible. That was the dichotomy of his nature, which kept people wondering and guessing and always a little off balance. Gino was an operator. But in the end, Eva always got her answers; she was the only one, except his wife, who knew everything—but never until Gino was ready.

After she hung up, Eva spent a few minutes speculating about Gino's little secret, looking over the schedule for the next day when the rest of the cast and crew would arrive and realized that everything was going as smoothly as on any set. Had this just been *any* set, Eva would be making plans to leave. Her reason for being here was over. It was time to go, but she was making no move to do so. And she knew why.

The schedules weren't keeping her here, placating the crew and townspeople wasn't keeping her here; neither was Gino's land search—she could do that in a day. She could have already done it if she'd been working at her usual pace. The reason was obvious. Reese Benedict.

As the night crept along, Eva realized that she wasn't going to be able to sleep. She threw a robe on over her teddy. It covered more, but was only a flimsy layer of cool ivory chiffon. Eva shrugged. Beau was out with the crew, and he'd let the servants off, so she was alone in the empty, quiet house. She headed for the kitchen, poured herself a glass of milk and sat drinking it slowly at the oak table, hoping for a miracle of lethargy to flow through her.

It didn't work. She was more wide awake than ever. Through the back windows she could see the gazebo. Its white latticework, glowing eerily in the moonlight, seemed to beckon to her. Responding adventurously she slipped out the back door and headed across the sweep of lawn, moving languidly and lazily in the heavy Carolina night.

Eva shivered a little in the warm air. The sense of mystery and otherworldliness that Gino wanted for *Glory Road* would certainly be easy to achieve with long hot summer nights like this when the past was a part of the present. Eva could feel the ghosts of the Southern belles from the stories Reese and Beau had told. She could imagine Louise Ross milking the mood for all it was worth and bringing the audience in with her. Louise wouldn't even have to act. Magic was in the air.

Eva climbed the three steps to the gazebo and turned to look back across the panorama of moonlit lawn to the eerie live oaks festooned with gray moss. The voice that came from behind her didn't even startle Eva; it seemed to fit the moment. It was a low, soft voice, Reese's voice.

"I couldn't sleep, either," he said gently. Eva turned. He'd stopped before reaching the steps and leaned against the side of the gazebo, both hands pushed down into the pockets of his white cotton pants. He was barefoot and shirtless and looked like a young boy with his dark hair tousled. "I felt restless," he added.

"Yes." Eva didn't know what to say next, but she was determined not to get into a conversation like the one earlier in the day when she'd said everything she didn't mean and nothing she meant. Better to keep quiet, she decided.

Obviously he'd made the same decision because he didn't attempt to speak again, and the silence between them stretched out endlessly, made more obvious by the sound of crickets and cicadas and night frogs. It was a palpable thing, the silence, and tension floated on it. Eva knew she had to end it even if she said the wrong thing.

"Reese, about last night—"

"Eva, I want to talk to you—"

They both spoke at once and shattered the silence and then laughed nervously. "You first," Reese said.

"No, you." Eva was suddenly tongue-tied. He hadn't come any closer, but even from where he stood she could feel the nearness of him, the force, the magnetism.

"All right," Reese said, almost with resignation. "I'll begin." But he paused again, shifted his weight from one foot to the other and took a step toward her. Eva felt herself start, and he must have seen the little jerk of her body because he stopped at once. "I felt totally inept this afternoon, trying to talk to you and wondering what you were thinking—wondering if I'd made a fool of myself."

Eva shook her head, and for the first time since they'd been together the night before, said what she meant. "No," she told him, "you could never be a fool."

Reese read the emotion in her voice and knew her words were spoken in earnest. "Thanks for that... confidence," he said, "but you'll find that it's not true. I can and do behave like a fool. Often," he added, remembering. "Just today, saying I was sorry about what happened between us. Good God," he said with fervor in his voice, "last night was the best thing that's ever happened to me."

Eva felt her whole body go weak with relief. No matter what she'd told herself, there was one thing she couldn't deny. "I feel the same way," she said softly. "But I was so afraid that you had regrets, that it had all been a whim...."

"You a 'whim'? No more than the stars or the moon." Reese reached out his hand toward her, and Eva stood up, took a step forward and placed her hand in his.

They stood as motionless as statues, Eva just inside the gazebo, Reese with one foot on the bottom step, reaching up to her. For a moment in the moonlight, neither of them moved. Then he was suddenly beside her, and she was in his arms. They didn't kiss; they just held each other with deep relief that caught like a sigh in Eva's throat. She felt so secure in his arms that she wanted nothing more, until she saw his lips opening to her, saw the slight smile playing across his mouth as he leaned forward, closer and closer.

She closed her eyes expectantly, but before his mouth touched hers, he spoke again. "Last night was wonderful," he said, voicing the truth they'd both meant to say earlier. She started to answer, but it was an answer he felt and didn't need to hear as his mouth came down on hers, softly, sweetly and then more deeply. His arms closed around her with a protective loving strength that would last through the night and into the next day when they would still be together.

## Chapter 8

"Get me out of this contraption," Lacy demanded as Reese pushed her up the stairs and across the front porch of Diligence Hall in the hospital wheelchair. "I want to walk into my own house."

Eva stood at the door while Reese, ignoring his mother, increased his speed and piloted the chair past Eva into the foyer and down the long hall. "As soon as we get to the porch, we'll move you into a regular chair."

"I'm not interested in regular chairs; I want to walk. Where's my cane?"

"Mother, you have to make the progression slowly. First the chair, then crutches, *then* a cane."

"Nonsense," Lacy objected as Reese carefully maneuvered the chair onto the porch. "For your information," she continued with a smug look on her face, "I've already mastered the wheelchair and the crutches and am quite adept at walking with a cane.

The doctor must have neglected to mention that to you."

"He must have," Reese said agreeably. "Now let me help you onto the chaise."

"Don't change the subject," Lacy said as he lifted her out of the wheelchair. "Where's my cane?"

"In the car," Reese answered with a sigh just as Eva appeared at the door carrying the crutches and cane. Without a word she placed them beside the chaise where Lacy was settled. Her expression told Reese to humor his mother. Lacy was wise enough to follow the doctor's instructions; she merely wanted the pleasure of having her walking aids nearby.

Lacy smiled at Eva and nodded with satisfaction, but as Eva had predicted, made no move to get up. Instead she looked around her for the first time. The porch had been turned into a bed-sitting room. "Oh, my," she said, amazed.

"Since this is your favorite room, and since you won't be able to go up and down the stairs for a while, I thought you'd like to stay down here, near the action," Reese added with a grin.

"Thank you, dear," Lacy said, shaking her head happily at the transformed room, complete with a sofa that turned into a comfortable bed for sleeping, a small chest, a wardrobe with her clothes and other personal belongings inside, her bookcase—and on top of it a collection of pictures of Beau and Reese through the years. "You brought down everything, even my perfume."

"And didn't break a bottle," Reese reminded her.

"I'm sorry for all the fuss, dear, and I do appreciate your efforts. Why, this must have taken all day."

Reese shook his head. "It was a cinch. I had help."

"Not from the servants, surely; they're only slightly more mobile than I."

Reese laughed. "No, I had a strong young helper." He nodded toward Eva, who was pouring a glass of iced tea for Lacy.

"Well, I might have known," Lacy said, "and I think it's about time I apologized for all the trouble I've put Eva to. She's here to see that an important film gets made, and she's spent most of her time battling storms, driving to the hospital and moving furniture—all for me."

"Well, she hasn't spent *all* her time that way," Reese said with a wink at Eva.

She turned away quickly, trying not to blush. While Lacy and Reese chatted on, she thought about the way she and Reese had spent the morning moving Lacy's room downstairs with the help of two grips from *Glory Road*, who surprisingly had shown up bright and early, ready to work.

"There's not much to do in Corinth, South Carolina, on a Sunday" had been their explanation.

"All the local girls seem to disappear before we're even out of bed."

Reese laughed at that. "They're in church, boys," he explained.

The grips glanced at each other, and Eva could have sworn she saw light bulbs go off over their heads.

"About how long do you think this job'll take us?" one of the boys asked.

Reese smiled. "I should think you'll be finished about the time church services are getting out all over town—if you work fast," he added.

They did just that, and after they left, Reese collapsed on the porch beside Eva, who inhaled the damp scent of a man who'd been exerting himself. There was a sheen of perspiration in the hollow of his throat. "South Carolina heat finds its way inside no matter how we build better and better air-conditioners to prevent it," he said as he leaned back on the porch swing.

His conversation was light and casual, but Eva was too aware of his physical presence to notice. Her breath came out raggedly long after she'd rested from the move, and a little shiver ran across her skin despite the heat and her effort to control what was happening to her.

Eva reached out as he talked and rested her hand on his forearm, and Reese noticed the little shiver that shook her body and worked its way through her fingertips. He felt it on his damp skin, and he knew what she was thinking. She wanted him. She was telling him as boldly as if she'd said the words. He looked over, and their eyes locked.

"Reese," she began.

"I know," he answered.

Suddenly Eva became embarrassed by her need. Never had she let her feelings take such complete control. Never had she been the one to initiate lovemaking. She looked down, away from him, her cheeks reddening.

"Oh, Eva," he said, taking her into his arms, "what an extraordinary woman you are. First you give me such a seductive, subtle signal, then you blush!" With that he'd lifted her into his arms and carried her upstairs where they'd made love in her canopied bed at Diligence Hall in the middle of the day, and for both of them it had been unlike anything before.

Eva smiled to herself as Lacy chatted on with Reese. Finally she managed to come out of her reverie to listen.

"I always seem to be thanking you, Eva," Lacy was saying.

"I really didn't help that much," Eva responded. "Reese did the heavy work with help from a couple of crew members."

"Mother was thanking you for the flowers you sent, Eva," Reese said with a half smile, aware that Eva's mind had been somewhere else. He was pretty sure he knew where, because he'd been thinking of the same early afternoon event.

"Oh," Eva said, trying to compose herself, "you're very welcome, Lacy."

"They were so beautiful," Lacy continued, "First you rescue me, then send flowers, then help Reese get me moved. Yes, I'm certainly glad that Marchetti Films came to Corinth."

"So am I," Eva said before realizing that there was more to those words than she'd meant. Everything seemed to be tinged with thoughts of Reese.

Lacy didn't notice, or she pretended not to notice; Eva wasn't sure which. However, she *was* sure that Lacy had a very observant nature, and if she hadn't seen what was going on between Eva and her son yet, she would soon. They'd all know soon, Eva thought, and then realized she didn't care. She'd never felt more self-indulgent in her life.

The next day shooting on *Glory Road* got into full swing with the entire cast and crew turning Diligence into an enormous movie set.

"It looks like a big Hollywood party," Lacy said from her perfect spot on the front porch. She was happy ensconced in her wheelchair, Eva observed.

"I expect when it's all over, you'll breathe a sigh of relief," Eva said.

"Well, maybe. I'm sure it'll be nice to have everything back to normal, especially since there'll be so many improvements for us to enjoy. But I'm certainly having a wonderful time while the movie lasts," she added with the enthusiasm of a real fan.

"So am I," came a voice from beside the steps as Reese appeared looking pleased with everything he saw, especially with Eva, whom he managed to kiss quickly when he came up behind her, out of his mother's view. "Are they shooting the ending now?" he asked.

Eva nodded as Reese glanced over her shoulder at the script she was holding.

"So tell us, does the girl stay with her Southern lover or does she go back to the life she left when he brought her to the Old South? Does love conquer all, Eva?" Reese asked. "Or does she realize that she'll never be able to adjust?" He tried to get a glimpse of the script, which Eva had moved out of his sight.

"You'll have to wait and see," she teased, trying to ignore the double meaning in his question. "It'll be a couple of days before we film the final scene."

"I'll wait in anticipation," Reese said, and something in his voice carried hope, as if two decisions would be made on the day the final scene was filmed. Eva shrugged away that thought; it was ridiculous. What happened in *Glory Road* had nothing to do with her and Reese.

"Here comes Louise Ross," Lacy chimed in and a quiet seemed to settle over Diligence as the movie's star emerged from her trailer and took her place in the scene.

"Who's the young man playing her husband?" Lacy asked.

"He's a newcomer to films," Eva explained. "Gino saw him in a play off-Broadway and cast him in *Glory Road.*"

"He's interesting looking, but not terribly handsome," Lacy declared.

Eva agreed. "But you'll change your mind, I think, when you see the finished film. Something in his acting shines through and makes him very appealing." Eva had seen the screen tests and known immediately that Gino had made a good choice. Even Mary, who'd resisted until the end, had had to agree.

When Louise's first scene was completed, she went directly to her trailer with her makeup man following close behind. Eva left Reese and his mother deep in a discussion of the plantation to join Beau and offer a little comfort. "I warned you," she said. "Louise isn't accessible."

Beau laughed. "That's putting it mildly. I believe we say in show biz that she's a prima donna. And only twenty-five."

"Stardom doesn't have anything to do with years," Eva reminded him. "Besides, you wouldn't like her anyway; she really is a little dumb, Beau."

"Oh, I probably could accept that," Beau said with a grin. "Besides, people can change."

"She's never going to get any smarter," Eva said.

Beau laughed. "That's not what I'm talking about. Oh, well," he added with a sigh. "At least I'm near her in my job."

"Which you're doing exceptionally well," Eva complimented him. "It's a great deal of help for us to have Mary freed up to start on the new picture. She really put her trust in you, and you're living up to her expectations. The extras for tomorrow's scene at the stable are perfect."

Beau smiled his thanks. "This job really means a lot to me, Eva."

"I know."

"Well, you know a little but not everything." Beau became unaccustomedly serious. "I never have found any job that really interested me. I'd begun to think that running Diligence was the only thing I'd ever be able to do."

"And now?" Eva asked.

Beau was silent for a while as he looked out across the lawn at the crew setting up for the next shot. The atmosphere was charged with an excitement that was reflected on Beau's face, and Eva remembered the first time she'd ever walked onto a Marchetti set. She'd known from the first moment that she was where she belonged. Beau didn't have to explain what was going on inside him; she could tell that he felt the same.

"Even my brother seems to be accepting all this," Beau said. "I don't know what's come over him."

"Maybe he sees that we're not threatening him or his way of life."

Beau shook his head. "No, there's more. You've made the change in Reese, Eva."

"How would you know that?" she countered. "You haven't even been around."

But Beau didn't hear her. The director had motioned to him, and with Eva still waiting for his response, Beau was off across the lawn with his clipboard and a grin that was becoming permanent. Eva shook her head and gave a word of silent thanks to the job that was keeping Beau so busy he hadn't stopped to figure out what was going on between Eva and his brother.

* * *

Late in the day Eva and Reese finally managed to break away from the others and walk over to the gazebo. "It's the only quiet spot for miles around," Reese said. "Nobody can hear us."

"But they can see us," she reminded him as he kissed her neck quickly, causing Eva to move a little way and sit down on the bench inside the gazebo where they were partially hidden by the latticework. There he kissed her again.

"They don't have to see me kiss you to know."

Eva couldn't disagree with that.

"So let's really give them something to talk about," Reese said with a playful leer as he reached out for her and then looked a little hurt when once more Eva managed to squirm away. "All right," he relented, "how about meeting me at my cottage?" He looked at his watch. "Say, in five minutes."

"Reese," Eva began.

"I'll go the back way and you can saunter over. But don't wait any longer than five minutes," he added. "I want to touch you, take you in my arms, hold you and kiss you..." He laughed a little, bewildered at the words and the yearning.

"Looking at you is wonderful," he said, taking in the vision of Eva sitting a little uneasily on the bench in her beige pleated skirt and overblouse. "It's a very pretty, very businesslike outfit. But I want to get it off you! Five minutes," he reminded her as he started down the steps of the gazebo.

"Reese, I can't. They're ready to begin the next scene."

"Which they can shoot perfectly well without you," he reminded her. "Not that I mean to make light of your job."

Eva laughed. "Actually, my job is just about over here."

"I know," he told her, stopping at the bottom of the stairs. There really wasn't any reason for her to be here, except for what was happening between them. Reese didn't want to talk about that now because—like the movie that was being filmed nearby—he didn't know the ending. "Five minutes," he said again over his shoulder as he quickly walked away.

Eva watched him go, thinking of all that was unsaid between them, thinking that whenever they talked, what really mattered was never spoken. She wanted to get inside his thoughts, but that hadn't been possible: so much of Reese was closed to her. Then Eva realized that she'd been as silent about herself as Reese had been about himself. Soon, they'd *have* to talk but not yet, not now. Now was the time to satisfy a longing so strong that in the middle of the day, before the shooting ended and not even five minutes after he'd left, Eva got up and followed Reese to the cottage.

Eva was purposefully on the set early the next morning so that she could avoid any knowing looks from the assembling cast and crew. But her mind was wandering. The AD made a comment to her, complaining about the screening room where they would be looking at the rushes, and waited patiently for an answer before asking the question again. Eva agreed to do what she could, and not until he'd walked away satisfied did she realize that she couldn't remember what she'd promised and had to run after him to get the details.

It was like that all day—she was the last one to notice the helicopter. It hovered over Diligence, turned and came in lower, and finally when it was almost overhead, she heard the engines and looked up. As everyone watched, hands shading their eyes against the blazing sun, the helicopter touched down, and she knew who would get out. They all knew, with the possible exception of Beau, Lacy and Reese. No, she decided, searching for him, Reese also knew because he understood the mind of the man who was the helicopter passenger. Gino Marchetti always kept his eyes on his investments and never did anything the usual way. There was no doubt about it; Gino Marchetti had style.

After meeting with the director in the middle of the lawn and agreeing to stay over until the first day's footage was flown in from the lab in Atlanta, Gino was ready to get back into the helicopter, but not alone.

"Get your file, Eva, and let's go. I wanna see what you've found for me." He'd taken a moment to give her a big bear hug, removing his cigar when he kissed her cheek, but with those amenities over, he was ready to move on.

"You plan to go in the helicopter?" Eva asked after she'd returned his hug and kiss.

"Naturally. We'll need a topography map," he added, looking at her expectantly.

"I have a map," she assured him.

"Then let's go."

"Gino," Eva stalled. "It's going to take me a few minutes to get everything ready. I assumed that when you decided it was time to have a look, first you'd let me know you were coming."

Gino laughed. "Since when did I have to let you know, *cara*? You've learned to sense those things."

"And secondly," Eva continued, ignoring him because she had in fact sensed that he'd arrive today, "you'd be willing to get to the properties in a more usual way—by car, for example."

"I considered that," Gino said, as if driving had been one of the least interesting possibilities. "But I like to see from above first. We'll put down and look around on foot, too, of course."

"Of course," Eva repeated.

Gino grinned and waved his cigar toward the director. "Finish the scene. I didn't mean to interrupt." From the moment he'd landed, shooting had stopped, and the crew was still on a break, taking advantage of his presence to loaf a little in the shade. Eva couldn't blame them. The heat was intense. Gino, however, didn't seem to notice, although Eva could see perspiration forming around the edges of his wavy gray hair. He wiped his forehead with a cotton handkerchief and was immediately as fresh as ever, in spite of the way he was dressed—formally, as usual, in a dark blue pin-striped suit.

Once Eva had everything ready for the trip, she was still reluctant to get in the helicopter. "I'll meet you at the sites in my car," she suggested, but Gino just laughed.

"Always my little scaredy-cat," he said, shaking his head. "Each time you get weak knees, I have to humor you past your fears."

"I'm not sure that humoring will be enough this time, Gino," Eva countered. "I just don't like the looks of that thing. It's inhospitable, not to mention insubstantial."

Gino paid no attention as he grabbed her hand and headed for the helicopter. "Conquer your fears, Eva," he said, "I'm always having to tell you to conquer your fears."

He called up to the pilot, "My friend here is a confirmed coward, so let's make the flight enjoyable for her." He hadn't even considered Eva's proposal that she follow in the car; he'd simply helped her, still protesting, into her seat.

After seeing three of the four sites that she'd scouted for him, Eva was beginning to get used to the helicopter but not to the noise. Climbing back in beside Gino for the final trip, she closed her eyes and tried to drown out the combined thudding of motor and blades as Gino bent over the map. So far he'd been uniformly negative about what he'd seen.

"If only you'd tell me what you want this land for," Eva shouted toward him over the noise, "I might have been able to find more suitable properties."

"No, *cara*, what you've found for me is in the ballpark, just not quite right for—" He clamped his cigar in his mouth as if to stem the explanation, and Eva couldn't help smiling. Gino was enjoying his little power play. "When the time comes, you'll know," he said, and then added, "If you think about it, you'll know now. Use your head."

Eva started to respond when the helicopter gave a shudder, and she forgot about everything except her fear of flying as she tightened her seat belt. They were landing again, this time on the lot Reese had shown her.

Following Gino around the property, Eva tried to figure out what he'd meant when he told her to think about it and she'd know why he wanted the land in Corinth. Gino was silent, waving his cigar in the air. The smoke, he'd informed Eva, provided a good screen against mosquitoes and gnats.

Eva put her mind to work. She hadn't really thought about it before, except to wonder vaguely why anyone would want to buy land here, particularly the cosmopolitan Gino Marchetti. Certainly he wasn't planning to build a house in Corinth, not when he owned a lovely apartment in Rome, a villa in Capri, a beach house in Southern California and the co-op in New York.

Even without so many homes, South Carolina would hardly be the place for Gino. He didn't care for the lazy, easy life. Between films he still wanted to be where the action was. Only on the island of Capri did he get away from it all, and then he brought enough people with him to fill the villa and overlap into guesthouses; still it was too quiet. He never stayed longer than a week at a time. No, Eva decided, Gino Marchetti wasn't about to build in Corinth, South Carolina.

Trudging across the valley behind him, Eva continued to rack her brain, irritated now that he'd suggested she *should* know. He wasn't much of a speculator, leaving it to his broker to buy and sell in bonds and stocks to a limited degree, and except for his homes, Gino owned very little other property, declaring that the only sure investment was a good film. That left only business . . .

"This is it, *cara*. This is the property I told you to find, and by God, you found it," Gino called out to her as he made another sweep around the perimeter of the little valley. Bent slightly at the waist, he was walking rapidly in black leather shoes that were meant only for the sidewalks of New York and Rome, and his cigar trailed a thin line of smoke after him. "This is the one I want."

"How can you be sure?" Eva asked as she attempted to keep up with him.

"Look at it," he answered, "a flat, open area close enough to a main access road but not right on the highway. It's perfect. Hell, I'll hardly have to excavate . . . just level it off and—"

Suddenly, as if by some sort of curious telepathy, Eva realized just why Gino wanted the land. "Gino, you're not going to—"

"Well, it's about time, Eva. I don't know where your brain has been this past week; I'll have to look into that." He laughed. "Yes, *cara*, I'm going to build a film studio here, the most complete studio in the country, right here in Corinth, South Carolina."

"Gino, why . . ."

"Eva, I'm seriously beginning to worry about you," Gino said almost merrily. "You know *why*. Union contracts," he said patiently. "Labor, wages, production costs. Eva, Eva, everything is less expensive in this part of the world. I can cut five million off a twenty-million-dollar film. Think about that," he said finally, putting his cigar back into his mouth and heading for the helicopter. Then for added emphasis, he called over his shoulder, "Even the extras. In Hollywood extras cost close to a hundred dollars a day. What do we pay here?" He didn't wait for a response. "You know damn well what we pay. Less than half. Multiply that by the entire film. Do that, Eva," he said as he hoisted himself into the helicopter.

Eva climbed in after him, a little dismayed. As they ascended, she found herself raising her voice above the noise to argue with him. "Corinth is such a quiet and sleepy little town. I'm sure the people—"

"The people will be crazy for it, Eva. I've had an economic survey done of this region. I'm not getting into this on a whim, you know,'' he reminded her. "This area is depressed, especially since the textile industry is losing so much business to overseas competitors. They need money here as much as anywhere in the country. This studio will mean housing for the people we bring in and jobs for the ones we hire locally. Don't tell me they won't want it. They'll want it,'' he said positively as he strapped himself into the seat and gave a thumbs-up signal to the pilot.

"Not everyone,'' she reminded him.

Gino eyed her sagely. "I know who you mean. Your Benedicts.''

Eva glanced at him, caught the laughter in his eyes and pointed out, "They're not *mine*, Gino. In fact, if there's ever been a family of individuals who owed nothing to anyone, it's the Benedicts. They're independent, and they're hardheaded. This land is so close to theirs. They aren't going to like it,'' she added emphatically, if needlessly.

Gino shrugged philosophically. "Even the Benedicts can't stop progress.''

Eva had to agree. "Marchetti International here in Corinth,'' she mused aloud, "that's going to make some waves. It's certainly going to be big news.''

"News not to be shared,'' Gino said. "Not with anyone. You understand that, Eva?''

She nodded.

"I don't want any publicity on this until I meet with the Graydon family and their lawyers. Until this is on paper, no leaks, *capisce*?''

*"Capisco,"* Eva answered. "But Gino—''

"What, Eva?'' he asked.

"Reese said that the Graydons didn't want to sell.''

*"Reese* said,'' Gino repeated, his smile broadening. "Let's talk about what Gino says. Gino says that

the Graydons are no different from anyone else. They have a price."

Just before they landed, Gino told Eva, "I'm spending one night here, maybe two, so I can see the first day's rushes when they get in from the lab. I'm staying in Charles Town—"

"Charleston?" Eva questioned and then realized that she couldn't have imagined Gino at the Corinth Columns Motel. "Of course," she said then.

"Tomorrow night I'll take those Benedicts—of yours," he added just to be contrary, "to dinner."

Eva shook her head. "Lacy's just out of the hospital; she can't walk."

"Then I'll have to make it easy for her, won't I?" he asked enigmatically, as if, having given up one secret, he needed another one just to keep his hand in. Then with a smile he touched her face a little awkwardly. "Don't be upset, my little Eva. Everything will work out, and when the deal is made, I'll let you be the first to tell your Benedicts. But not before, promise?"

She promised.


Gino *did* make it easy for Lacy. He flew dinner in from Charleston and had it served by two white-coated waiters under a blue-and-white tent set up on their back lawn.

"Of course, we'll have the lawn resodded after the film wraps," Gino assured Lacy as he personally wheeled her chair up to the long table that was covered with a white linen cloth and decorated with a centerpiece of summer flowers.

"Mr. Marchetti," Lacy said effusively, "this is all so—"

"Please," Gino insisted, touching her arm lightly, "call me Gino."

Across the lawn, Eva and Reese approached the tent. "I guess you could call this the icing on the cake," Reese said under his breath. "First he pays good money for the use of Diligence, agrees to make expensive improvements and then flies in a catered dinner."

Eva glanced over at him. "Which I plan to enjoy," she said.

Reese responded with a smile and admitted that he had the same intention. "But your boss might have *asked* before he arrived with the tent and the waiters and the dinner."

"He doesn't think, Reese; he just acts. That's part of his Latin charm—assuming that everyone will react favorably to his plans, especially when they're so extravagant. Most people do," she added as they walked under the tent to join Gino, Lacy and Beau, who was reveling in the sumptuous evening. "Of course, you're not most people," Eva added.

"But I'm going to like everything on the menu," Reese responded with a smile when they had taken their places at the table.

Eva breathed a little sigh. It was going to be all right, she decided; the evening wasn't going to deteriorate into a battle of wills between two strong men with very different views about everything.

"I was just saying to Mr.—Gino," Lacy corrected, "that we've certainly been well compensated for the use of Diligence, and all this wasn't really necessary," she said with a sweeping gesture that included the tent and everything under it.

Gino responded gallantly. "I've always preferred the personal touch in my business transactions, and since you are sharing your lovely home with Marchetti Films..."

Eva glanced at Reese, waiting for him to say that they'd had very little choice. The words formed on his lips, she was sure, but instead of voicing them, he lifted his champagne glass and said, "To Diligence—now, during the filming, and afterward, when we who cherish it return to the peaceful quiet of being nonentities again."

As Gino drank the toast, Eva noticed that he watched Reese carefully, meeting his eyes above the champagne flute, measuring and, Eva suspected, seeing the steeliness and deciding to back away. He'd heard the unsaid words in the toast, but this wasn't the time for a confrontation.

Nor was Reese about to confront Gino. *Glory Road* was shooting at Diligence, and there was nothing Reese could do about it. But as he sipped the champagne—a very good year, he noted—Reese felt a frown quivering at his forehead and knew something was wrong. What was done was done, and still Gino Marchetti had ordered this feast, accompanying it with all his Latin charm, even though he'd gotten what he needed from them. That, Reese decided, wasn't Gino's style. What, he wondered, was the reason for all this?

"Business is business," Gino was saying, "but our aim is to make everything as pleasant as possible for everyone while we're here. How have we done so far?" he asked Lacy.

She didn't hesitate. "It's been a lovely experience, especially because of Eva. Without her..." She looked at Eva, who'd had very little to say as she watched, somewhat nervous about the makeup of the party and still wondering about Gino and Reese at the same table.

"Ah, my Eva, she is something, isn't she?" Gino smiled benignly and glanced not at Lacy but at Reese. Eva happened to look at him at the same time, and both she and Gino saw his jaw tighten. *My* Eva. Reese hadn't liked that at all. Eva knew why; Gino could guess.

Beau, enjoying the food and the wine and oblivious to the nuances, joined the conversation. "All of us are grateful to Eva. Without her I wouldn't have my job." It took a full three seconds for him to realize that Gino might not know about the work he'd been assigned on *Glory Road*, and if he didn't know, or even if he did, might not be entirely happy about it.

But it was okay with Gino. "I've heard good reports about you, Beau. In fact, I've been thinking that maybe it's time for you and me to have a little talk."

Beau's face lit up as Reese's darkened. Eva watched Reese while Gino and his brother talked. She knew that he wanted what was best for Beau, but she could see that he still wasn't able to accept Gino Marchetti—not in his home and certainly not wooing Lacy and his brother, which was exactly Gino's plan.

"But we won't talk business at dinner," Gino told Beau. "Tomorrow before I leave, we'll discuss this." He smiled and raised his glass in a final toast as the dinner was cleared away and dessert and coffee served.

Gino was well aware that he hadn't charmed everyone at the table and turned his attention to Reese. He seemed a little unsure to Eva—as well he should have been. Reese wasn't an easy one to charm, and she almost wondered why Gino was bothering; then she decided it was the challenge. He couldn't resist giving everyone a try.

"Tell me, Reese," he said, lighting a cigar after Lacy gave him permission to smoke. "Will we see you on television again?"

Reese shook his head. "That part of my life is over," he said flatly.

Gino nodded. He understood a man who made such a decision and stuck by it. He knew that when his time came, he would also get out fast. But that time was way in the future. Eva could tell from his puzzled look that he thought Reese had bowed out too early.

"I imagine you're working at something else?" Gino offered.

Reese shook his head and smiled blandly, a smile that didn't light his eyes. "No, I'm quite happy here at Diligence. It's the kind of life I need now, quiet, with no false values, with no..." His voice drifted off. He'd been about to belittle his profession and in doing so belittle Gino's, as well. Reese stopped just short of doing that, and Eva breathed a sigh of relief. These two men were the most important men in her life. They could continue their sparring and in doing so make it uncomfortable for everyone. But they let the moment pass.

Gino offered Reese a cigar; Reese accepted it, and the evening ended as it had begun, warmly.

But that night when Eva lay in Reese's arms, she could feel an uneasiness in him. He was quiet, withdrawn.

"What's the matter?" she asked. "Is it Gino?"

He nodded against her forehead. "I can't like him, Eva, and I know why. I don't trust him."

Eva tried not to be defensive about Gino. "I can understand that. Not everyone is impressed by his aura of power."

"Well, he certainly made two converts this evening, my mother and my brother. But it's not the power that puts me off. God knows I've been around enough of that in my life. I suppose at one time I had a little of it myself," he added.

"More than a little," Eva remembered. "But power has to be handled well."

"That's what bothers me. I don't trust his motives."

Eva settled more comfortably into Reese's arms. "In many ways—in most ways, I think—Gino is a good man. I certainly wouldn't be where I am without him."

Reese stroked her hair and nodded. "Your ties to him are very deep, aren't they?"

"Yes," she said softly. "He gave me my job and believed in me. But there's more," she said, suddenly wanting to tell Reese, wanting to open up to him and share the hurt she'd once experienced, hoping, perhaps, that in time he could share part of himself, too.

"We've been through a lot of pain together because of Franco."

"Tell me," Reese said. His hand comforted her cheek.

"It wasn't so terrible," she answered, knowing that even now after all the years that had passed, all the time she'd had to get over it, she'd never really forgotten the hurt. And she was still wary of everyone, even of Reese. "Time heals," she murmured.

"Yes," Reese agreed. He was also thinking of himself; time *had* begun to heal his pain—time and Eva. He hadn't had a nightmare in almost a week. But he had the feeling that Eva wasn't telling the whole truth. "Time—and someone to share the pain," Reese said quietly.

"It *was* terrible," Eva amended.

"You were very young," Reese reminded her.

"Oh, yes. I don't think anyone has ever been so young, innocent and trusting. I was the first woman he'd ever introduced to his parents, and he'd had many girlfriends. The Marchettis took that as a good sign, an indication that Franco was settling down at last."

"How old was he?"

"Thirty-five," Eva said. "And I was twenty."

Reese shook his head and Eva said, "I know. That's a big age difference, but it didn't matter. Nothing mattered."

"How long did it last?"

"A year," Eva told him. "I later found out that I held the record in that, too. He'd never stayed with anyone for so long. But it was over long before. He started staying out later and later and coming home drunk, if he came home at all. One night he brought a girl in with him."

"Oh, Eva." Reese held her close.

"It was terrible.... But you know, I believe he'd actually forgotten that I lived there; he was so drunk. But I was humiliated. I'll never forget that night as long as I live. Or the next morning."

"What happened, Eva?" Reese asked, and he found himself feeling an empathy for her that he couldn't remember ever having felt for anyone.

"He hit me," she said.

Reese flinched.

"I don't think he meant to," she said quickly. "Franco had too much; yet he never had enough. He was striking out at anything and everything that he thought had made him the way he was. I just happened to be there."

"I'm sure that's true," Reese said, hoping with his words to ease her pain.

"He passed out then, and I ran. I didn't even take anything with me, I just ran to Gino. I threw myself at him, begging for the money to leave, to get out of there. The next day I started work at Marchetti Films. Within a week I was in California. It was all over."

"Except that it's never really over," Reese sympathized.

"Until so much time passes that it all becomes blurred, until you can open up and face what happened and—"

"Find someone to share it with," Reese finished for her. "Thank you, Eva, for sharing it with me."

# Chapter 9

Eva drove Reese's car to the airport two days later; she drove fast and let the wind whip her hair back wildly. It was a beautiful day, not as steamy and humid as usual, and she was enjoying the drive. Reese had thought about taking her but decided to let her have the car and go alone when Eva told him what the trip back from the airport to town would probably be like.

It would be terrible, she reminded herself again. Well, maybe not terrible but certainly bothersome. She was going to the airport to meet Dan Morrow, and she'd have less than an hour to get him into a reasonably good mood—a difficult if not impossible task given Danny's attitude about returning to Corinth to make set changes.

"Nonsense," he'd said on the phone when she'd called him in New York and woken him at eight o'clock in the morning. "That bar-restaurant looks perfect. I worked with the designer on it for days, and I drew the sketches myself. Joey overpaid the guy for letting us change the mirror behind the bar. For the rest, you've got my sketches, Eva. What are the set decorators for? Let *them* dress up the set.''

Eva had let him go on for a while longer before telling him that he didn't have any choice. The director had been adamant. He needed Danny. It was an important scene, one that set the mood for the end of the film, and he wasn't happy with the way it looked.

''It's a good thing you're still on this location, Eva,'' Dan said as he tossed his bag in the back of the car and got in. ''Though why you're still here is beyond me. I've never known you to hang around this long after the shooting began. But if you hadn't, my dear, I wouldn't have been on that plane. I did it for you,'' he said, settling back against the seat. ''I must say the weather is a little cooler, and I do like this car. I can't remember seeing any convertibles at the rental place,'' he added, changing the subject to the relief of Eva, who knew, however, that he'd quickly get back to complaining. This was just a verbal side trip.

''I didn't rent it. This is a Benedict car,'' Eva told him.

''Which Benedict?''

''Reese,'' Eva answered.

Dan thought that one over but didn't comment on it. That, too, would come later, Eva suspected. Dan stored those things up and then brought them out at the oddest times. Anticipating his conversational direction could be mind-boggling.

''There *is* a scenic artist on this film, isn't there?'' he asked.

''Yes,'' Eva responded.

"Say that again, darling. The wind blew your answer away," Dan shouted as he placed his panama hat more firmly on his head. "If this chapeau blows off and gets lost alongside a South Carolina highway, I'll never forgive you, the director or our darling producer. You said *yes*, I believe," he continued.

Eva nodded and stepped on the gas as she passed a line of cars.

"You've become a rather dangerous driver since I left. And you look gorgeous, so I surmise you're having a thing with the elder Benedict son, but more about that later," Dan said. "If there is a scenic designer, why couldn't he just look at my sketches and *find* the mood? It was there. Anyone with any talent could re-create it."

Eva came to a stop at a light on the outskirts of Corinth and turned to Dan. "That's exactly what he did, Danny, but it's not quite right; it needs something more—your finishing touch. That's the consensus. The scene has to be just right because it's pivotal."

The light changed, Eva stepped on the gas again, and Danny changed the subject. "Actually, I already knew about you and Reese Benedict. Mary told me when I talked to her a few days ago."

"Mary has a good imagination."

"On the contrary, darling. Mary has no imagination at all. She's total reality, facts and specifics, as you well know. Why are you trying to deny this little romance?"

Eva didn't answer.

"Hmm," Dan said. "Maybe because it's more than your typical location love affair," he decided as they drove down Main Street and approached the local bar that was the subject of the day's shooting—and the day's problem.

Eva slowed down and considered Dan's remark. This *wasn't* just another location love affair; it was more, much more. When she noticed Reese standing on the corner talking to a couple of kids from the crew and saw his face light up at the sight of her, Eva felt sure she was right. Location romances were fleeting and ended when the movie ended. Theirs was different. But where would it go from here?

Eva and Dan got out of the car at the spot where everyone was waiting. Eva flashed a wide smile at Reese as she passed him and went into the bar. He was still there waiting for her a few minutes later when she sneaked away. "Drive around the corner," she said in a conspiratorial voice straight from a movie itself. "I have about ten minutes, I've figured, until Danny gets into a row with the set decorator."

Reese laughed, started the car and drove away from the action to a quiet side street. "I thought Danny would solve the problem."

"He will. As I expected, Danny took one look at the set and decided what was wrong. Thank the Lord for our Marchetti geniuses," she said with a sigh. "But it's going to take all day and some tempers are going to flare. I wanted to tell you not to wait, and I wanted—"

"This?" he asked as he stopped the car, turned off the engine and took her in his arms. Their kiss was not a daytime kiss at all; it was a kiss that belonged in the moonlight. "I wish tonight was here," Reese said, his lips still touching hers.

"It will be soon," Eva murmured.

Reese smiled, gave her a hug and tried to forget the moonlight. "You enjoy all this, don't you?"

"Mmm. Of course."

"I mean the movie business," he said with a laugh.

"Yes," Eva admitted, "especially when I know that I can run off for a few minutes with you—" she kissed him softly "—and at the end of the day's shooting, you'll be there. You will be there, won't you?"

"Absolutely," Reese said, looking lovingly at her. She was full of life and laughter, and excitement seemed to go with her everywhere. He felt a little envious because he knew that some of the excitement was for her job. But he was just as sure that the rest was for him. "I have some special plans for tonight."

From down the street, a crew member called out, "Eva, they want you." She moved a little away from him so Reese could start the car, but not before they exchanged one more quick kiss.

"What plans?" she asked.

Reese shook his head. "I'm not telling." He turned the car around and headed back.

"Oh, please. I hate secrets," she said.

"This isn't a secret," Reese replied, pulling up to the bar. "It's a surprise. There's a big difference."

Eva got out of the car and leaned over with her arms on the door, looking at him. "That explains everything," she said. "I love surprises. And I can't wait."

"Good," Reese said, satisfied. "I'll see you tonight."

As he drove away, Eva stood on the sidewalk and watched him while half the crew stood nearby and watched her. When she turned around, they all made a special effort to look busy until she laughed, and they knew she was on to them.

"Eavesdroppers," she said as she walked past them into the bar, getting the innocent looks she expected. Gossip was one of the mainstays of a location shooting. Eva had surprised herself by deciding to live with it rather than fight it; she knew that was a wise decision. But she was still wondering whether this *was* a location romance. As she walked into the bar, closed the door behind her and joined the mayhem surrounding Dan and the artistic designer, she still didn't have the answer. But she had at least the night—and a surprise—to look forward to.

Reese drove fast, faster than Eva, as he headed back toward Diligence, but when he reached the intersection, he changed his mind and turned away from the house toward the direction of Charleston. He hadn't been there since he'd returned to South Carolina, but it was still, architecturally, one of his favorite towns. Even during the house party weekends in his high school days, Reese had enjoyed getting away from his friends to walk through the streets and admire the gracious old homes.

Charleston hadn't changed much. It was still a town, instead of a city, still a good place to explore the narrow side streets and old churches and museums and walk along the Battery where as a boy he'd spent imaginative hours climbing the Civil War cannons. Charleston had experienced a refreshing cultural renaissance with the arrival of the Spoleto Festival, but otherwise it was much the same.

Reese drove slowly through the streets of his memory. Today he wasn't here to explore; he was here to shop. He parked the car and got out, filled with a sort of excitement that he couldn't remember having felt in years. He walked down streets crowded with sightseers and shoppers on this unusually mild summer day, and he found himself smiling.

Eva had done something to him, all right, Reese thought. Not just had the nightmares stopped, but he'd found himself enjoying the strangest things—

strange to him, anyway. Today it was the scent of flowers in the parks and the smiles on the faces of tourists lingering with delight in front of famous old homes, the damp feel of ocean air on his skin.

Shaking his head, Reese entered a department store. He was wrapped up in Eva; there was no doubt about that. Why else should he be inhaling the perfume of Charleston with such delight? He headed for the lingerie department, aware that he'd never shopped for a woman in his life. He'd left that to Barbara or to his mother. Over the years on Barbara's birthday or at Christmas Lacy had mailed packages that had eventually caught up with them, often in some remote area, boxes that were battered and falling apart but filled with the kind of feminine, frothy lingerie Reese had in mind right now.

"May I help you?" a voice asked. While Reese cleared his throat and searched for a way to explain what he was looking for, the salesgirl peered at him over the top of her glasses. "Why, you're Reese Benedict, the newscaster," she exclaimed, and Reese was quickly reminded of why he had always tried to stay near home. In Corinth he was considered a neighbor, albeit a rather odd one. Everywhere else he was still a celebrity.

"What can I do for you, Mr. Benedict?" she effervesced.

Rather than being irritated, Reese found himself confiding in the older woman, leaning close and describing, as best he could, the nightgown he wanted.

"Well, I'm not sure we have anything exactly like that," she responded with a slight purse of the lips that told Reese he might have been a little too explicit in his description. "But I'll show you what we have. Do you know the size?"

Reese's answer consisted of curvy hand gestures from which the salesclerk was able to get a vague idea. "Smallish, I suppose," she said as she went about selecting gowns for him to choose from.

Systematically Reese rejected each one, beginning with a pink cotton gauze gown with layers of lace and ribbon that he considered too girlish, a satiny nightshirt that was too uninteresting and a soft paisley print that was too prim.

"How about that one," he said, indicating a splash of red on a hanger behind the counter. It was cut low in the front with tiny straps and a lacy top that crossed the skirt diagonally. The clerk held it up, and Reese had no trouble at all mentally filling it with Eva, but in his picture she wasn't standing before him. She was stretched out on the bed, her blond hair tangled around her head, her creamy breasts barely contained by the lacy top of the gown, her slim body, which had once seemed so coolly fragile to him, curled into seductive curves, her dark eyes staring up at him widely with an innocence that didn't hide the desire.

"That's the one," Reese said, forcing himself to blink away the sultry vision.

The gown was just the beginning of his purchases. He left the lingerie department and went upstairs where he bought a bright blue jumpsuit with palazzo-style pants and a wrap-around jersey belt. "She looks great in bright colors," he told the woman who waited on him, remembering the one colorful outfit she'd worn since he met her and telling himself that the whites and beiges were just a part of her job. Now that she—they—were breaking out a little and enjoying themselves, Reese was sure she'd like the jumpsuit, so sure that he added a fuchsia silk shirt and a pair of tight black pants and a bottle of perfume to his purchases.

Driving back to Diligence in the late afternoon, he couldn't help smiling to himself. Two years had passed during which Reese had begun to think he never would want to join the human race again, and during that time the nightmares had continued. No matter how far he'd withdrawn from the people and places that saddened him, he'd remained sad. In two weeks, Eva had changed that. The nightmares were over; she'd made him smile again, laugh again, love again. The night when she had told him about Franco, he'd felt compassion for someone besides himself.

After she'd shared her feelings with him, Reese had been overcome by a sudden urge to share something of his life with her. He'd pulled back, though, not knowing where or how to begin. But soon, Reese told himself, he'd be able to open up and tell her everything that had happened to him—and what was happening now. When Gino had asked, Reese hadn't mentioned that he had any plans for himself; in fact, he hadn't told anyone, not even Lacy or Beau. He'd tell Eva. It was because of her that he'd made the decision.

"Beau," Lacy called, "come here, Beau." He'd wheeled her onto the front porch half an hour ago to enjoy the late afternoon breeze, and Beau went down the hall toward her voice, assuming that she was ready to come in and couldn't get the chair turned around.

He was wrong. "Look," she said, indicating the car that had driven up the driveway and then turned onto the side road leading toward the cottage.

"It's just Reese, Mom," Beau said, ready to turn her chair around.

"I know that, Beau, for goodness' sake. But did you see what was in the back of the car?"

"Packages."

"Those weren't just packages. They were all wrapped up with bows and ribbons. Don't turn me around," she ordered. "I want to sit here awhile longer. It's not Christmas."

"No, that's absolutely true. What are you getting at, Mom?"

"And it's not anyone's birthday that I know of."

"True," Beau agreed, giving up and sitting down beside her on the brick steps.

"Now who do you suppose he's bought all those gifts for? I'll tell you who," she said, answering her own question. "They're for Eva."

"Eva?" Beau looked up at her.

"That's right," she said. "I haven't missed all the signs that something was going on between them, even if you have."

"Actually, I haven't, either," Beau admitted, "although I can't understand why Eva wouldn't prefer me. I'm much younger."

"Beau, darling, you seem to think that youth is the answer to everything. Maturity is very appealing."

"Well, I'm not sure there's anything so mature about dropping out of life like Reese did."

Lacy raised her eyebrows and smiled, looking toward the cottage. "From the looks of things, I'd say your brother has decided to join the human race again. I'm so glad," she added with a sigh, "for both of them."

Beau pondered that for a moment and then said, "But Eva's totally wrapped up in Gino Marchetti's world. Reese sure didn't get along with Gino at dinner the other night. He's probably jealous of him, and I don't suppose I can blame him. She's loyal to Gino."

"Well, of course," Lacy snapped. "She works for him, dear. Besides, Gino and his wife have been like family to her after the way their son treated her."

Beau raised his eyebrow. He'd always suspected Eva had something a little scandalous in her past.

"A very sad love affair," Lacy said and then added, "I do hope that if this affair is what I think it is, that they are both serious, or both frivolous. I wouldn't want either of them to get hurt again," she said, shaking her head as Beau got up to push her back inside.

"Don't worry about it, Mom. They're both grown up. It's *my* breaking heart you should be concerned about—that Eva chose Reese over me."

"Why, Beau," Lacy said, turning her head to look back over her shoulder at him, "I thought you had your eyes on Louise."

"Well, Mother, a man can have two love interests—at my age."

Reese threw a cover over the packages in the back of his car and went inside. He'd been gone all day, and the dogs were frantic for their walk, but he turned them out alone. "I'll make it up to you tomorrow, girls," he said as he closed the door behind them, fixed a drink and took it into his room. There was just time for a shower before meeting Eva, but there was one more thing Reese wanted to do first.

He took a big swig of the drink, put it on the bureau and opened his closet door. He stood there for a full minute looking up at the typewriter on the top shelf before he took it down, pushed aside a stack of books, put it on his desk and removed the cover. Then he took another drink and stood looking down at the machine.

It was an old portable that had been with him since college and all through his years as a commentator. It had seen a lot of action from the barren sands of Ethiopia to the teeming streets of Shanghai and the hot spots in between. Once, after a night in a bar in some nameless town in the Middle East, it had been stolen right off the table, and Reese, along with a couple of his reporter cronies, had chased the thief into the dark forbidden recesses of the town's slums and finally run him down. They'd grabbed the type-writer and left, not bothering to call the authorities.

Reese smiled, reached out and tapped a couple of keys. Still in good shape. There was a worn spot on the space bar from the millions of spaces made by his thumb in a career of scripts revised and revised again before broadcast. But for two years now, the machine had seen no action. That was about to change. Reese touched the gray metal once more and went in to take a shower.

"I'm going to write it all down," he said to Eva hours later. "All those years in broadcast, everything that happened, to me and to the people I came in contact with all over the world."

"Oh, Reese," Eva said, "what a wonderful idea." She leaned up on one elbow and looked down at him. He was lying in bed on his back, staring at the ceiling, his eyes narrowed thoughtfully, and Eva felt like she could see something change in him as he spoke of his plans for the future. Up until he'd met Eva, it had seemed far in the distance, not even reachable from the present, where he'd been content to remain. Now he could look forward and see himself there in the future, *with* a future for the first time in two years.

"It won't be easy," he said thoughtfully.

"No," she answered, well aware of the scope of the task.

"And possibly I won't even want to publish it after it's all put down."

"I'm sure you will," Eva disagreed. "There are thousands of people who would be interested in reading it."

He didn't seem to be listening. "But even if I write it only for myself, that'll be good enough. Just getting it down…" His voice trailed off, and Eva settled back quietly beside him as he began to think aloud about the experiences he wanted to relate. A little thrill went through her as she listened. When their evening together had begun, she'd known it would be a lovely evening, a glorious evening. That thought had kept her going through a difficult day of shooting. But she never dreamed that he would talk to her of himself at last.

Reese had picked her up at eight-thirty at Diligence Hall, with Lacy very much in evidence. She had mastered her crutches, decided they were too much trouble and returned to her chair. "In a few days I'll be ready for the cane. Meanwhile, I've learned to manipulate this thing myself," she told Reese as she expertly wheeled herself into the front parlor. "Eva will be down shortly; she just went upstairs to get her purse," Lacy informed him.

"Why, thank you, Mother," Reese said, amused. "Are you now going to grill me about my suitability to take Eva to dinner?"

"Actually, I did have something of the sort in mind. Eva is a lovely girl, and I expect you to treat her accordingly."

Reese bowed slightly from the waist. "Yes, ma'am."

"By the way, isn't it a little late for dinner?"

"I hope so," he said with a smile. "We'll have the restaurant to ourselves."

"Now, Reese," Lacy scolded, "I don't know how serious this relationship between you and Eva is, but it's beginning to sound very serious indeed. I just want to tell you that if that's the case, it's perfectly all right with me. I can't think of anything I'd like better than to have Eva at Diligence permanently."

Reese started a little and wondered if he'd actually had the same thought himself. He'd certainly been dreading the day Eva would finally leave, but he'd always accepted that day as inevitable; now his mother was talking like there was another choice. Reese shook his head. "Eva has her career, Mother. She works for Gino Marchetti, and her life is in Los Angeles. Our life here in Corinth isn't for her," he said, but wondered as he spoke the words if he could possibly be wrong.

"Then we'll just have to enjoy the time she has left with us," Lacy said.

"Yes," Reese agreed with a smile as Eva came down the stairs.

Once out of the house and out of Lacy's hearing, Reese said, "I think my mother approves of us."

He opened the door, and Eva got into the car without noticing the mysterious-looking lump under a cover in the back seat. "Thank heavens," she said. "Without her approval I, for one, wouldn't be able to walk out that door with you."

"Me, either," Reese admitted with a laugh. "But, happily, tonight we are blessed."

Eva wasn't surprised when they ended up at the restaurant on the pier where they'd spent their first evening together; in fact, she'd hoped that was what Reese had in mind for them.

It was late for dining in South Carolina, but Reese— long used to European habits—had chosen the hour for another reason. "I didn't mind all the friendliness and camaraderie when we were in here the first time, but tonight I'm interested in a quiet table in the corner with no one to bother us, a lot of good seafood and you. Not necessarily in that order," he added.

Reese got what he wished for. The restaurant was almost empty, the food was good, and from their corner table Reese and Eva had a view of the midnight blue ocean illuminated by lights from the restaurant roof. The only other light came from the candle on their table. It put an added glow on their already glowing faces.

"Let's close the place," he suggested.

"I'd love to."

They did. At eleven o'clock there was no one left except the bartender, dozing with his arms on the counter, their waiter and the owner, who were out of sight at the far end of the restaurant tallying up the evening's receipts. Reese and Eva held hands across the table and looked into each other's eyes with wonder and something like disbelief. Whatever was happening, they'd both decided not to question it or try to analyze it or even think past where this moment would lead them. And that Reese had already planned.

"Back to room 12," he said.

"What?"

"Don't tell me you've forgotten the number of our room."

"The motel next door . . ."

"Yes."

"We're going back there tonight...."

"Yes. That is, if you want to." The candle on their table flickered. "*Now*, I think," he said as the candle went out.

"That's the surprise..." All of Eva's thoughts had hung in the air, like this one, to be finished by Reese.

"That's *part* of the surprise." He pressed her hand warmly. "What do you think?"

Eva smiled. "I'd like nothing better."

Hand in hand they walked through the empty restaurant, past the waiter and owner, who looked up with smiles that Reese interpreted for Eva as soon as they were out of the door.

"You might think those were romantically approving glances, but in fact they were smiles of relief," he said. "I think they were beginning to wonder if we'd ever leave, but you know Southerners, too polite to say anything."

Eva shook her head. "It's certainly different here from the rest of the world," she said.

"Is this a world you fit into?"

"I think so," she said.

"But you aren't sure? I'll wait to see how the movie ends," he added with a wry smile as they got into the car for the short drive to the motel down the road. But Reese had stored her response in his mind without pursuing it any further.

As soon as he unlocked the door of number 12, Reese turned on the lights, ushered Eva in and left her standing in the middle of the room with a quick "Wait here." He returned with an armful of packages.

"Reese, what in the world?"

"It's nothing—just our anniversary," he said with the smile of a schoolboy. "No, no," he told her as she excitedly reached for a package. "You have to open them in order. This one first." He put the boxes down and handed her the smallest one. "It's perfume," he said.

"Reese! You aren't supposed to tell me what's inside," she scolded.

"Oh, that's right." He laughed. "I'm not very good at this sort of thing." In fact, he'd never done anything like it in his life. Spontaneous gift giving wasn't Reese Benedict's style.

She opened the perfume. It was her favorite, which she wore all the time.

"I didn't know the name," he told her, "but I recognized the scent immediately. Now for the rest." He handed her another present.

She opened them one by one and tried them on for his approval while Reese lay back on the bed, enchanted.

Finally she stood in the middle of the little room wearing the nightgown, her hair a golden mass around her head, her eyes shining in delight. Spontaneously, she threw herself on the bed beside Reese. He gathered her in his arms, and they began to laugh, tears rolling down their cheeks.

"Fuchsia," she said, "periwinkle blue, ruby red. Are you trying to tell me something, Reese?"

"Not at all. I'm crazy about beige and white," he said, filling his hands with her wild hair. "For rugs and sofas. But not for beautiful women like you."

"Everything fits perfectly," she said between his kisses, which began gently but were quickly becoming more passionate. "How did you know my size?"

After another long kiss he whispered against her cheek, "I described perfectly this beautiful body that I'm holding. I remembered every inch of it," he said, his hands roaming down the satiny gown and slipping beneath it. "Now, enough of that. As pretty as it is, I want what's under this red gown."

Her arms tightened around his neck as she responded to his kiss, running her tongue along the outline of his lips, nibbling at the clean-shaven skin of his chin and cheek, letting her tongue slide easily into the smoothness of his mouth. "Then take it off," she murmured provocatively.

He reached down to her thighs and grabbed a handful of satin and pulled it up to her waist. Then he slipped his hands beneath the gown and lovingly caressed the soft skin of her hips and moved upward to her waist, working the gown to her breasts. He lingered a long moment to rub the dark pink nipples, taut and ready for his touch, before he pulled the gown over her head and tossed it, a red splash, onto the floor.

She stretched out beneath him on the bed, and there was no false modesty in her pose. She didn't try to hide herself but instead lay languidly beneath his gaze in the dim light of the motel room lamp.

Without taking his eyes off her, Reese stood up and removed his clothes, paying no attention to the task except to get it over with so he could get back to her, kneel beside the alabaster goddess who was always more beautiful than any of his fantasies of her. He reached out and caressed her slowly and watched in the lamplight as the emotions he'd hoped for, expected, floated across her face—pleasure and desire. With equal slowness he lowered his head and began to kiss her. His lips grazed the hollow between her breasts. He ran his tongue over each round orb, and Eva gave a little sigh as she pulled his head closer so that his mouth could capture one eager nipple.

As his tongue teased her, Eva's flesh grew warm and flushed; she seemed to melt and dissolve beneath him. She held him tightly, bound by the dual pleasures of his mouth at her breast, sucking, teasing, tantalizing, and his hand drifting downward until he found the welcoming honeyed moistness that awaited him.

Reese's breath quickened, and he wondered if his lungs would be able to get enough air. His brain whirled, filled with Eva, her beauty, her passion. Each time he made love to her, he wanted her more, and now he could only wonder if he would ever get enough of her, if this obsession would ever end.

When he paused, lifting his head away from her tantalizing breast for a moment, she reached up and found his lips with her moist open mouth. He fell back on the bed with Eva on top of him, suffused by a glowing warmth that permeated the core of his being as her tongue sought the inner recesses of his mouth and her hands roamed the hard planes of his body. His blood raced and pounded, burning a hot trail through him that was no more fiery than Eva's touch.

Her hands moved over the hard muscles of his thighs, the line of his hipbone, the flatness of his abdomen. The sensations they caused were almost unbearable, the pleasure intense and building, spiraling inside him. He didn't know how much longer he could control himself. Then her hand moved to caress him, stroking, driving him to the edge. Suddenly he captured her hand in both of his and held it fast. "Eva," he said in a voice that sounded hoarse.

"I know," she said, for she, too, was on passion's edge. She moved her hand away, no longer touching him, allowing him—and herself—to pause for an instant.

Reese looked down at her, and his heart gave a lurch. Her face was radiant, her hair spread around her like a golden halo, her eyes were filled with need. He knew that there was so much more to making love to Eva than the joining of their physical bodies.

There was something deep and almost spiritual that made him feel a part of her. His head was swimming and his heart was racing as he gazed down on her, but the feeling of desire, powerful as it was, couldn't touch that other feeling. It was love, and it possessed him completely, as completely as she possessed him.

Slowly, slowly, still trying to stay in control until they were truly one, Reese knelt above her. But she was as eager as he, and she arched toward him. He met her with a force that caught them both by surprise as his manhood filled her, and his power coursed through her. Together they moved with a rhythm that was perfectly matched in its nearly frantic pace. Still together, still one, she dug her fingers into his flesh and flung back her head. With each thrust he brought her closer, closer to the pinnacle of ecstasy where fulfillment awaited her.

Reese gripped her shoulders, and she tried to hold him, but her hands slipped on his damp skin, across his back, down his shoulders and finally caught on his arms where the muscles bulged just above his elbow. Holding on as if for life, faster and faster they moved until in one agonizingly perfect moment, she was there—he was there—they were one.

They held each other, hot bodies wet with love and locked together. Finally they relaxed, grew limp and collapsed into each other's arms.

"Reese—"

"Eva—" he answered, and together they said the same words. *"I love you."*

Later, lying beside her half asleep, half awake, Reese realized that the words he'd spoken to her had been true: he *was* in love with Eva. That thought mingled with the sensations of pleasure and desire that were even now so much a part of his feeling for her. He loved her, but she belonged to a different world. In fact, from what he'd seen during Marchetti's visit, the man had her more closely under his thumb than ever. There was more: Reese was never going to enter that world again.

He sighed deeply and kissed the top of her golden head. He would have to be content with having her with him for a while. For now, that was all he could ask.

"What's the matter?" Eva asked him, opening her eyes and looking up into his troubled gaze.

"I was thinking how little time we have left before you have to leave. It's borrowed time now," he said.

"Yes," she admitted.

"I was thinking that I want to spend it all with you." He reached down and grabbed her hand, almost fiercely.

"You will, Reese," she said, "but let's not talk about it. It frightens me."

"I'm sorry," he replied. "I'm just regretful for what happened in the past." He still held on to her hand. "I was selfish with time. Barbara suffered because of that."

"I'm sure she understood," Eva soothed. "I'm sure—"

"Yes, she did understand, and that's what makes it so much more painful. I thought I had it all under control, when in reality I couldn't control anything. I was such a superstar that I thought nothing of subjecting my wife to the kind of life I led, thinking it was the life for her, too.''

"Maybe it was," Eva said, "because you were there to share it with her.''

Reese smiled wryly. "Some of the time. The sad part is that's probably true. But she didn't choose the life; *I* chose it.''

"You're too hard on yourself. She chose you." Eva challenged.

Reese shook his head. "No, I always knew what she wanted: a home here in Corinth. I never wanted that, and now, strangely enough, I'm back here.'' Eva realized that it wasn't because of Barbara he was back. It was because of something in him, something he was searching for.

It was much later when he told her about the book. "The sudden knowledge that I was going to write it, that I *could* write it, came over me so strongly. Then just now, the urge to tell you was almost as strong." Reese looked at her. Her body was pressed close to his, one leg thrown over his calf, porcelain against his tanned skin, feminine and masculine overlapping. Reese smiled.

"I want to stay here all night," he said, "stay awake all night here in room 12 and talk to you.''

Eva curled up against him happily. He'd never talked with her about himself, never opened up. She wanted to stay all night, too, and listen to him, share his past and his plans for the future.

"Ah, yes," he said as if to reinforce his earlier words. "I do love you.''

Eva felt her heart quicken, for now she knew that the words spoken at the height of passion had been true for him, as they were for her.

Reese kissed her and then reached down and pulled the sheet over her, tucking it beneath her chin and kissing her again. "You've been good for me," he said. "I'm coming alive again, and I owe that to you, Eva."

Now, Eva thought, everything was perfect. The night stretched before them, a time to be together and to share as never before.

# Chapter 10

I used to have nightmares," Reese told Eva.

She lay quietly beside him as he spoke, feeling closer to him than ever before. This was the man who'd roamed the world in search of news stories until that terrible day two years ago when he'd stepped out of the human race. Now he was coming back. It would be a long journey, but he'd taken the first steps. He'd begun to communicate, and not just with Eva. He'd stopped recently to listen to crew members on the set and even to talk a little.

They'd weathered Gino's arrival and departure and somehow become closer for it. She'd told him about Franco; he'd told her about Barbara and the book. She'd fallen in love with him.

"In the nightmares I see Barbara's death," he said to her quietly. "But that's not all. I see myself. Standing there, doing nothing."

"There was nothing you *could* do," Eva insisted.

"I mean doing nothing to prevent it before it happened, nothing to get her out of there, away from that life."

"Reese—"

"I know. It was her choice, too, and I can't go on living with the guilt. It's over now," he said, "and it's time for me to start living again. You've taught me that, Eva."

Reese had settled her comfortably against him, and their naked bodies were stretched out languidly under the cool sheet. Yet even after their lovemaking, when they were spent and exhausted and in a peaceful sort of haze, the desire was still there; it rose in them with each touch, each tender kiss that always seemed to deepen into much more.

"Ymmm," Eva mouthed a sound that was part satisfaction, part excitement. "It's so good to touch you, feel you, so good to talk to you. For a long time, we didn't really talk at all. Well, we *talked*..."

"But we couldn't seem to say what we meant, what we wanted to say," Reese responded thoughtfully.

"Now we can," Eva said. "I feel as if I can tell you anything."

He gathered her even closer with an audible sigh that held both relief and happiness. Turning his head a little, he kissed her. Eva's mouth opened under his, and as she felt his tongue slip inside, the excitement grew within her. Only a few minutes had passed since he'd made love to her, but Eva knew that very soon things would begin again.

Reese wanted her now, but they had all night, and the kisses would be enough to satisfy them for a while. Right now, he needed the talk as much as the lovemaking.

"I want you to share everything with me," he said. "Always." For a moment he was silent, his lips still close to hers. "There's so much I want to share, too," he said. "I've been thinking about teaching."

"Oh, Reese..."

"There's no broadcast department at the local college."

"You could set one up." Eva was intrigued. "You could get involved."

"Yes," Reese said as he stroked her hair, which was still a little damp from their lovemaking. "It's a good school, and I'd like to think I could contribute something. The academic rating is high, but putting some well-known people on the faculty can't hurt. And I'm still pretty well known," he said.

Eva laughed. "Yes, I'm afraid you are. But let's not forget your talent, Reese. It's so exciting to think of you sharing all that knowledge and experience."

Reese nodded. "It's only fair, I guess, to share what I've learned, especially with those people who have the same roots. I left this part of the world very early, but it's always stayed with me. Now I'm back for good. You know, this isn't a bad future, living in Corinth, writing my book and teaching at the college." He smiled contentedly. "Maybe I'll even get that land from Graydon and build myself a house."

Eva could feel her heart quicken. The Graydon land. She'd never told Reese about Gino's plans. She'd promised Gino to say nothing, and it hadn't occurred to her not to keep that promise, particularly since Reese had never mentioned the land again. She'd almost forgotten about his interest; now Eva felt confused.

"A house," she said thoughtfully. "I understood you were interested in the land as a buffer zone, something to keep you separated from the rest of the world. Now that you've decided to join the world again, you don't even need the solitude."

Reese laughed. "Oh, yes I do. I'm planning to start living again, but that doesn't mean that I want to lose my privacy. And I certainly can't stay where I am forever. That's my mother's guest cottage, after all. Diligence belongs to Lacy; I need a home of my own."

"But the Graydon land . . ."

"It's an ideal spot. I've always been drawn to it, and ever since I took you there I've been thinking about it more seriously. It's unspoiled, beautiful. Graydon has priced it way over the market value, totally out of sight, but I have time to negotiate with him. Meanwhile, I don't imagine he'll sell to anyone he doesn't know."

Very softly Eva answered, "I hope you're right."

The tone of her voice was so strained that Reese glanced at her sharply. Her face was pale with bright splotches of color in her cheeks.

"What's the matter, Eva?"

She tried to snuggle closer to him, to somehow burrow into him. But she couldn't hide from this.

"Eva?"

"I showed it to Gino," she answered in a voice that was muffled because she was still in his arms with her face against his chest.

"You what?" Reese was sure that he must not have heard correctly.

"I showed it to to Gino when he was here.

"Why in God's name did you do that?" Reese's voice sounded stunned, but there was no anger in it yet, just surprise.

"He'd asked me to look for some property for him. I found several possibilities, but he didn't seem interested in any of them. I just happened to mention the Graydon land—"

"Just *happened*?" Reese had moved away slightly to sit up against the headboard, propping a pillow behind his back. His eyes were cold, but the anger was still held in check.

"You didn't tell me not to mention it, Reese. I wasn't aware that the property was forbidden to everyone else." She tried to defend herself from his anger, which she realized was building and which was so unexpected. Or was it? Maybe, Eva realized, this was why she hadn't told him. She hadn't wanted to endanger what they had together. If only this conversation could have come later, Eva felt her heart cry out, later, when they understood each other better, believed in each other more. Now their relationship was just beginning; it was so fragile.

Although Eva had avoided looking at him, she felt Reese move again on the bed and knew he was getting up. She reached out to touch his shoulder, but he'd already swung his legs over the side of the bed and was out of her reach—or he'd seen her hand and purposefully moved away just in time to avoid her touch.

Reese pulled on his pants, and when he turned back to her, she saw the anger at last. Somehow that was a relief. "What the hell does Marchetti want with Graydon's land?" He reached for his shirt.

Gino had asked her not to discuss his plans. She was caught between two sets of values, and for a moment she hesitated.

In that moment Reese caught on. "He swore you to secrecy, and like the perfect flunky, you did his bidding."

"I'm not his flunky," Eva said, and for the first time her own anger began to show. She got out of bed, too, and started dressing. Obviously, the evening they'd both looked forward to with such joy was over. "Gino *did* ask me not to discuss his plans...."

Reese tucked his shirt into his pants carefully, waiting. When she didn't continue, he looked across at her, his eyes steely gray.

Eva sighed. He was daring her to tell him, almost sure that she wouldn't. For a moment she thought of doing as he expected and keeping her promise to Gino—choosing Gino over Reese, which is how Reese would interpret it. But she'd already made her decision: she would tell him, and she would tell him for her own reasons. She wanted him to trust her; she wanted to preserve what was between them.

"He wants to build a film studio." Her words were almost inaudible, and Eva knew why. Even now, even the way she felt about Reese, her loyalty to Gino was strong.

Reese's oath was low and profane. Eva tried to ignore it as she continued. "He plans to build the studio here in Corinth, but it may not be on the Graydon property. Don't you see, Reese, we have no idea if Graydon will be interested in selling to him...."

"A film studio," Reese repeated, paying no attention to anything else Eva was saying. "The only thing that could be worse than a studio in Corinth would be that same studio in my backyard, on the Graydon property, on the land where I want to build a home of my own. That's all that could be worse, Eva, and you've managed that, too."

"I haven't managed anything, Reese," she shouted, unable to believe that he could accuse her of being responsible for what was only a plan in Gino Marchetti's head. "You're jumping to conclusions. You have no idea what's going on."

He looked at her for a moment and then nodded. "That's absolutely correct, Eva. But I'm going to find out." He reached for the telephone.

"Reese, it's past midnight—"

His look silenced her. Shaking her head as much in sadness at what had happened between them as in confusion over Reese's reaction, Eva sank down on the bed.

"Information for Asheville, North Carolina," Reese said curtly into the phone. "Charles Graydon." As he listened to a voice Eva couldn't hear, he stared at her, his eyes filled with accusation even as he hung up and said, "The number's not listed."

Immediately he dialed again. "Beau, this is Reese. Yes, I know, but you've been keeping late hours recently so I didn't think you'd be asleep. I need Graydon's phone number. The one who moved to Asheville. Charles Graydon. It should be in the address book on the hall table. Yes, Beau, downstairs," he said curtly. "I'll wait."

By the time Reese got the number and dialed, Eva had taken her clothes into the bathroom to finish dressing. She didn't want to hear the conversation.

Five minutes later he shouted, "You can come out now, Eva. I'm sure you know what Graydon told me."

Through the door she answered, "I have no idea what he told you, Reese."

"Well, I imagine you can guess."

Eva opened the door. He was picking up the clothes he'd given her. They were scattered around the room, on chairs and over the bureau. Their bright splashes of color looked like the remains of a costume party that had dragged too long. Eva turned her eyes away. She didn't want to look at the clothes. While he talked, Reese put them into boxes.

"Graydon closed the deal with your boss. The land belongs to Marchetti Films International. He told me that the great man was planning to build a film studio," Reese added with a bitter smile. "So now it's out; you don't have to keep silent any longer."

"Reese, I'm sorry. I didn't know. . . ." she began.

"What do you mean, you 'didn't know'?"

"I didn't know how much you wanted it." Her words were softer now, but they did nothing to soften the look on Reese's face.

"I took you there; I showed it to you," he said as if that had been a monumental decision. And it had been. Now, when she understood him better, Eva knew that.

"All you talked of was a buffer zone, Reese. That's all you told me. I can't read your mind."

He raised one eyebrow as if somehow he'd expected her to understand without words what the land meant to him.

"I didn't realize how much you cared for it," she said. "You acted so casually, as if it were another site on your tour, different only because it was near Diligence. How was I to know, Reese? We didn't talk then. The words we said weren't the words we meant."

"Maybe they weren't tonight, either," Reese answered sharply. "Maybe I was right when I categorized you as the cool hatchet wielder for Marchetti. Somehow, though, I got lost along the way in the idea that you cared for me and for Corinth."

Eva ignored the hurt his words inflicted when she answered. "I do, Reese. I love you and I do care."

Reese stacked the boxes by the door. Clearly, it was time to leave. "I don't think so, Eva. We're two different people from two different worlds. You thought nothing of showing the land to Marchetti so he could gobble it up. Well, I have news for you; that's not going to happen." Reese opened the door and took the packages out, tossing them into the back seat of the convertible. "You said 'get involved,'" he reminded her as he came back inside. "Well, now I'm really getting involved. I'm going to fight him and I'm going to win. Marchetti Films will never come to Corinth."

Late that morning, Reese and his dogs were emerging from the woods by the cottage when Beau caught up with him.

"Reese, what in the world was that phone call about?"

Coleen broke into a run toward Beau, jumping up, paws on his chest, ready for the expected attention, which she got. "Hello, old girl, I'm flattered by your attention," he said, rubbing her head before returning to his interrupted conversation. "I thought I'd never get back to sleep, I was so curious. *Why* were you calling old man Graydon in the middle of the night?"

"Have you been to town today, Beau?" Reese asked enigmatically.

"No, they're just shooting some pickup scenes. I'm not needed. Why?"

Reese laughed. "That explains it, although I can't imagine that the news hasn't carried out here on the tom-toms."

"What are you talking about?" Beau queried. His brother had headed toward the cottage, and Beau followed him, both dogs now playing at his heels.

"I called Graydon about his property down on the river road," Reese said over his shoulder.

"Come on, Reese. You've been interested in that land since you moved back here. Are you telling me that you called him in the middle of the night to find out that Graydon wouldn't come down on his price?"

"I suppose he figured that if he held out long enough, someone would meet his price," Reese said without answering Beau's question.

"Don't tell me you bought it?"

"Nope. Gino Marchetti bought it," Reese said flatly. "He plans to build a film studio there—over my dead body," he added emphatically. "Come on, girls." The dogs left Beau's side immediately and followed Reese into the house. He closed the door behind them, leaving Beau standing in the middle of the yard, totally perplexed.

When Beau returned to Diligence Hall, Lacy was getting out of her car, leaning on the cane and helped by one of the servants, who'd accompanied her to town.

"Mom, have I got news for you," Beau called out.

Lacy chose to ignore his excitement. "You see, Beau," she responded, "I've learned to walk with my cane quite well." She reached the top step, shooed the servant away and refused Beau's help.

"I can see that, Mom," Beau said, walking ahead to open the door. "But wait till you hear what *else* happened."

"Beau, dear, I know what's happened," she responded. "As you can see, I've just been to town." The servant returned, pushing Lacy's wheelchair. "All right," she said, settling into the chair, "but only to the end of the hall. I can get around on the porch with just my cane. Walking a long distance still tires me a little," she admitted to Beau.

"Mom—"

"I know, dear. Marchetti Films is moving to Corinth."

Beau sighed. "How'd you find out?"

"It's all over town, and it's causing quite a stir, let me tell you. I'll walk from here." Lacy, with help on both sides, rose from the wheelchair and walked onto the porch aided only by her cane.

"Yes, there's apparently going to be a film studio located right here in Corinth," Lacy added. Iced tea had already been placed on the table. Lacy sat down carefully in her wing chair and poured a glass for herself and Beau.

"What do you think about the idea, Lacy?" Eva had appeared at the door, dressed in one of her beige business outfits.

"Oh, Eva, dear. I'm so glad you didn't go to town for the filming. Come out here and talk to us. I don't know how I feel about this news, and that's the truth." Lacy poured another glass of iced tea that Eva accepted as she sat down beside the older woman.

"It will bring changes to Corinth. There's no doubt about that," Eva said.

"I know," Lacy agreed. "We're such a sleepy little town."

"Which is exactly why it's time for Corinth to move into the twentieth century. Sleepy little towns finish last," Beau said adamantly.

"Well, I guess I know how *you* feel," Eva responded with a laugh.

"You're right," Beau declared.

"Maybe I'm just too old to face change," Lacy contemplated aloud. "I thoroughly enjoy having a movie made at my house. I'm very fond of you, Eva, as you know, and I like the young people on the crew, even though some of them are a little strange, and Mr. Marchetti—Gino—is certainly a charming man. I just don't know if I'd like all this excitement day after day, with a Hollywood studio located practically in my backyard. Do you understand that, Eva?''

"Of course I do. I feel—"

"Look what's going on at the cottage," Beau interrupted. He'd pulled up the blinds at the end of the porch. "If I didn't know better, I'd say Reese was having a party."

"Eva, help me up," Lacy asked. "I want to see what's happening."

"So do I," Eva declared as she and Lacy made their way to the window.

Two cars had pulled into the driveway of the cottage, and another one was coming down the road. The dogs were barking excitedly.

"It's been a long time since they've seen anyone at the cottage," Beau said with a laugh.

"Who's that getting out of the gray car?" Lacy asked her son. "I can't see his face."

"I do believe it's the mayor, Mom, and that's one of the country commissioners in the other car. And look who's with him . . ."

"Who, Beau?" Lacy asked. She was intrigued.

"It's old Snake Eyes. Well, we can all guess what Reese is up to. He's marshaling his forces to fight Marchetti Films," Beau said.

"Yes," Lacy agreed. "That was the talk in Corinth this morning. The monthly town meeting is Wednesday night."

"Reese is getting all his big guns loaded."

Eva stood between them, peering out the window and watching as the group of men was greeted at the door by Reese and ushered into the cottage.

"Isn't this exciting?" Lacy asked. "It's like a movie itself. All the suspense. I wonder how it's going to end."

"It'll end at the town meeting, when the people of Corinth let their elected officials know what they want."

"What do you think that'll be?" Eva asked curiously.

"I don't know," Beau answered honestly. "Reese can be very persuasive. On the other hand, he's going to confront a lot of people who aren't about to be persuaded—including his little brother."

As Eva went up to her room, she wondered what she would have said if she'd had a chance to tell Lacy her thoughts. When Beau had interrupted her, Eva had been about to express them, yet she hadn't really been sure of what she was going to say. She still wasn't sure. She knew what Gino wanted—perfect loyalty. She knew what Reese wanted—understanding. But Eva was torn. This issue, like a wedge, had been driven between her and the man she loved. A sort of sadness came over Eva, but it was short-lived. Reese was the one who didn't understand. Reese was the one who stubbornly insisted that Eva was responsible, that somehow she'd been plotting all along to bring outside forces into his life and disrupt his carefully organized tranquillity.

Work on *Glory Road* continued out of sequence, with the scene that would end the film being shot the next day at the train station. Eva didn't have to be there; she wasn't needed. But she *was* there, standing alone at the edge of the parking lot as a machine that would create train "steam" was moved into place. Gino knew how to establish poignancy and save money at the same time, Eva thought admiringly.

She watched and waited, wondering why she'd come here to witness this last farewell. As Reese had long ago guessed, Gino was going with the unhappy ending.

Only a few words of dialogue would be exchanged between Louise Ross and the actor who played her young husband. Unable to hear them from where she stood and not wanting to move closer, Eva followed along from her bound copy of the script.

A: There's still time to change your mind.
(He looks into the distance, hearing the whistle of the train.)
C: (Shakes her head.)
A: You'll come back. I know you will.
C: (Looks at him sadly. Her lips part as if to speak and then close. She shakes her head again and starts to walk toward the platform.)
A: I'll write to you.
C: No. Please. Don't. (She looks down the tracks as the train nears.)
A: (Calling over the noise.) I'll come after you. As soon as things get settled here, I'll bring you back. It'll be different, honey. You'll see.
Close-up of C: (Her face shows the sorrow, but there are no more tears.)

THE END

"Cut and print. I don't need another take," the director called out as the steam that had filled the station began to dissipate. "We'll see rushes on that tomorrow and start shooting at the house the next day. You two are free. Don't shave off your beard for the early scenes," he called after the actor. "Not until I see these rushes."

The crew members quickly scattered, lighting cigarettes and finding comfortable places to settle down for a break, but the director had other ideas. "Okay, let's move," he cautioned them. "We have the establishing shots to get to. Eva!" he shouted, seeing her standing in the distance. "Do you need to talk to me?"

"No," she answered. "I just wanted to watch the scene." She didn't explain further because she wasn't sure why she was here unless to inflict unnecessary pain on herself, adding to the sadness she was already feeling about two other worlds and two other very different sets of ideals.

As Eva turned away, she saw Reese. He'd been standing out of sight on the other side of the tracks. Eva wondered if he'd come here to watch the end of *Glory Road* for the same perverse reason—to remind himself of the very real differences between them. Almost two days had passed since she'd told him about the Graydon land. He'd made no effort to talk with her, and he made no effort now, although Eva was sure that he'd seen her.

Slowly she walked back to her car. The heat was already oppressive even at this early hour. Their cool respite was over. It was time for Eva to return to L.A.

Gino had different ideas. As usual, he knew what was happening in Corinth. The land he'd bought was in a residential area. A special permit would have to be issued to change the zoning to business. Gino hadn't imagined that would present any problems and had left the details up to his lawyer to handle with the authorities over the phone. Then Reese had taken action, and the whole scene had changed.

The telegram that Eva received that afternoon was wordy, as was Gino's style. There were some areas in which he saved money, big money. But he did have his extravagances, and sending telegrams was one. Gino composed for Western Union with all of his Italian pizzazz.

> Understand there's a little problem. Can't be there to solve it so must depend on you, *cara*. State our case at town meeting with all your charm and grace not to mention persuasiveness. You know why Marchetti Films will save that little hamlet; I don't have to go into it. Get up there and convince them and the next day hop a plane to L.A. We got other fish to fry. Gino

Armed with that telegram and what little optimism she could garner from it, Eva rode with Beau to the town meeting.

"Lacy's already left with Reese," he told her, a little embarrassed.

"So," Eva said. "We're dividing up along party lines."

Beau attempted to laugh. "Actually, I think Mom will come over to the right way of thinking. But these things do take time. You have to remember, Eva, she's lived here since she was nineteen, and not much has changed around her in that time. Progress just kind of overlooked our town, and that's a comfort to some of the older people. For them, Corinth is like an old shoe—comfortable, familiar, never changing except to get a little worn."

"I thought Lacy was more modern in her thinking than that," Eva mused aloud.

"She is. That's why I'm sure she'll come around when she hears your arguments. I do hope you have some good ones, Eva," Beau said.

"I haven't really prepared anything...."

"Eva—"

She laughed. "Well, I have a few notes in my head, but I seem to have more success when I speak extemporaneously."

Beau was concerned. "That's all right in high school, Eva, but tonight you'll be up against Reese Benedict. I'm sure you recall that he was a news commentator, and one of the best," Beau reminded her wryly.

"Which is precisely why I'm not preparing anything," she told a still perplexed Beau. "I can't fight Reese in his style, Beau. That would be ridiculous. I'm no match for the cool, collected television personality. I'll simply tell the people at the meeting what Marchetti Films in Corinth will mean for them—and answer their questions. That's all."

Beau moaned, which didn't help to put Eva any more at ease. She *was* nervous, although she'd never have admitted that to Beau. This was certainly not the most difficult position she'd been in as Marchetti Film's representative. She'd confronted groups far more powerful than the members of the Corinth town meeting. But she'd never had to stand up against the man she loved. However stubborn he was, however shortsighted and wrong-thinking—from Eva's point of view—one fact was still undeniable. She loved him. But tonight she was working for Gino, Eva told herself, and she wouldn't let her feelings show.

That determination lasted only until Eva walked through the door of the meeting hall and saw Reese standing up on the stage. He turned toward her when she and Beau entered the room, as if he'd known by some sort of magical telepathy that she was there. The expression on his face was unreadable, but for an instant she thought she saw love there, and desire. She knew he must have seen those dual emotions in her eyes, too, for there was no doubt about what she was feeling.

Reese was wearing cream-colored linen trousers and a green cotton polo shirt. He was surrounded by a group of people on the stage, but they seemed insignificant beside him, not just because he was taller and more handsome, which he certainly was, but because of the charisma. It made her tremble with trepidation. Beau had been right: she was up against the best tonight.

"I think we got a good turnout for our side," the man standing near Reese was saying.

"Depends on if that group from down by the highway comes," responded another one of Reese's allies.

Reese nodded at both observations but made no audible comment. When Eva and Beau had entered the meeting room, he'd forgotten for an instant about zoning and commissioners and votes. She was wearing the black pants and fuchsia shirt he'd given her, and very high heels. That threw Reese off completely. He'd expected the businesslike Eva, the representative of Marchetti Films who'd arrived in Corinth weeks ago and presented her boss's case so succinctly. She'd been cool and distant and very effective. That's the woman he'd expected tonight, the one he'd prepared himself to face in this battle over the future of Corinth.

The Eva who'd turned up instead would be more difficult to do battle with because she was *his* Eva, the one who'd given him a new life, the one he'd fallen in love with.

"Reese, don't you think it's time to get this started?" a man at his elbow asked.

Reese came out of his reverie promising himself not to let it happen again but not at all sure he'd be able to keep that promise. "Yes," he answered vaguely. "Why don't you see if you can get the mayor up here."

He looked down into the audience again and saw that some of the cast and crew from *Glory Road* had come to the open meeting and were sitting in the back of the hall, curious spectators to what they probably considered rather primitive goings on. Eva wasn't sitting with them, Reese noticed. She and Beau had taken places near the front among a group friendly toward Marchetti Films. A smart move, Reese imagined, presenting herself as one of the crowd rather than an oddity from the movie world. Reese thought that was probably only the beginning of her smart moves.

As the mayor climbed to the podium, the air was crackling with electricity. He had to bring down his gavel half a dozen times to get the silence he needed. Finally a hush came over the crowd, but the anticipation was in the silence, as it had been in the noise.

# Chapter 11

The town meeting for July 12 is called to order," the mayor said, bringing his gavel down with grave authority. "We'll follow parliamentary procedure tonight, so I'll need a motion that we forgo all other business and move onto this zoning problem since that's why we're all here."

The motion was made, seconded and passed quickly.

"Then we might as well get to it," the Mayor said. "Do I hear a motion that the zoning on Route 22 from the river bridge to the city limits be left residential?"

"He could have put it the other way" Eva whispered.

"Of course," Beau agreed, "but that would have sounded favorable to Marchetti. The mayor's no fool."

A woman sitting in front of them made the necessary motion, and when it was seconded, she smiled back over her shoulder with a look of satisfaction. Eva recognized her as the postmistress, who'd frequently informed Eva of her views of Corinth and of Reese. Things had changed.

"I thought we could count on her," Eva said to Beau, not bothering to whisper since everyone was deep in conversation, some with those nearby, others calling across the room.

"Are you kidding? She's married to the most conservative commissioner, the first one to jump into Reese's pocket."

"But she had some opinions that seemed very independent," Eva objected.

"Maybe," Beau agreed, "but she *votes* with her husband."

The mayor was pounding his gavel again, and a semblance of quiet was spreading through the room. "All right, folks, let's settle down. Looks like we've got a long night ahead of us, and we need to move right along. At this time, I'd like to recognize Reese Benedict, who has a suggestion to make that I think will be agreeable to everyone."

"Hmmm," Beau said, "that's a little departure from parliamentary procedure, isn't it?"

Eva shook her head. There wasn't much they could do about it; Reese was already on his feet.

His proposal was brief. "I'd like to be given the opportunity to state the case in favor of the motion. Afterward, the question will be open for discussion."

"What?" Eva said aloud, not even attempting a quiet voice. Beau looked over at her with a grin as she started to stand up.

She was about halfway out of her seat when Reese noticed her and quickly amended his suggestion. "Of course, the other point of view will also be argued—

before the discussion," he added when he saw Eva start to rise again, "by Miss Sinclair, representative of Marchetti Films."

"Does this sound agreeable, folks? the mayor asked. "Then let's have a motion."

The motion was made and seconded, and a din broke out once more during which Eva said to Beau, "Did he really think he'd get by with leaving me out completely?"

Beau laughed. "He was about to suggest that other opinions be a part of the open discussion. But to answer your question, no, he didn't expect to get away with it. He just wanted to make you fight, put you on the defensive right away."

"Which he did," Eva said.

"Umm," Beau mouthed. "So you'd better be prepared to wow 'em."

Again, Eva felt her nerves tighten. She managed to hide the fact from Beau and concentrate on Reese, who, with his first words, was greeted by the respectful silence that the mayor hadn't been able to achieve with his gavel.

Reese's voice was quiet and confidential, as if he were discussing a very personal subject with a very close friend. It was the right technique. He didn't preach to them; he didn't address them as a television personality; he took them into his confidence. It worked.

"Damn," Beau murmured. "This is going to be worse than I expected."

It *was* worse. Reese was taking them back in his memories, which were their memories, too. "I know most of you. Just about everyone in this room went from first grade through high school two blocks down the street. We got a fine education in that old brick building, and we had good times there, too. And I might as well mention those four winning football seasons in a row." Across the room, faces broke out in wide grins.

"Of course, we weren't always heroes, were we, boys?" Another ripple of laughter moved through the room. "Is Miss Phifer here?" he asked, knowing perfectly well that she was. "Well, she can vouch for the bad behavior," he said with a grin. "I guess I cleaned about as many erasers after school as anyone. And I probably cut class to go fishing more than anyone. No, I take that back," he amended. "Nookie Bourne outdid me in that department."

Laughter rippled, and from the back of the room, a voice called out, "High time you admitted that, Reese."

Reese waited for the laughter to die down and then said, "It was a good life," in a voice that Eva suspected he'd forced a tremor into. But whether the catch in his throat was real or not, it worked. "It was those memories of home that kept me going during all the years that I was away," he said. "Now that I'm back, I realize that this is the only place for me."

Reese paused to let that sink in. He was back with them for good; the pause emphasized the fact that he'd chosen Corinth over all the other places in the world.

"I'm sure that those of you who've stayed here and kept this way of life going feel the same. Plenty of our sons and daughters have left Corinth, looking for something else, something bigger, something better. That's fine," he said. "Some of us need a kind of stimulation that can't be found in a small town like Corinth. I understand that because for a long time I needed it, too. It can be found elsewhere, in Dallas or

Denver or Atlanta; in New York and L.A.; in Europe. But this kind of life, the easy, peaceful, uncorrupted and unspoiled life, can't be found too many places. It's here in Corinth, South Carolina. Let's keep it here," he said in a voice that was barely audible.

The room exploded in applause and cheers. Eva made the mistake of looking across at Lacy. She was sitting on the aisle seat, and her face was radiant, not unlike most of the faces around her. They beamed with pride. He was a son of Corinth, one who had made his way in the world and chosen to come back to them.

As Eva had warned Beau, her comments were brief, but they included some very real facts, some hard evidence about the state of affairs in Corinth, South Carolina, in the 1980s. "Sometimes looks can be deceiving," she said. "A quiet peaceful town can have a lot going on underneath—unemployment, need, even poverty. In some small towns there aren't enough jobs for everyone. Farmers aren't getting the prices for their crops that they'd counted on, fishermen aren't bringing in the catches they'd expected, and these hardworking people can't pay their bills at the stores or their loans at the bank." Eva's description was general, not specific. She didn't have to mention names. She'd touched many of the people in the room, and she knew it. So did they.

"One big company, one major industry, can change all that. It can create jobs for the people who need them and generate capital for the businesses that are in trouble. It can bring in extra revenue for the schools and highways. It can enable the parks and recreation departments to add summer programs in the arts and in science and athletics so the children can have all the advantages they deserve. That's what Marchetti Films can do for Corinth," she said fervently. "That's change, yes, but change for the good."

The applause, although not as zealous as the ovation that followed Reese's remarks, was more than polite; it satisfied Eva, and it gave renewed hope to Beau, who couldn't refrain from pumping Eva's hand in his enthusiasm. "That was great, Eva. Fabulous."

The discussion that followed was led by one of the county commissioners, the husband of the postmistress, Beau reminded Eva. The commissioner did his best to convince the gathering that a terrible "element" would come into Corinth with the studio.

"That's right," another supporter agreed. "Instead of helping our school kids with parks and classes and all that stuff, we'll be putting them right into the hands of the druggies."

"As soon as the those wild film people move here, they'll bring all their bad habits with them and turn this into a place like they came from."

"That's the truth," another voice called out.

"Wait a minute," Beau said, standing up. This was the first time he'd spoken during the town meeting, and the audience quietened, eager to hear what Reese's brother had to say.

"We don't know *who* will be coming here to work for the studio, but I suspect Mr. Marchetti will open with a staff willing to relocate in South Carolina, most of them family people who've been with Marchetti films for a long time."

"That's what you say, Beau," someone called out. "What does Marchetti say?"

"I believe I can speak for him," Eva answered. As she stood up, the noise lessened. "It's far too soon to announce staff plans, but I can tell you that in the past when Marchetti Films has opened new locations we've transferred only a skeletal staff of the production people, the film people you're concerned about. The rest are hired locally and trained.''

That sent a murmur of satisfaction through the crowd, but Beau wasn't quite ready to let the subject go. "Furthermore," he said emphatically, "I've worked closely with the production crew on *Glory Road* for the past few weeks, and I can tell you that these dedicated artists are interested in doing their jobs and doing them well and aren't here to tempt the children of Corinth into evil ways," he said, getting the expected laugh. "Tell me, have any of you had trouble with the members of the *Glory Road* crew?"

There was a silence in the crowd. Several heads were shaken. Then from the far side of the room a tall, thin man stood up uncertainly. "Well," he said, clearing his throat, obviously unaccustomed to speaking in public, "They're staying at my motel, and they do keep very strange hours. They don't seem to come and go like other folks."

"Have they disturbed anyone?" Beau asked.

"Why, no, Beau. I can't say they've *disturbed* anyone. They just act different, and they order funny kinds of food from all sorts of places out of town, as far away as Beaufort. Italian food."

"Well," Beau said, "I don't reckon a little Italian food can corrupt the morals of the minors in town, do you?"

Smiling crookedly, the motel owner shook his head and sat down.

"Anyway," someone else chirped up, "it's not the corruption of the people that worries me. I'm worried about the land."

"Yeah," another agreed. "We don't want some film studio coming in here and disrupting a quiet residential area."

"You know how big those studios are?" a loud voice asked. "I do. I've been out there to Hollywood, and I can tell you. They go on for acres and acres, big concrete things. I sure don't want to see one of those here in Corinth, especially not on that pretty piece of land down by the river. It won't fit in," he declared with finality, and there was plenty of agreement about that until another idea took precedence.

"Maybe the building'll be an eyesore, but people'll get hired on there. It's jobs that count nowadays."

"How do we know he won't bring most of the people with him? She said herself," somebody said, nodding at Eva, "that she didn't know the staffing plans. We got no guarantees."

"But even if he brings *everybody* with him," another responded, "they still have to buy houses or build them: they still need food and clothes. And *we* own the dry goods store and the grocery stores and the construction companies and—"

"Okay, okay, we get the point."

The battle continued to rage, and from what Eva was able to discern, the sides were pretty evenly divided. Then things began to get heated.

Ed, referred to by Beau and Lacy as Snake Eyes, was loud but not yet committed. "I'm all for bringing in new business," he said. "You've heard me on that subject before. But I'll tell you one thing, I'm not sure we need these Hollywood types coming in here and taking over our town. We want jobs, but I say we better be very careful about who we pick to move in...."

"Damn," said Beau. "I was counting on him."

Eva agreed. "I had the feeling he didn't like Reese's ideas at all," Eva said, remembering his vitriolic remarks at the general store.

Beau shook his head. "He was at the cottage for that meeting, though. He's never liked Reese, but that's probably because Reese has never paid any attention to him. Asking Ed to join the big shots at that meeting was a stroke of genius that I didn't even recognize at the time. Reese knows that if he can convert Ed, he's won. Yep, old Snake Eyes is our barometer, all right."

But they weren't going to get a reading that night. The meeting was getting out of hand.

"All right, Ed," a burly younger man shouted, pointing his finger in Ed's face, "you've been courted, that's what." He turned away from the man he was accusing and waved his big arms at the audience. "We all understand how Ed felt before, just like plenty of us who haven't had a steady job in years. He felt like it was time, and so did we. *We* still do, but Reese Benedict is trying to keep things the way he wants them. What does he care? He has plenty of money. He doesn't need to work. All he has to do is talk everyone else into thinking like him—"

"You're right, Bubba. He doesn't want to work, but we do."

"Exactly," the burly man whose name was Bubba agreed. "And we don't care whether it's for a movie company or a fertilizer company!"

The man beside him stood up, shaking his fist. "And we don't have time to sit around waiting for another business to move down here that suits him. We'll take what we can get. We'll take Marchetti!"

When another man in the group stood up, the mayor began pounding his gavel on the podium. "I knew it," Beau said. "He's going to stop the discussion just when our side is getting warmed up."

Beau was right. After getting everyone's attention, the mayor put a quick end to the meeting. "We can't decide the issue tonight," he told them. "So I'm going to suggest we take a couple of days breathing time. You all think this matter over and discuss it among yourselves. Then we'll hear from Reese and Miss Sinclair one more time—if that's all right with the two of you?"

Eva nodded, and the mayor didn't have to look at Reese, because, Eva suspected, this was Reese's idea. The breathing time could just as well be called campaign time. It would allow Reese to publicize his ideas, meet with his friends and those who opposed him to use his charm effectively.

"Don't we need a motion, Mr. Mayor?" Beau asked. Then he whispered to Eva, "Maybe if our side shouts loud enough we can bring this to a vote while we're ahead."

"You're sure we're ahead?"

"I'd rather take my chances now than wait for Reese to charm everybody."

But Beau's hopes were dashed by a voice vote that, according to the mayor, favored postponement.

"Just a minute," Beau shouted as everyone was getting up to leave. "I know you'll have a lot of questions to ask in the next couple of days and you know how to find Reese at the cottage, but maybe you don't all know that Miss Sinclair is staying with us at Diligence Hall. Everyone's welcome to call her there, aren't they, Mom?" Beau asked, looking across the aisle at his mother.

Eva, too, glanced Lacy's way for the second time that evening and found a look of agreement on her face. "Indeed, you're all welcome," she said, and Eva sat back with relief. Even if Lacy was unconvinced that Marchetti Films belonged in Corinth, at least she was willing to admit both sides deserved a fair hearing.

Eva wondered if Reese shared that sentiment. He was looking at her from his place of importance on the podium. She didn't know what the look meant and made a quick decision to find out. But it took a while for her to get to him.

As the group broke up and began, loudly, to leave the meeting hall, Eva was surrounded. She tried to forget about Reese and answer, comment on or dispute the remarks that came at her in rapid succession. By the time she and Reese stood side by side, almost an hour had passed.

Beau had seen them edging toward each other, and he'd also seen that his mother was tiring. "I'll take Mom home, Eva," he said. Before she could respond, Beau and Lacy were on the way out of the hall, and Eva and Reese were left in the middle of the finally dispersing crowd. She couldn't decide whether to rush after Beau or stay and confront Reese. The decision was made for her.

He didn't grab hold of her arm; he merely touched it. But the touch was a detaining one. It stopped her. "Your remarks were very impressive," he said sincerely, and she could tell that he was a little surprised.

"Thank you," she answered. "You did quite well yourself. It's good to see you back in public."

Reese smiled ruefully. "I knew you'd somehow change my life, but I didn't know it would be like this." His hand remained on her arm. "I still don't know what's going to happen to us."

"I don't, either," she admitted.

They walked toward the door of the hall. No one was left except a maintenance man closing up for the night. "I think I can keep Marchetti out of Corinth, Eva." She didn't answer, but for a wild moment she almost hoped he was right—for their sake. "I can sure as hell put up a good battle," Reese assured her. Again, Eva didn't answer. She suddenly realized that she, too, could put up a battle, and she was going to, not because Gino needed Corinth but because Corinth needed Marchetti Films.

The streets of the little town were almost empty. Reese took her hand, and they walked along under the soft glow of the streetlights. They walked in silence. On the block where Reese had parked, the streetlight was out, and they didn't notice what had happened until they reached the car.

"Reese—"

He let go of her hand and looked around quickly before he took another step toward the car. The top was up—what was left of it. It had been slashed deliberately and violently until it hung in shreds.

After looking around once more, Reese reached inside the car, turned the ignition with his key and put the top down. "I hope you don't mind a little night breeze in your hair," he said with a bitter smile.

"Reese, what in the world—"

"Marchetti's work, I imagine."

"Why on earth would you say that?" Eva asked, amazed.

He turned to her with narrowed eyes. "I've lived all over the world. I know what power is. I know how easily a command can be given from one place and carried out elsewhere. It's strong arm stuff. I've seen enough of it in my time, God knows."

"Reese—"

"Go on, get in," he said, ignoring her. "They've done their damage for the night. We're safe enough."

Obediently Eva got into the car. "You're wrong about him," she said as they drove off. "Gino's not that kind of person." But her voice lost its conviction. She'd had similar thoughts about Gino, and now here she was defending him.

"Loyal to the end, eh?"

"Does it have to be like this, Reese? An all-out battle?" Before he could respond, she said, "Gino didn't have anyone slash the car top. He doesn't operate like that. He's certainly a wheeler-dealer, but he's also a compromiser. I'm sure there are a lot of compromises that can be made over the film company moving to Corinth—"

"The film company isn't coming to Corinth, Eva, and I'm not interested in compromises."

"I guess that's the way it is with you, Reese—all or nothing." The wind whipped in Eva's hair, and she tried to keep it out of her face as she turned to him and said, "Isn't that the way it was with you and Barbara? Your way or not at all?" She knew that the words were cruel, but she also knew they were true. "I'm sorry," she added, wondering if he'd heard the apology over the wind.

Even if he didn't hear it, Reese was ready to hit back, ready to wound. "And what do you have to show for your life by your great compromises? An indebtedness to Gino Marchetti, who's a conniver at best and a crook at worst. Who the hell do you believe in, Eva—you or Gino Marchetti?"

He'd hit a nerve. Eva quickly and adamantly came to her own defense. "I can think for myself," she said. "Gino doesn't tell me what to do."

Reese looked over at her with a frown. "He told you to find the land."

"That was part of my job, Reese. I didn't know what he wanted it for, and I didn't know how much you wanted it."

"He told you to represent Marchetti Films at the town meeting," Reese continued. "Of course, that's part of your job, too."

"Yes, it is, but even if it weren't I'd still feel the same." They turned into Diligence and drove past the house to the cottage.

He stopped the car, and they both got out. Eva was still responding to his remarks. "I'm not being bullied into this by Gino."

Reese made a noise that was clearly doubtful.

Eva shot back, "And I won't be bullied by you. *I* believe that Marchetti Films will be good for Corinth."

He'd unlocked the door to the cottage, let the dogs out and closed the door behind them before Eva had time to realize what was happening. They were alone in the darkness. Reese didn't turn on the lights.

"I meant to get out at the house," she said.

"I meant to stop there," he answered.

Tension hung in the air, still mixed with anger. But somehow, suddenly, they were in each other's arms, kissing with a passion that was tinged with their anger. It was wild and abandoned, that kiss, and it didn't end when she tried to pull away or even when he relaxed his hold on her. It went on, their mouths exploring, tasting, their tongues probing deeply with a need that was nearly frantic. They'd ached for days to hold each other again, and now there was a rough desperation in the way they clung together, as if to release each other now would somehow mean to lose each other for good.

Eva wasn't even aware of the fury with which her nails dug into the back of his neck as she held his mouth to her; Reese didn't know the force with which his hand had locked on her shoulders from the moment when he'd first spun her around and into his arms.

They fell backward together onto the little sofa in the living room and struggled with their clothes, still kissing, still clinging with a need that dictated their movements. They managed to remove some of their clothes although Eva's bra was only pulled away so that Reese could capture her breast in his eager mouth while her hands tore at his shirt.

All at once, she was lost in him. She felt his hot tongue probing her mouth, felt his hands rake across her body, felt his chest crush against her, and through it all, over and above it all, felt the force of Reese within her. Eva moved as he moved, wildly and with abandon. Her whole body was consumed by him.

From the time they'd stepped inside the door of his house and he'd taken her into his arms, Reese hadn't let go of Eva for an instant, and now he was holding her, filling her, taking her with him to a place that was beyond reality, beyond where they'd ever been before. The force of their passion was so strong that Reese thought he'd lose control. He held on to her, feeling her hot, damp skin beneath his fingers, grasping her with all his might.

Just as tightly, Eva held him as they reached the pinnacle together, cried out together, found the very limit of their passion together and then fell apart, crumpled against the sofa, struggling for breath.

Nearly an hour later, as Reese slept, Eva untangled herself from his arms and got up. Standing beside the sofa, she looked down at him, confused by what they'd shared. She found her rumpled clothes and put them on. She'd never left him in the night, but it was different now. She still loved him and knew he loved her, but the caring, the friendship, the understanding had been missing tonight. She wondered if that would ever return. She wondered, as she silently went out the door into the warm, heavy night, if they'd ever make love again.

"Well, there you are finally," Beau called out to Eva as he met her on the steps of Diligence Hall. "I've been looking for you all morning."

"I've been on the phone," Eva explained. "Half the people in town took your advice. They've barraged me with questions."

"Which you answered to their satisfaction, I hope," Beau said and then added, "I know you did, Eva. After your talk at the meeting last night, I'll never have any doubts again," he complimented. "You were terrific, and when you left with Reese, I figured the battle was over. Did you convince him, too?"

"Hardly," Eva said. They sat down beside each other on the steps. "But someone tried to. Have you seen his car?"

Beau nodded. "Not a very smart move. Probably made by a member of our contingent." Eva refrained from voicing Reese's theory, and Beau added, "But that shouldn't affect you and Reese. You two are crazy about each other, right?"

"Before all this happened I guess you might have said that, but now I don't know. The feelings are still there, but what's come between us is very important to Reese. He's made this his cause; it's brought him back to the mainstream."

"And you oppose him. I hope you believe in what you're doing and aren't just doing it because it's what Gino wants and it's your job.

"Of course not. Why do you say that, Beau?" He, like Reese, seemed to think she was under Gino's thumb.

"No reason. Just a sudden thought. We need you on our side in this battle, but it would be a shame for you and Reese to split over something that you're doing for Gino."

"I'm doing it because I think it's right, Beau," Eva assured him, "certainly right for Corinth."

"And if the studio's built, *when* it's built," he amended with a grin, "will you relocate here?"

Eva shook her head. "I'll still work out of the L.A. office. Gino will want me to travel...."

"And whatever Gino wants—"

Eva tried to laugh that off, but she realized that Beau and Reese were right about one thing: Gino Marchetti had a powerful influence over her life. She loved Reese, but she'd done nothing to break the hold Gino had over her. "Maybe I haven't been tested yet," she said as much to herself as to Beau. "So far, everything Gino's wanted, I've wanted, too."

"Well, the test is bound to come someday."

Eva nodded. "I suppose so. What about you, Beau? Are you going to work for him?"

Beau shook his head. "Nope."

Eva looked up with surprise. "Didn't he offer you a job?"

"Yes, he did. He said I could work in the casting department, but I'm not going to. I want to help bring the studio to Corinth; after that I want to go out and get a job on my own."

"This would be a sure thing," Eva reminded him.

"I know, but I like independence—or think I do. Since I've never had it, we'll have to wait and see. I have a good eye for talent, and I'm going to try my hand in New York, working for a theatrical agency. I'm willing to start at the bottom, so it shouldn't be difficult to get something."

"I don't know about that, Beau."

Beau grinned. "Well, I'm not totally foolish. I wouldn't strike out without any support. Mary's going to make some calls, open some doors for me. She's very well respected as you know.

"Even with her help, it's a big step. I'm proud of you for taking it, Beau."

He gave her a loving smile. "It's all your fault. You're the one who insisted that Mary take me on. You started it." He leaned over and kissed her cheek. "Thanks, Eva."

"What about Lacy?"

"She'll be all right. She's never really needed me here, and I'm even more unnecessary now that Reese is back for good. I always told myself I was staying here for her, but I think I really stayed because I was afraid to go. I'm not afraid now." He paused and looked at Eva with a sheepish grin. "Well, actually I'm scared to death, but it's an exciting fear. I *will* miss Mom, though. Even Reese."

"So will I," said Eva softly.

## Chapter 12

On the afternoon of the next town meeting, Eva went for a walk in the woods, remembering to wear long pants and a long-sleeved shirt to protect herself from chiggers, ticks and poison ivy.

"It's a real battlefield out there," Beau reminded her as she set out, adding, "Take this walking stick to beat off the snakes." He flashed her a grin that, Eva hoped, indicated the absurdity of his words.

Beau had asked to go along, but she'd put him off politely; she hadn't felt like company. Eva needed to face what was happening to her and Reese. So far, it was wrenching. If the vote went in favor of Marchetti, it might mean the end of their relationship.

Eva followed a bridle path that led to the river and sat down on the bank. Beneath the trees the air was cool, and the water flowed by slowly, lazily. She even saw a fish jump. This was unspoiled country, Eva thought. Maybe a film studio would desecrate its natural beauty; maybe Gino should find another place to save himself millions and leave the people of Corinth alone.

What she really meant was *leave Reese alone*, protect Reese and thereby protect her relationship with him. But if their relationship was unable to confront problems and still stand, it was probably so fragile it wouldn't have survived anyway.

Suddenly the two Irish setters came bounding out of the woods, red flashes cutting through the green. Eva laughed as they jumped around her. She threw a stick into the river, and they both plunged in, Coleen somewhat cautiously. After retrieving the stick a few more times, Bridget grew bored with the game and went off to explore on her own, and Coleen, wet and tired, found a spot beside Eva.

While the dogs played around her, Eva had been watching for Reese, expecting that he, too, would come out of the woods. When he didn't appear, she wondered if he'd let the dogs out on their own or if he'd walked with them, seen her and turned back. Yes, she told herself, shaking her head in perplexity, she was unsure of him, and all because of what was happening in the local town meetings. Eva sighed deeply, confused and yet still determined. She couldn't stand beside Reese to fight the studio when she knew it would be good for the town.

That night the meeting hall was crowded, packed with the faces from two days before and many, many more. All the seats were taken, and dozens of people stood in the back. The two cars from Diligence had arrived early; Eva and Beau driving in together as before and, as before, Lacy arriving with Reese.

Reese had made sure that his mother was comfortably settled in her aisle seat before joining the dignitaries at the long table on stage. But as soon as he walked away, Lacy motioned to Beau. "Help me up," she said in a rather loud voice, which caused Reese to turn and look around when he reached the stage. "I think it's ridiculous for me to be sitting over here alone," she said while Beau quickly did as he was asked, "especially since I'll be voting with you two."

Eva's mouth dropped open. She and Lacy hadn't discussed the vote during the two days that had elapsed, although they'd dined together pleasantly at Diligence Hall. Eva had presumed that Lacy's mind hadn't changed.

"Yes," Lacy continued as Eva attempted to modify her expression, "I've been doing some serious soul searching, and I find that this isn't a family problem, and I don't have to side with one son or the other. This is Corinth's future, and it's just plain ridiculous for me to rob my town of a future because I'm an old so-and-so who can't accept a little change. Shoot," she said, coming as close as she ever came to cussing, "I *like* change. I like having the film crew around my house; I can't wait until they film more of the party scenes; I'll be lonely when everyone leaves. Furthermore, I'll be glad to see some of them come back to Corinth when the studio gets built."

"Does Reese know this?" was Beau's only question.

"No, he doesn't, and there isn't any reason why he should. This is a matter of conscience, and my conscience is my own, dear." With that, Lacy grasped Eva's hand. "Whatever happens tonight, you're absolutely right about change for the good."

The mayor was wielding his gavel, and the room was beginning to quieten so that Beau's remarks to Eva, which began loudly, ended in a whisper. "By rights," he said, "you should speak first tonight since Reese led off last time. But mark my words, this little bit of fairness won't happen to occur to the good mayor."

Beau was right. At that moment, the gavel having done its job, the mayor introduced Reese.

As Eva expected, Reese's words were less neighborly than before. He was committed now. Even his voice changed. The affable tone became more demanding as he urged everyone to stand beside him in his fight to "save" Corinth.

Listening to him decry Marchetti Films' planned move to South Carolina, Eva tried to form answers for each of his arguments and told Beau, "I'm *glad* that I have the chance to speak last. I'll be able to use my time as a rebuttal."

"After which, the mayor will allow Reese to respond to your arguments."

"And if he does, I'll ask for equal time," she said with a smile. "After all, this is a parliamentary meeting."

"So we're told," Beau responded.

Reese was expounding on the environmental dangers that would be created by Marchetti when Eva had a brainstorm. She'd been trying to think of a commitment that she could make, in the name of Marchetti Films, to Corinth. In a phone conversation that morning with Gino, she'd asked about the staff, looking for assurances that a large percentage of the production people would be hired locally.

"Eva, how do I know what my staff will be? The place hasn't even been built yet. Hell, I don't even have the right to build yet, but I will by tonight, huh?"

When she agreed, with her fingers crossed to cover herself, Gino continued, "Tell them whatever they want to hear about the staff. Tell them we won't send any kids—all gray-bearded grandfathers; tell them we'll hire six hundred local people. Promise anything. We can always change our minds."

Eva couldn't do that, but now she knew something that she could do, and Gino would just have to go along with her. She wouldn't give him any choice. Eva listened to the rest of Reese's speech without the sense of doom that she'd experienced during most of the meeting. She was sure she had an answer to one of the major stumbling blocks. It would be a compromise of sorts, and even Reese would realize the good that could come from it. Eva felt a flush of excitement that didn't fade with the ovation greeting Reese's final words. She was ready.

Standing at the podium, referring occasionally to her notes, Eva tried to respond to some of the points Reese had raised. She did so effectively enough that a few audible sounds of agreement spread around the hall. But she saved her main point for last, hoping it would be the pièce de résistance that would win the votes needed to bring Marchetti Films to Corinth. Her side had gained ground, but Reese was still ahead—as Beau had so infuriatingly reminded Eva when she'd climbed the podium. Now was the time to catch up.

"Progress must come," she told them. "Change is inevitable. Perhaps it can be avoided for a while, put off, resisted, but it will come in time. Why not now?" she tempted. They seemed to be holding a collective breath in the packed hall, expecting something. Well, Eva thought, they were going to get it.

"Let's not wait," she said. "Let's start now and make that change for the good. Here's what I propose.'' Again she paused, and even Reese seemed to lean forward. "The land where Marchetti Films will be located is beautiful, but of course it won't be the same after the studio is built. Some wildlife habitats will be disturbed...." She let them make noises of agreement. "Many trees will be sacrificed...." Again Eva waited for the groans and accompanying comments. "But building doesn't have to be destructive. It can be beautiful; it can contribute." This time her pause was greeted with total, anticipatory silence.

"Much of the land won't be built on, and we can preserve the habitats of the birds and animals of the area. The land was used and lived on before. Marchetti Films wants to bring the land back into use and retain its beauty and graciousness with landscaping, a boulevard of flowering trees that would recapture some of the plantation's past glory. We can return to Corinth far more in the way of trees, foliage and wildlife than we take away, because we'll make it successful. That's what I promise." Her last pause was the most dramatic. "I hope that is acceptable."

There was no silence this time. Eva's final words were followed by immediate and abundant applause after which, as Beau had predicted, the mayor recognized Reese again.

"I have only one question," he said curtly, glancing at Eva and then looking away, out into the audience. "Mr. Marchetti," he said, and the three syllables seemed to take on an ominous connotation, "has never been known as an environmentalist—unless I'm mistaken." He looked over at Eva again, waiting for her to dispute his words. Around the room she heard a few snickers and considerable agreement. "My question is: has Marchetti agreed to your beautifica-

tion plans? Have you in fact even discussed this idea
with him?''

Eva addressed her answer to the crowd. ''I haven't
discussed it with him yet, but I will and—'' The din
was too loud for her to continue.

The mayor used his gavel again, and when the noise
quietened, Reese asked pointedly, ''Don't you think it
would be a good idea to *ask* Mr. Marchetti before
making such an outrageous offer?'' He turned to the
mayor. ''That's all I have to say. I believe it's time for
the vote.''

''Wait a minute,'' Eva said. She was out of order,
but no more so than Reese had been. ''I would appreciate the opportunity to answer the question that was
just put to me.'' She paused, knowing they couldn't
refuse her now. ''I can speak for Mr. Marchetti in the
matter of the environmental improvements. You have
my *word*; the improvements will be made.'' While the
audience responded to that, Eva turned to the mayor.
''I believe it's time for the vote,'' she told him, echo-
ing Reese's words and getting a smattering of laughter.

Neither of them got their way, however, for the discussion period dragged on until everyone who'd had
a thought on the subject expressed it—or tried to—
over the roar of the crowd. Finally no more voices
called out to be recognized, and there was nothing left
to do but vote. Wisely, the mayor decided against a
show of hands. There was still too much dissension in
the air.

Three volunteers from each side of the question
were chosen to count the written votes, and a party
atmosphere began to take over the hall as the crowd
broke up into small groups, laughing and talking.
They'd let go of the subject that had obsessed them for

the past few days and relaxed now that the voting was over. The talk turned to baseball, weather, the crops, the usual topics that occupied their conversation.

Even after the vote was announced, the camaraderie continued, and everyone left the hall in good spirits, those who'd lost and those who'd won. What was done was done, and they were all ready to pull together. Even though the majority was a slim one, the vote was final. It was over.

For everyone except Reese. He left the hall alone, going out a side door without a word to Eva or a glance in her direction.

"He'll get over it," Lacy told Eva the next day as they sat sipping iced tea on the porch.

"I wonder," Eva said contemplatively. He'd lost; Marchetti Films International was moving to Corinth. Reese wasn't taking defeat well, and he'd told Beau that he believed Gino responsible not only for the vandalism of his car but also for buying votes among the townspeople of Corinth. Eva knew she had to find out the truth of those accusations, but she wondered if the answer would even interest Reese. Whatever his reaction, she'd be on the West Coast by then, and Reese would be here. That, Eva realized, was how it was going to remain.

"I tried to compromise," Eva told Lacy, "but that wasn't enough."

"No," Lacy agreed. "Reese has never been much for compromises." She shook her head sadly. "Will you see him before you leave?" she asked in a voice filled with hope that quickly faded when Eva shook her head.

"I can't go to him now, Lacy. I have nothing left to say. If only he could have accepted the decision..."

"That saddens me, of course," Lacy said, "but it's over and done, and our town will be better off for it. But what makes me as mad as an old hatter is the effect all this has had on you and Reese. I almost wish it had never happened."

"Then Reese and I might never have known what our relationship could withstand. It's better to find out now," Eva said, but her look and her words were wistful. Like Lacy, she almost wished that Gino had stayed away from Corinth, South Carolina.

Lacy forced herself to cheer up, and she could always find a way to counter problems. She had one now. "Reese will come around," she assured Eva. "You'll see. In fact—" she smiled broadly "—I think I'll just ask him to join us for dinner tonight since you'll be leaving in the morning. That way—"

"No, Lacy, please," Eva asked. "If I see him before I leave, I want it to be his choice. Don't force him."

"But Eva—"

"He'll come if he wants to."

Reese didn't come, and the following day Eva returned to Los Angeles, where she was on her own again. This time she was determined to be her own person. She took that determination to her meeting with Gino.

Naturally he was pleased with the outcome of the town meeting, which he'd known about moments after it ended. "Of course, I counted on you to convince those locals. You did a great job, *cara*."

"I did what I believed was right. The studio will be good for that town, Gino. They can use the business all the new people will generate, and they can certainly use the jobs. I do hope you'll hire freely from among those who apply in Corinth.''

"We'll see," he said disinterestedly as he lit a cigar. "Anyway, you did it for me, Eva."

"I did it for myself," she shot back, causing him to look up through the smoke screen he'd created.

"*Cara*, that was your job," Gino said, waving the smoke away so he could see her better.

"But I have to believe in my job, Gino, or I can't be effective. I believed in this. I was my own person this time."

"Haven't you always been?" he asked, and now that the smoke was clearing, he looked at her very closely, trying to read what was going on.

Eva shook her head. "No, I've been your person. I've done what you wanted for so long that I forgot I have a mind of my own. I'm going to have to start using it, Gino."

Gino's eyes narrowed, and Eva could see that he'd just decided what was going on. "Benedict," he said, lodging the cigar firmly in one corner of his mouth, satisfied that he'd found the answer. "Benedict's gotten to you."

"No," Eva denied. "In fact, I came to your defense when he accused you of using strong-arm tactics."

Gino's black eyebrows shot up. "What tactics?"

"His car was vandalized during the first town meeting."

Gino's mouth turned down as his shoulders went up in a kind of shrug.

"He also claims that you bought votes to assure that you'd win."

Again the mouth went down and the shoulders up. "Your Reese Benedict knows me better than I thought."

"Gino, you didn't—"

"Nope," he said, "In fact, my sources tell me they found out who did a job on the car, a local guy called Bubba," Gino said with a grin.

Eva remembered the man from the town meeting.

Gino's next words were brutally honest and took Eva by surprise. "Vandalism is for guys like Bubba. Give me credit for a little more brains. In the first place, Benedict wouldn't be scared away by it; in the second place, none of that stuff was necessary, but don't fool yourself, Eva. I would have found a way to get the votes if I'd needed them. We're talking about millions of dollars, *cara*. With stakes like that, I play by my own rules. Fortunately for everyone concerned, I didn't need to. I had you."

Eva realized, perhaps for the first time, that he meant what he said. While he'd been like a father to her, and she still loved him and always would love him, Gino had used her. She'd been manipulated by him, not just in Corinth, but all along. And it was her own fault, not Gino's, because she'd let it happen. Except this time, at the end, she'd taken matters into her own hands and spoken promises that it would be up to Gino to keep. She'd done so not for him, but for Corinth.

"Gino, I have something to tell you," Eva said softly.

Twenty minutes later, after she'd explained everything that had happened at the last town meeting with special emphasis on the promises she'd made to the people of Corinth, Eva sat back in her chair and asked in an unfaltering voice, "What are you going to do about it?"

"Nothing." Gino removed the cigar from his mouth, put it in an ashtray and stood up. "I'm gonna do nothing. You spoke without my backing, Eva."

"But what I promised is only fair, Gino. You'll be giving back some of what you take away."

"No, positively not. Do you realize what all that 'beautification' you promised would cost me? No," he repeated as he circled the room once, sat back down and picked up his cigar, signaling that he'd made the decision.

"If you don't support me on this, Gino, my own credibility will be gone. No one will trust me in negotiations again. I'll be useless to you." She caught his attention with that, and she kept it with what came next. "I might as well resign."

"Don't be ridiculous, Eva. You can't resign. I depend on you."

"I won't go back on my word to the people of Corinth, Gino. If you don't back me on this, I'll quit." Her chin lifted with what seemed to be outright defiance.

"That sounds like a threat, *cara*."

Eva shook her head. "I'm just presenting the facts," she said coolly, although her heart was pounding. She'd never stood up to him before, and she was scared.

Gino looked at her long and hard, but when Eva's gaze didn't falter, he sat back, put his feet on the desk and puffed imperiously on his cigar. In spite of his authoritative attitude, Eva could see his mind working. That was encouraging; Gino was considering her proposition.

"You know what I'm thinking?" he asked finally and then answered his own question. "I'm thinking that this could work to my advantage." Eva looked up a little startled but kept silent. "Yes, it could work for me. For a change, those guys down in the publicity department could do something to earn their fancy salaries." Eva began to catch on. "Marchetti—the environmentalist," Gino said with delight, "turns a two-bit town into a showplace." He looked at Eva with a smile wrapped around his cigar. "Okay, I'll do it; I'll look like a good guy. But you have to get things started for me."

"I can't, Gino."

That seemed to surprise him more than her earlier remarks. "Why not?" I thought you wanted to go back there; I thought you were crazy for that Benedict character."

"I did, and I was. But no more. I'll find someone to do a good job with the planning, but I want to stay in L.A."

"Women! Can't ever make up their minds. I always figured you were different, Eva, but I guess not," Gino said, resigned and secretly happy that he'd have her back with him in L.A.

"Would you really have bought votes, Gino?" she asked.

He shrugged. "Would you really have quit?"

On the morning that Eva left Corinth, Reese had gotten up early but not with the intention of seeing her off or even telling her goodbye; he'd been there at the window of the cottage for some other perverse reason that he tried not to dwell on.

They hadn't talked at all since the last town meeting. They hadn't *really* talked since the night he'd brought her home and they'd made love with such passion and fury. She'd slipped away while he slept, as if to reinforce her feelings that there was nothing left for them but the passion. He'd awakened at dawn, not surprised to find her gone.

Since then, they'd exchanged few words. Once she'd asked about his book, and he'd lashed out, angry that she knew about something so close and personal now that their own understanding seemed to have vanished. He didn't want to be reminded of what he'd shared with her; more than that, Reese admitted to himself at last, he didn't want to be reminded of the book at all. He hadn't begun it; he couldn't begin it. Something kept him from putting the first sheet of paper in the typewriter.

Later that morning, long after she'd gone, Reese had sat down at his desk and forced himself to begin. She was out of his sight and would soon be out of his mind. But not out of his heart, Reese admitted, not for a long time.

He'd remained at the desk for the rest of the morning and well into the afternoon, making a few stabs at a first chapter, working for a while on an outline, giving that up and writing half a page of a preface. It was nearly twilight when he put the cover on his typewriter and took the dogs out for a walk.

"This is a terrible time to get writer's block," he said quite seriously to Coleen, "before the book even begins." But he *knew* what he was going to write. The outline was in his head and so was the first chapter and the preface. He didn't have writer's block at all; he was obsessed with something else.

During the next days Reese did everything he could to exorcise Eva from his mind. Then he finally gave up and went into town. It was no longer possible for him to live secluded in the cottage; she'd taken that privilege away. He'd been glad at the time, but later when he tried to retreat into his shell, Reese realized that he was out for good. He also realized that as long as he was out, he might as well make himself useful.

He let it be known that he was willing to work with the committee on environmental planning for the film studio. Contact had already been made with Marchetti's office in Los Angeles, and a group was forming locally. He was immediately put in charge of it. That wasn't enough, though. More than Corinth was on Reese's mind.

When the phone in her apartment rang while Eva was heating a bowl of soup for dinner, she thought of ignoring it. She'd just about given up hope of hearing from Reese, and no other call interested her. On the sixth ring, she picked up the receiver.

"I just wanted to tell you that I'm heading up the local planning committee."

For a moment, Eva was stunned, less by Reese's news than by the sound of his voice.

"Eva..."

"I'm glad, Reese." She reached over and turned off the burner and tried to think of something else to say.

"We got the go-ahead from Marchetti's office."

"I know," Eva responded. She was having trouble regaining her composure, but Reese thought the silence was directed at him.

"Eva, I realize that I took a long time to come around, to see that you were right, but I don't like to be bested."

"I know that, too, Reese," she said, and something of her composure returned. They were talking again; he'd called.

"You asked about my book..."

"You said it was none of my business," Eva said.

"I needed an excuse not to answer. I hadn't started anything. I still haven't."

"Well, sometimes it takes a while to get back into writing. You've been away from it so long, you—"

"Those were my reasons, too," he interrupted, "until I decided to face the truth." When she didn't respond, he explained, "My mind is elsewhere, Eva. I can't write when I'm thinking of you all the time, and I'm going to continue thinking of you all the time until... Eva, I want to see you."

Eva sat down on a stool at the kitchen counter. "We're on different coasts, Reese," she said. "I don't expect to go back to Corinth."

"Even to work with the planning committee?"

"No, I—I'm sending my assistant," Eva said, cursing herself for making those plans.

"While the studio is being built?"

"No," she said.

"When it's completed and the staff arrives?"

"I'll be in L.A.," Eva said, wishing she'd never made the deal with Gino, wishing she could start all over from that last day in Corinth, wondering what she could do to change what had happened.

Reese had no such worries. "Then I'll have to come up now," he said.

"What?" Eva was perplexed.

"I'm downstairs in the lobby. I'll be right up."

Eva was still standing in the kitchen, holding the phone in a hand that seemed to have become instantly paralyzed, when the door buzzer rang. "It's unlocked," she said in a voice that couldn't possibly have carried down the hall. But Reese was already inside. She heard the door close, heard his footsteps on the parquet floor. She'd put down the telephone finally and was absently stirring the now-cold soup when he walked into the kitchen.

Firmly but lovingly, he removed the wooden spoon from her hand and took her into his arms. They didn't kiss; they just held each other.

"Dear Eva," he said huskily, "I've missed you so much. This living on two coasts is going to have to end. I want you back in Corinth."

"Reese—"

"I know. We have some problems to work out—one of them is me. I'm stubborn, uncompromising and arrogant."

"Oh, I wouldn't say arrogant," Eva disputed.

Reese laughed, lifted Eva up onto the kitchen stool, put his arms around her waist and kissed her hard. "But you'll agree with the other two adjectives?"

"Stubborn and uncompromising . . . yes," she said.

"Well, I'm changing fast."

"So am I," Eva said. "You were right about Gino. He's been using me for years until you showed me I had to be my own person."

"You're still very influenced by him."

"Maybe I'll quit," she said rashly.

Reese laughed. "You don't really want to quit, do you Eva?"

She shook her head. "I must admit that I'm a born working girl. I love my job, but I told Gino I didn't want to work in Corinth. I told him to keep me in the L.A. office."

"I guess you'll just have to change your mind," Reese said, putting his arms around her.

Eva smiled to herself. "I guess I will." Then she looked at him with a glint in her eye. "Are you propositioning me, Reese Benedict?"

He shook his head, and his face became serious, the look in his eyes so loving that Eva felt a shiver race through her body. "No, dear Eva," he said, "I'm proposing. Don't answer until you've had time to think about it," he said quickly, and she realized that he was not sure what her answer would be.

"Oh, Reese, Reese," she said, slipping from the stool and into his arms, "I don't have to think about it. The answer is *yes*."

He kissed her with relief and with passion. "Where's the bedroom?" he asked, picking her up in his arms.

Eva pointed over his shoulder and down the hall. "That way," she said and with a half smile added, "This was certainly an easy compromise."

"That's my style from now on," Reese answered as he pushed open the bedroom door. "Except when it comes to how much I love you—on that I'll never compromise."